THIRTEEN O'CLOCK

Stories of Several Worlds

THIRTEEN O'CLOCK

O'CLOCK

Stories of Several Worlds

by

STEPHEN VINCENT BENÉT

Short Story Index Reprint Series

BOOKS FOR LIBRARIES PRESS
FREEPORT, NEW YORK

INTERNATIONAL STANDARD BOOK NUMBER:
0-8369-3793-7

LIBRARY OF CONGRESS CATALOG CARD NUMBER:
78-152935

PRINTED IN THE UNITED STATES OF AMERICA

TO LAURENCE VINCENT AND
MARGARET COX BENÉT WITH
MANY SALUTES

CONTENTS

I

II

III

IV

I

BY THE WATERS OF BABYLON

THE north and the west and the south are good hunting ground, but it is forbidden to go east. It is forbidden to go to any of the Dead Places except to search for metal and then he who touches the metal must be a priest or the son of a priest. Afterwards, both the man and the metal must be purified. These are the rules and the laws; they are well made. It is forbidden to cross the great river and look upon the place that was the Place of the Gods—this is most strictly forbidden. We do not even say its name though we know its name. It is there that spirits live, and demons—it is there that there are the ashes of the Great Burning. These things are forbidden—they have been forbidden since the beginning of time.

My father is a priest; I am the son of a priest. I have been in the Dead Places near us, with my father—at first, I was afraid. When my father went into the house to search for the metal, I stood by the door and my heart felt small and weak. It was a dead man's house, a spirit house. It did not have the smell of man, though there were old bones in a corner. But it is not fitting that a priest's son should show fear. I looked at the bones in the shadow and kept my voice still.

Then my father came out with the metal—a good, strong piece. He looked at me with both eyes but I had not run away. He gave me the metal to hold—I took it and did not die. So he knew that I was truly his son and would be a priest in my time. That was when I was very young—nevertheless, my brothers would not have done it, though they are good hunters. After that, they gave me the good piece of meat and the warm corner by the fire. My father watched over me—he was glad that I should be a priest. But when I boasted or wept without a reason, he punished me more strictly than my brothers. That was right.

After a time, I myself was allowed to go into the dead houses and search for metal. So I learned the ways of those houses—and if I saw bones, I was no longer afraid. The bones are light and old—sometimes they will fall into dust if you touch them. But that is a great sin.

I was taught the chants and the spells—I was taught how to stop the running of blood from a wound and many secrets. A priest must know many secrets—that was what my father said. If the hunters think we do all things by chants and spells, they may believe so—it does not hurt them. I was taught how to read in the old books and how to make the old writings—that was hard and took a long time. My knowledge made me happy—it was like a fire in my heart. Most of all, I liked to hear of the Old Days and the stories of the gods. I asked myself many questions that I could not answer, but it was good to ask them. At night, I would lie awake and listen to the wind—it seemed to me that it was the voice of the gods as they flew through the air.

We are not ignorant like the Forest People—our women spin wool on the wheel, our priests wear a white robe. We do not eat grubs from the tree, we have not forgotten the old writings, although they are hard to understand. Nevertheless, my knowledge and my lack of knowledge burned in me—I wished to know more. When I was a man at last, I came to my father and said, "It is time for me to go on my journey. Give me your leave."

He looked at me for a long time, stroking his beard, then he said at last, "Yes. It is time." That night, in the house of the priesthood, I asked for and received purification. My body hurt but my spirit was a cool stone. It was my father himself who questioned me about my dreams.

He bade me look into the smoke of the fire and see —I saw and told what I saw. It was what I have always seen—a river, and, beyond it, a great Dead Place and in it the gods walking. I have always thought about that. His eyes were stern when I told him—he was no longer my father but a priest. He said, "This is a strong dream."

"It is mine," I said, while the smoke waved and my head felt light. They were singing the Star song in the outer chamber and it was like the buzzing of bees in my head.

He asked me how the gods were dressed and I told him how they were dressed. We know how they were dressed from the book, but I saw them as if they were before me. When I had finished, he threw the sticks three times and studied them as they fell.

"This is a very strong dream," he said. "It may eat you up."

"I am not afraid," I said and looked at him with

both eyes. My voice sounded thin in my ears but that was because of the smoke.

He touched me on the breast and the forehead. He gave me the bow and the three arrows.

"Take them," he said. "It is forbidden to travel east. It is forbidden to cross the river. It is forbidden to go to the Place of the Gods. All these things are forbidden."

"All these things are forbidden," I said, but it was my voice that spoke and not my spirit. He looked at me again.

"My son," he said. "Once I had young dreams. If your dreams do not eat you up, you may be a great priest. If they eat you, you are still my son. Now go on your journey."

I went fasting, as is the law. My body hurt but not my heart. When the dawn came, I was out of sight of the village. I prayed and purified myself, waiting for a sign. The sign was an eagle. It flew east.

Sometimes signs are sent by bad spirits. I waited again on the flat rock, fasting, taking no food. I was very still—I could feel the sky above me and the earth beneath. I waited till the sun was beginning to sink. Then three deer passed in the valley, going east—they did not wind me or see me. There was a white fawn with them—a very great sign.

I followed them, at a distance, waiting for what would happen. My heart was troubled about going east, yet I knew that I must go. My head hummed with my fasting—I did not even see the panther spring upon the white fawn. But, before I knew it, the bow was in my hand. I shouted and the panther lifted his head from the fawn. It is not easy to kill a panther with one arrow but the arrow went through his eye and into his brain. He died as he tried to spring—he rolled over, tearing at the ground. Then I knew I was meant to go east—I knew that was my journey. When the night came, I made my fire and roasted meat.

It is eight suns journey to the east and a man passes by many Dead Places. The Forest People are afraid of them but I am not. Once I made my fire on the edge of a Dead Place at night and, next morning, in the dead house, I found a good knife, little rusted. That was small to what came afterward but it made my heart feel big. Always when I looked for game, it was in front of my arrow, and twice I passed hunting parties of the Forest People without their knowing. So I knew my magic was strong and my journey clean, in spite of the law.

Toward the setting of the eighth sun, I came to the banks of the great river. It was half-a-day's journey after I had left the god-road—we do not use the god-roads now for they are falling apart into great blocks of stone, and the forest is safer going. A long way off, I had seen the water through trees but the trees were thick. At last, I came out upon an open place at the top of a cliff. There was the great river below, like a giant in the sun. It is very long, very wide. It could eat all the streams we know and still be thirsty. Its name is Ou-dis-sun, the Sacred, the Long. No man of my tribe had seen it, not even my father, the priest. It was magic and I prayed.

Then I raised my eyes and looked south. It was there, the Place of the Gods.

How can I tell what it was like—you do not know. It was there, in the red light, and they were too big to be houses. It was there with the red light upon it, mighty and ruined. I knew that in another moment the gods would see me. I covered my eyes with my hands and crept back into the forest.

Surely, that was enough to do, and live. Surely it was enough to spend the night upon the cliff. The Forest People themselves do not come near. Yet, all through the night, I knew that I should have to cross the river and walk in the places of the gods, although the gods ate me up. My magic did not help me at all and yet there was a fire in my bowels, a fire in my mind. When the sun rose, I thought, "My journey has been clean. Now I will go home from my journey." But, even as I thought so, I knew I could not. If I went to the place of the gods, I would surely die, but, if I did not go, I could never be at peace with my spirit again. It is better to lose one's life than one's spirit, if one is a priest and the son of a priest.

Nevertheless, as I made the raft, the tears ran out of my eyes. The Forest People could have killed me without fight, if they had come upon me then, but they did not come. When the raft was made, I said the sayings for the dead and painted myself for death. My heart was cold as a frog and my knees like water, but the burning in my mind would not let me have peace. As I pushed the raft from the shore, I began my death song—I had the right. It was a fine song.

"I am John, son of John," I sang. "My people are the Hill
   People. They are the men.
I go into the Dead Places but I am not slain.
I take the metal from the Dead Places but I am not
   blasted.
I travel upon the god-roads and am not afraid. E-yah! I
   have killed the panther, I have killed the fawn!
E-yah! I have come to the great river. No man has come
   there before.
It is forbidden to go east, but I have gone, forbidden to go
   on the great river, but I am there.
Open your hearts, you spirits, and hear my song.
Now I go to the place of the gods, I shall not return.
My body is painted for death and my limbs weak, but my
   heart is big as I go to the place of the gods!"

All the same, when I came to the Place of the Gods,
I was afraid, afraid. The current of the great river is
very strong—it gripped my raft with its hands. That
was magic, for the river itself is wide and calm. I could
feel evil spirits about me, in the bright morning; I
could feel their breath on my neck as I was swept down
the stream. Never have I been so much alone—I tried
to think of my knowledge, but it was a squirrel's heap
of winter nuts. There was no strength in my knowledge
any more and I felt small and naked as a new-hatched
bird—alone upon the great river, the servant of the
gods.

Yet, after a while, my eyes were opened and I saw.
I saw both banks of the river—I saw that once there
had been god-roads across it, though now they were
broken and fallen like broken vines. Very great they
were, and wonderful and broken—broken in the time

of the Great Burning when the fire fell out of the sky. And always the current took me nearer to the Place of the Gods, and the huge ruins rose before my eyes.

I do not know the customs of rivers—we are the People of the Hills. I tried to guide my raft with the pole but it spun around. I thought the river meant to take me past the Place of the Gods and out into the Bitter Water of the legends. I grew angry then— my heart felt strong. I said aloud, "I am a priest and the son of a priest!" The gods heard me—they showed me how to paddle with the pole on one side of the raft. The current changed itself—I drew near to the Place of the Gods.

When I was very near, my raft struck and turned over. I can swim in our lakes—I swam to the shore. There was a great spike of rusted metal sticking out into the river—I hauled myself up upon it and sat there, panting. I had saved my bow and two arrows and the knife I found in the Dead Place but that was all. My raft went whirling downstream toward the Bitter Water. I looked after it, and thought if it had trod me under, at least I would be safely dead. Nevertheless, when I had dried my bow-string and re-strung it, I walked forward to the Place of the Gods.

It felt like ground underfoot; it did not burn me. It is not true what some of the tales say, that the ground there burns forever, for I have been there. Here and there were the marks and stains of the Great Burning, on the ruins, that is true. But they were old marks and old stains. It is not true either, what some of our priests say, that it is an island covered with fogs and enchantments. It is not. It is a great Dead Place—

greater than any Dead Place we know. Everywhere in it there are god-roads, though most are cracked and broken. Everywhere there are the ruins of the high towers of the gods.

How shall I tell what I saw? I went carefully, my strung bow in my hand, my skin ready for danger. There should have been the wailings of spirits and the shrieks of demons, but there were not. It was very silent and sunny where I had landed—the wind and the rain and the birds that drop seeds had done their work—the grass grew in the cracks of the broken stone. It is a fair island—no wonder the gods built there. If I had come there, a god, I also would have built.

How shall I tell what I saw? The towers are not all broken—here and there one still stands, like a great tree in a forest, and the birds nest high. But the towers themselves look blind, for the gods are gone. I saw a fish-hawk, catching fish in the river. I saw a little dance of white butterflies over a great heap of broken stones and columns. I went there and looked about me—there was a carved stone with cut-letters, broken in half. I can read letters but I could not understand these. They said UBTREAS. There was also the shattered image of a man or a god. It had been made of white stone and he wore his hair tied back like a woman's. His name was ASHING, as I read on the cracked half of a stone. I thought it wise to pray to ASHING, though I do not know that god.

How shall I tell what I saw? There was no smell of man left, on stone or metal. Nor were there many trees in that wilderness of stone. There are many pigeons, nesting and dropping in the towers—the gods must have loved them, or, perhaps, they used them for sacrifices. There are wild cats that roam the god-roads, green-eyed, unafraid of man. At night they wail like demons but they are not demons. The wild dogs are more dangerous, for they hunt in a pack, but them I did not meet till later. Everywhere there are the carved stones, carved with magical numbers or words.

I went North—I did not try to hide myself. When a god or a demon saw me, then I would die, but meanwhile I was no longer afraid. My hunger for knowledge burned in me—there was so much that I could not understand. After awhile, I knew that my belly was hungry. I could have hunted for my meat, but I did not hunt. It is known that the gods did not hunt as we do —they got their food from enchanted boxes and jars. Sometimes these are still found in the Dead Places— once, when I was a child and foolish, I opened such a jar and tasted it and found the food sweet. But my father found out and punished me for it strictly, for, often, that food is death. Now, though, I had long gone past what was forbidden, and I entered the likeliest towers, looking for the food of the gods.

I found it at last in the ruins of a great temple in the mid-city. A mighty temple it must have been, for the roof was painted like the sky at night with its stars —that much I could see, though the colors were faint and dim. It went down into great caves and tunnels— perhaps they kept their slaves there. But when I started to climb down, I heard the squeaking of rats, so I did not go—rats are unclean, and there must have been many tribes of them, from the squeaking. But near there, I found food, in the heart of a ruin, behind a door that still opened. I ate only the fruits from the jars —they had a very sweet taste. There was drink, too, in bottles of glass—the drink of the gods was strong and made my head swim. After I had eaten and drunk, I slept on the top of a stone, my bow at my side.

When I woke, the sun was low. Looking down from where I lay, I saw a dog sitting on his haunches. His tongue was hanging out of his mouth; he looked as if he were laughing. He was a big dog, with a grey-brown coat, as big as a wolf. I sprang up and shouted at him but he did not move—he just sat there as if he were laughing. I did not like that. When I reached for a stone to throw, he moved swiftly out of the way of the stone. He was not afraid of me; he looked at me as if I were meat. No doubt I could have killed him with an arrow, but I did not know if there were others. Moreover, night was falling.

I looked about me—not far away there was a great, broken god-road, leading North. The towers were high enough, but not so high, and while many of the dead-houses were wrecked, there were some that stood. I went toward this god-road, keeping to the heights of the ruins, while the dog followed. When I had reached the god-road, I saw that there were others behind him. If I had slept later, they would have come upon me asleep and torn out my throat. As it was, they were sure enough of me; they did not hurry. When I went into the dead-house, they kept watch at the entrance—doubt-less they thought they would have a fine hunt. But a dog cannot open a door and I knew, from the books, that the gods did not like to live on the ground but on high.

I had just found a door I could open when the dogs decided to rush. Ha! They were surprised when I shut the door in their faces—it was a good door, of strong metal. I could hear their foolish baying beyond it but I did not stop to answer them. I was in darkness—I found stairs and climbed. There were many stairs, turning around till my head was dizzy. At the top was another door—I found the knob and opened it. I was in a long small chamber—on one side of it was a bronze door that could not be opened, for it had no handle. Perhaps there was a magic word to open it but I did not have the word. I turned to the door in the opposite side of the wall. The lock of it was broken and I opened it and went in.

Within, there was a place of great riches. The god who lived there must have been a powerful god. The first room was a small ante-room—I waited there for some time, telling the spirits of the place that I came in peace and not as a robber. When it seemed to me that they had had time to hear me, I went on. Ah, what riches! Few, even, of the windows had been broken —it was all as it had been. The great windows that looked over the city had not been broken at all though they were dusty and streaked with many years. There were coverings on the floors, the colors not greatly faded, and the chairs were soft and deep. There were pictures upon the walls, very strange, very wonderful— I remember one of a bunch of flowers in a jar—if you came close to it, you could see nothing but bits of color, but if you stood away from it, the flowers might have been picked yesterday. It made my heart feel strange to look at this picture—and to look at the figure of a bird, in some hard clay, on a table and see it so like our birds. Everywhere there were books and writings, many in tongues that I could not read. The god who lived there must have been a wise god and full of knowledge. I felt I had right there, as I sought knowledge also.

Nevertheless, it was strange. There was a washing-place but no water—perhaps the gods washed in air. There was a cooking-place but no wood, and though there was a machine to cook food, there was no place to put fire in it. Nor were there candles or lamps— there were things that looked like lamps but they had neither oil nor wick. All these things were magic, but I touched them and lived—the magic had gone out of them. Let me tell one thing to show. In the washing-place, a thing said "Hot" but it was not hot to the touch—another thing said "Cold" but it was not cold. This must have been a strong magic but the magic was gone. I do not understand—they had ways—I wish that I knew.

It was close and dry and dusty in their house of the gods. I have said the magic was gone but that is not true—it had gone from the magic things but it had not gone from the place. I felt the spirits about me, weighing upon me. Nor had I ever slept in a Dead Place before—and yet, tonight, I must sleep there. When I thought of it, my tongue felt dry in my throat, in spite of my wish for knowledge. Almost I would have gone down again and faced the dogs, but I did not.

I had not gone through all the rooms when the darkness fell. When it fell, I went back to the big room looking over the city and made fire. There was a place to make fire and a box with wood in it, though I do not think they cooked there. I wrapped myself in a floor-covering and slept in front of the fire—I was very tired.

Now I tell what is very strong magic. I woke in the midst of the night. When I woke, the fire had gone out and I was cold. It seemed to me that all around me there were whisperings and voices. I closed my eyes to shut them out. Some will say that I slept again, but I do not think that I slept. I could feel the spirits drawing my spirit out of my body as a fish is drawn on a line.

Why should I lie about it? I am a priest and the son of a priest. If there are spirits, as they say, in the small Dead Places near us, what spirits must there not be in that great Place of the Gods? And would not they wish to speak? After such long years? I know that I felt myself drawn as a fish is drawn on a line. I had stepped out of my body—I could see my body asleep in front of the cold fire, but it was not I. I was drawn to look out upon the city of the gods.

It should have been dark, for it was night, but it was not dark. Everywhere there were lights—lines of light —circles and blurs of light—ten thousand torches would not have been the same. The sky itself was alight —you could barely see the stars for the glow in the sky. I thought to myself "This is strong magic" and trembled. There was a roaring in my ears like the rushing of rivers. Then my eyes grew used to the light and my ears to the sound. I knew that I was seeing the city as it had been when the gods were alive.

That was a sight indeed—yes, that was a sight: I could not have seen it in the body—my body would have died. Everywhere went the gods, on foot and in chariots—there were gods beyond number and counting and their chariots blocked the streets. They had turned night to day for their pleasure—they did not sleep with the sun. The noise of their coming and going was the noise of many waters. It was magic what they could do—it was magic what they did.

I looked out of another window—the great vines of their bridges were mended and the god-roads went East and West. Restless, restless, were the gods and always in motion! They burrowed tunnels under rivers—they flew in the air. With unbelievable tools they did giant works—no part of the earth was safe from them, for, if they wished for a thing, they summoned it from the other side of the world. And always, as they labored and rested, as they feasted and made love, there was a drum in their ears—the pulse of the giant city, beating and beating like a man's heart.

Were they happy? What is happiness to the gods? They were great, they were mighty, they were wonderful and terrible. As I looked upon them and their magic, I felt like a child—but a little more, it seemed to me, and they would pull down the moon from the sky. I saw them with wisdom beyond wisdom and knowledge beyond knowledge. And yet not all they did was well done—even I could see that—and yet their wisdom could not but grow until all was peace.

Then I saw their fate come upon them and that was terrible past speech. It came upon them as they walked the streets of their city. I have been in the fights with the Forest People—I have seen men die. But this was not like that. When gods war with gods, they use weapons we do not know. It was fire falling out of the

sky and a mist that poisoned. It was the time of the
Great Burning and the Destruction. They ran about
like ants in the streets of their city—poor gods, poor
gods! Then the towers began to fall. A few escaped—
yes, a few. The legends tell it. But, even after the city
had become a Dead Place, for many years the poison
was still in the ground. I saw it happen, I saw the last
of them die. It was darkness over the broken city and
I wept.

All this, I saw. I saw it as I have told it, though not
in the body. When I woke in the morning, I was
hungry, but I did not think first of my hunger for my
heart was perplexed and confused. I knew the reason for
the Dead Places but I did not see why it had happened.
It seemed to me it should not have happened, with all
the magic they had. I went through the house looking
for an answer. There was so much in the house I could
not understand—and yet I am a priest and the son of
a priest. It was like being on one side of the great river,
at night, with no light to show the way.

Then I saw the dead god. He was sitting in his chair,
by the window, in a room I had not entered before
and, for the first moment, I thought that he was alive.
Then I saw the skin on the back of his hand—it was
like dry leather. The room was shut, hot and dry—no
doubt that had kept him as he was. At first I was afraid
to approach him—then the fear left me. He was sitting
looking out over the city—he was dressed in the clothes
of the gods. His age was neither young nor old—I could
not tell his age. But there was wisdom in his face and
great sadness. You could see that he would have not
run away. He had sat at his window, watching his city

die—then he himself had died. But it is better to lose one's life than one's spirit—and you could see from the face that his spirit had not been lost. I knew, that, if I touched him, he would fall into dust—and yet, there was something unconquered in the face.

That is all of my story, for then I knew he was a man —I knew then that they had been men, neither gods nor demons. It is a great knowledge, hard to tell and believe. They were men—they went a dark road, but they were men. I had no fear after that—I had no fear going home, though twice I fought off the dogs and once I was hunted for two days by the Forest People. When I saw my father again, I prayed and was purified. He touched my lips and my breast, he said, "You went away a boy. You come back a man and a priest." I said, "Father, they were men! I have been in the Place of the Gods and seen it! Now slay me, if it is the law—but still I know they were men."

He looked at me out of both eyes. He said, "The law is not always the same shape—you have done what you have done. I could not have done it my time, but you come after me. Tell!"

I told and he listened. After that, I wished to tell all the people but he showed me otherwise. He said, "Truth is a hard deer to hunt. If you eat too much truth at once, you may die of the truth. It was not idly that our fathers forbade the Dead Places." He was right —it is better the truth should come little by little. I have learned that, being a priest. Perhaps, in the old days, they ate knowledge too fast.

Nevertheless, we make a beginning. It is not for the metal alone we go to the Dead Places now—there are the books and the writings. They are hard to learn. And the magic tools are broken—but we can look at them and wonder. At least, we make a beginning. And, when I am chief priest we shall go beyond the great river. We shall go to the Place of the Gods—the place new-york—not one man but a company. We shall look for the images of the gods and find the god ASHING and the others—the gods Licoln and Biltmore and Moses. But they were men who built the city, not gods or demons. They were men. I remember the dead man's face. They were men who were here before us. We must build again.

II

THE BLOOD OF THE MARTYRS

THE man who expected to be shot lay with his eyes open, staring at the upper left-hand corner of his cell. He was fairly well over his last beating, and they might come for him any time now. There was a yellow stain in the cell corner near the ceiling; he had liked it at first, then disliked it; now he was coming back to liking it again.

He could see it more clearly with his glasses on, but he only put on his glasses for special occasions now—the first thing in the morning, and when they brought the food in, and for interviews with the General. The lenses of the glasses had been cracked in a beating some months before, and it strained his eyes to wear them too long. Fortunately, in his present life he had very few occasions demanding clear vision. But, nevertheless, the accident to his glasses worried him, as it worries all near-sighted people. You put your glasses on the first thing in the morning and the world leaps into proportion; if it does not do so, something is wrong with the world.

The man did not believe greatly in symbols, but his chief nightmare, nowadays, was an endless one in which, suddenly and without warning, a large piece of glass would drop out of one of the lenses and he would grope around the cell, trying to find it. He would grope very carefully and gingerly, for hours of darkness, but the end was always the same—the small, unmistakable crunch of irreplaceable glass beneath his heel or his knee. Then he would wake up sweating, with his hands cold. This dream alternated with the one of being shot, but he found no great benefit in the change.

As he lay there, you could see that he had an intellectual head—the head of a thinker or a scholar, old and bald, with the big, domed brow. It was, as a matter of fact, a well-known head; it had often appeared in the columns of newspapers and journals, sometimes when the surrounding text was in a language Professor Malzius could not read. The body, though stooped and worn, was still a strong peasant body and capable of surviving a good deal of ill-treatment, as his captors had found out. He had fewer teeth than when he came to prison, and both the ribs and the knee had been badly set, but these were minor matters. It also occurred to him that his blood count was probably poor. However, if he could ever get out and to a first-class hospital, he was probably good for at least ten years more of work. But, of course, he would not get out. They would shoot him before that, and it would be over.

Sometimes he wished passionately that it would be over—tonight—this moment; at other times he was shaken by the mere blind fear of death. The latter he tried to treat as he would have treated an attack of malaria, knowing that it was an attack, but not always with success. He should have been able to face it better than most—he was Gregor Malzius, the scientist—but that did not always help. The fear of death persisted, even when one had noted and classified it as a purely physical reaction. When he was out of here, he would be able to write a very instructive little paper on the fear of death. He could even do it here, if he had writing materials, but there was no use asking for those. Once they had been given him and he had spent two days quite happily. But they had torn up the work and spat upon it in front of his face. It was a childish thing to do, but it discouraged a man from working.

It seemed odd that he had never seen anybody shot, but he never had. During the war, his reputation and his bad eyesight had exempted him from active service. He had been bombed a couple of times when his reserve battalion was guarding the railway bridge, but that was quite different. You were not tied to a stake, and the airplanes were not trying to kill you as an individual. He knew the place where it was done here, of course. But prisoners did not see the executions, they merely heard, if the wind was from the right quarter.

He had tried again and again to visualize how it would be, but it always kept mixing with an old steel engraving he had seen in boyhood—the execution of William Walker, the American filibuster, in Honduras. William Walker was a small man with a white semi-Napoleonic face. He was standing, very correctly dressed, in front of an open grave, and before him a ragged line of picturesque natives were raising their muskets. When he was shot he would instantly and tidily fall into the grave, like a man dropping through a trap door; as a boy, the extreme neatness of the arrangement had greatly impressed Gregor Malzius. Behind the wall there were palm trees, and, somewhere off to the right, blue and warm, the Caribbean Sea. It would not be like that at all, for his own execution; and yet, whenever he thought of it, he thought of it as being like that.

Well, it was his own fault. He could have accepted the new regime; some respectable people had done that. He could have fled the country; many honorable people had. A scientist should be concerned with the eternal, not with transient political phenomena; and a scientist should be able to live anywhere. But thirty years at the university were thirty years, and, after all, he was Malzius, one of the first biochemists in the world. To the last, he had not believed that they would touch him. Well, he had been wrong about that.

The truth, of course, was the truth. One taught it or one did not teach it. If one did not teach it, it hardly mattered what one did. But he had no quarrel with any established government; he was willing to run up a flag every Tuesday, as long as they let him alone. Most people were fools, and one government was as good as another for them—it had taken them twenty years to accept his theory of cell mutation. Now, if he'd been like his friend Bonnard—a fellow who signed protests, attended meetings for the cause of world peace, and generally played the fool in public—they'd have had some reason to complain. An excellent man in his field, Bonnard—none better—but, outside of it, how deplorably like an actor, with his short gray beard, his pink cheeks and his impulsive enthusiasms! Any government could put a fellow like Bonnard in prison—though it would be an injury to science and, therefore, wrong. For that matter, he thought grimly, Bonnard would enjoy being a martyr. He'd walk gracefully to the execution post with a begged cigarette in his mouth, and some theatrical last quip. But Bonnard was safe in his own land —doubtless writing heated and generous articles on The Case of Professor Malzius—and he, Malzius, was the man who was going to be shot. He would like a cigarette, too, on his way to execution; he had not smoked in five months. But he certainly didn't intend to ask for one, and they wouldn't think of offering him any. That was the difference between him and Bonnard.

His mind went back with longing to the stuffy laboratory and stuffier lecture hall at the university; his feet yearned for the worn steps he had climbed ten thousand times, and his eyes for the long steady look through the truthful lens into worlds too tiny for the unaided eye. They had called him "The Bear" and "Old Prickly," but they had fought to work under him, the best of the young men. They said he would explain the Last Judgment in terms of cellular phenomena, but they had crowded to his lectures. It was Williams, the Englishman, who had made up the legend that he carried a chocolate éclair and a set of improper post cards in his battered brief case. Quite untrue, of course— chocolate always made him ill, and he had never looked at an improper post card in his life. And Williams would never know that he knew the legend, too; for Williams had been killed long ago in the war. For a moment, Professor Malzius felt blind hate at the thought of an excellent scientific machine like Williams being smashed in a war. But blind hate was an improper emotion for a scientist, and he put it aside.

He smiled grimly again; they hadn't been able to break up his classes—lucky he was The Bear! He'd seen

one colleague hooted from his desk by a band of deter-
mined young hoodlums—too bad, but if a man couldn't
keep order in his own classroom, he'd better get out.
They'd wrecked his own laboratory, but not while he
was there.

It was so senseless, so silly. "In God's name," he said
reasonably, to no one, "what sort of conspirator do you
think I would make? A man of my age and habits! I
am interested in cellular phenomena!" And yet they
were beating him because he would not tell about the
boys. As if he had even paid attention to half the nonsense! There were certain passwords and greetings—a
bar of music you whistled, entering a restaurant; the
address of a firm that specialized, ostensibly, in vacuum
cleaners. But they were not his own property. They
belonged to the young men who had trusted The Bear.
He did not know what half of them meant, and the one
time he had gone to a meeting, he had felt like a fool.
For they were fools and childish—playing the childish
games of conspiracy that people like Bonnard enjoyed.
Could they even make a better world than the present?
He doubted it extremely. And yet, he could not betray
them; they had come to him, looking over their shoulders, with darkness in their eyes.

A horrible, an appalling thing—to be trusted. He
had no wish to be a guide and counselor of young men.
He wanted to do his work. Suppose they were poor and
ragged and oppressed; he had been a peasant himself,
he had eaten black bread. It was by his own efforts that
he was Professor Malzius. He did not wish the confidences of boys like Gregopolous and the others—for,
after all, what was Gregopolous? An excellent and un-

tiring laboratory assistant—and a laboratory assistant he would remain to the end of his days. He had pattered about the laboratory like a fox terrier, with a fox terrier's quick bright eyes. Like a devoted dog, he had made a god of Professor Malzius. "I don't want your problems, man. I don't want to know what you are doing outside the laboratory." But Gregopolous had brought his problems and his terrible trust none the less, humbly and proudly, like a fox terrier with a bone. After that—well, what was a man to do?

He hoped they would get it over with, and quickly. The world should be like a chemical formula, full of reason and logic. Instead, there were all these young men, and their eyes. They conspired, hopelessly and childishly, for what they called freedom against the new regime. They wore no overcoats in winter and were often hunted and killed. Even if they did not conspire, they had miserable little love affairs and ate the wrong food—yes, even before, at the university, they had been the same. Why the devil would they not accept? Then they could do their work. Of course, a great many of them would not be allowed to accept—they had the wrong ideas or the wrong politics—but then they could run away. If Malzius, at twenty, had had to run from his country, he would still have been a scientist. To talk of a free world was a delusion; men were not free in the world. Those who wished got a space of time to get their work done. That was all. And yet, he had not accepted—he did not know why.

Now he heard the sound of steps along the corridor. His body began to quiver and the places where he had been beaten hurt him. He noted it as an interesting reflex. Sometimes they merely flashed the light in the cell and passed by. On the other hand, it might be death. It was a hard question to decide.

The lock creaked, the door opened. "Get up, Malzius!" said the hard, bright voice of the guard. Gregor Malzius got up, a little stiffly, but quickly.

"Put on your glasses, you old fool!" said the guard, with a laugh. "You are going to the General."

Professor Malzius found the stone floors of the corridor uneven, though he knew them well enough. Once or twice the guard struck him, lightly and without malice, as one strikes an old horse with a whip. The blows were familiar and did not register on Professor Malzius' consciousness; he merely felt proud of not stumbling. He was apt to stumble; once he had hurt his knee.

He noticed, it seemed to him, an unusual tenseness and officiousness about his guard. Once, even, in a brightly lighted corridor the guard moved to strike him, but refrained. However, that, too, happened occasionally, with one guard or another, and Professor Malzius merely noted the fact. It was a small fact, but an important one in the economy in which he lived.

But there could be no doubt that something unusual was going on in the castle. There were more guards than usual, many of them strangers. He tried to think, carefully, as he walked, if it could be one of the new national holidays. It was hard to keep track of them all. The General might be in a good humor. Then they would merely have a cat-and-mouse conversation for half an hour and nothing really bad would happen.

Once, even, there had been a cigar. Professor Malzius, the scientist, licked his lips at the thought.

Now he was being turned over to a squad of other guards, with salutings. This was really unusual; Professor Malzius bit his mouth, inconspicuously. He had the poignant distrust of a monk or an old prisoner at any break in routine. Old prisoners are your true conservatives; they only demand that the order around them remains exactly the same.

It alarmed him as well that the new guards did not laugh at him. New guards almost always laughed when they saw him for the first time. He was used to the laughter and missed it—his throat felt dry. He would have liked, just once, to eat at the university restaurant before he died. It was bad food, ill cooked and starchy, food good enough for poor students and professors, but he would have liked to be there, in the big smoky room that smelt of copper boilers and cabbage, with a small cup of bitter coffee before him and a cheap cigarette. He did not ask for his dog or his notebooks, the old photographs in his bedroom, his incomplete experiments or his freedom. Just to lunch once more at the university restaurant and have people point out The Bear. It seemed a small thing to ask, but of course it was quite impossible.

"Halt!" said a voice, and he halted. There were, for the third time, salutings. Then the door of the General's office opened and he was told to go in.

He stood, just inside the door, in the posture of attention, as he had been taught. The crack in the left lens of his glasses made a crack across the room, and his eyes were paining him already, but he paid no attention to that. There was the familiar figure of the General, with his air of a well-fed and extremely healthy tomcat, and there was another man, seated at the General's desk. He could not see the other man very well—the crack made him bulge and waver—but he did not like his being there.

"Well, professor," said the General, in an easy, purring voice.

Malzius's entire body jerked. He had made a fearful, an unpardonable omission. He must remedy it at once. "Long live the state," he shouted in a loud thick voice, and saluted. He knew, bitterly, that his salute was ridiculous and that he looked ridiculous, making it. But perhaps the General would laugh—he had done so before. Then everything would be all right, for it was not quite as easy to beat a man after you had laughed at him.

The General did not laugh. He made a half turn instead, toward the man at the desk. The gesture said, "You see, he is well trained." It was the gesture of a man of the world, accustomed to deal with unruly peasants and animals—the gesture of a man fitted to be General.

The man at the desk paid no attention to the General's gesture. He lifted his head, and Malzius saw him more clearly and with complete unbelief. It was not a man but a picture come alive. Professor Malzius had seen the picture a hundred times; they had made him salute and take off his hat in front of it, when he had had a hat. Indeed, the picture had presided over his beatings. The man himself was a little smaller, but the picture was a good picture. There were many dictators in the world, and this was one type. The face was white, beaky and semi-Napoleonic; the lean, military body sat squarely in its chair. The eyes dominated the face, and the mouth was rigid. I remember also a hypnotist, and a woman Charcot showed me, at his clinic in Paris, thought Professor Malzius. But there is also, obviously, an endocrine unbalance. Then his thoughts stopped.

"Tell the man to come closer," said the man at the desk. "Can he hear me? Is he deaf?"

"No, Your Excellency," said the General, with enormous, purring respect. "But he is a little old, though perfectly healthy. . . . Are you not, Professor Malzius?"

"Yes, I am perfectly healthy. I am very well treated here," said Professor Malzius, in his loud thick voice. They were not going to catch him with traps like that, not even by dressing up somebody as the Dictator. He fixed his eyes on the big old-fashioned inkwell on the General's desk—that, at least, was perfectly sane.

"Come closer," said the man at the desk to Professor Malzius, and the latter advanced till he could almost touch the inkwell with his fingers. Then he stopped with a jerk, hoping he had done right. The movement removed the man at the desk from the crack in his lenses, and Professor Malzius knew suddenly that it was true. This was, indeed, the Dictator, this man with the rigid mouth. He began to talk.

"I have been very well treated here and the General has acted with the greatest consideration," he said. "But I am Professor Gregor Malzius—professor of biochemistry. For thirty years I have lectured at the university; I am a fellow of the Royal Society, a corresponding member of the Academy of Sciences at Berlin, at Rome,

at Boston, at Paris and Stockholm. I have received the
Nottingham Medal, the Lamarck Medal, the Order of
St. John of Portugal and the Nobel Prize. I think my
blood count is low, but I have received a great many
degrees and my experiments on the migratory cells are
not finished. I do not wish to complain of my treatment,
but I must continue my experiments."

He stopped, like a clock that has run down, surprised to hear the sound of his own voice. He noted,
in one part of his mind, that the General had made a
move to silence him, but had himself been silenced
by the Dictator.

"Yes, Professor Malzius," said the man at the desk,
in a harsh, toneless voice. "There has been a regrettable
error." The rigid face stared at Professor Malzius. Professor Malzius stared back. He did not say anything.

"In these days," said the Dictator, his voice rising,
"the nation demands the submission of every citizen.
Encircled by jealous foes, our reborn land yet steps
forward toward her magnificent destiny." The words
continued for some time, the voice rose and fell. Professor Malzius listened respectfully; he had heard the
words many times before and they had ceased to have
meaning to him. He was thinking of certain cells of
the body that rebel against the intricate processes of
Nature and set up their own bellicose state. Doubtless
they, too, have a destiny, he thought, but in medicine
it is called cancer.

"Jealous and spiteful tongues in other countries
have declared that it is our purpose to wipe out learning and science," concluded the Dictator. "That is not
our purpose. After the cleansing, the rebirth. We mean

to move forward to the greatest science in the world—our own science, based on the enduring principles of our nationhood." He ceased abruptly, his eyes fell into their dream. Very like the girl Charcot showed me in my young days, thought Professor Malzius; there was first the ebullition, then the calm.

"I was part of the cleansing? You did not mean to hurt me?" he asked timidly.

"Yes, Professor Malzius," said the General, smiling, "you were part of the cleansing. Now that is over. His Excellency has spoken."

"I do not understand," said Professor Malzius, gazing at the fixed face of the man behind the desk.

"It is very simple," said the General. He spoke in a slow careful voice, as one speaks to a deaf man or a child. "You are a distinguished man of science—you have received the Nobel Prize. That was a service to the state. You became, however, infected by the wrong political ideas. That was treachery to the state. You had, therefore, as decreed by His Excellency, to pass through a certain period for probation and rehabilitation. But that, we believe, is finished."

"You do not wish to know the names of the young men any more?" said Professor Malzius. "You do not want the addresses?"

"That is no longer of importance," said the General patiently. "There is no longer opposition. The leaders were caught and executed three weeks ago."

"There is no longer opposition," repeated Professor Malzius.

"At the trial, you were not even involved."

"I was not even involved," said Professor Malzius. "Yes."

"Now," said the General, with a look at the Dictator, "we come to the future. I will be frank—the new state is frank with its citizens."

"It is so," said the Dictator, his eyes still sunk in his dream.

"There has been—let us say—a certain agitation in foreign countries regarding Professor Malzius," said the General, his eyes still fixed on the Dictator. "That means nothing, of course. Nevertheless, your acquaintance, Professor Bonnard, and others have meddled in matters that do not concern them."

"They asked after me?" said Professor Malzius, with surprise. "It is true, my experiments were reaching a point that——"

"No foreign influence could turn us from our firm purpose," said the Dictator. "But it is our firm purpose to show our nation first in science and culture as we have already shown her first in manliness and statehood. For that reason, you are here, Professor Malzius." He smiled.

Professor Malzius stared. His cheeks began to tremble.

"I do not understand," said Professor Malzius. "You will give me my laboratory back?"

"Yes," said the Dictator, and the General nodded as one nods to a stupid child.

Professor Malzius passed a hand across his brow.

"My post at the university?" he said. "My experiments?"

"It is the purpose of our regime to offer the fullest

encouragement to our loyal sons of science," said the Dictator.

"First of all," said Professor Malzius, "I must go to a hospital. My blood count is poor. But that will not take long." His voice had become impatient and his eyes glowed. "Then—my notebooks were burned, I suppose. That was silly, but we can start in again. I have a very good memory, an excellent memory. The theories are in my head, you know," and he tapped it. "I must have assistants, of course; little Gregopolous was my best one——"

"The man Gregopolous has been executed," said the General, in a stern voice. "You had best forget him."

"Oh," said Professor Malzius. "Well, then, I must have someone else. You see, these are important experiments. There must be some young men—clever ones— they cannot all be dead. I will know them." He laughed a little, nervously. "The Bear always got the pick of the crop," he said. "They used to call me The Bear, you know." He stopped and looked at them for a moment with ghastly eyes. "You are not fooling me?" he said. He burst into tears.

When he recovered he was alone in the room with the General. The General was looking at him as he himself had looked once at strange forms of life under the microscope, with neither disgust nor attraction, but with great interest.

"His Excellency forgives your unworthy suggestion," he said. "He knows you are overwrought."

"Yes," said Professor Malzius. He sobbed once and dried his glasses.

"Come, come," said the General, with a certain bluff

heartiness. "We mustn't have our new president of the
National Academy crying. It would look badly in the
photographs."

"President of the Academy?" said Professor Malzius
quickly. "Oh, no; I mustn't be that. They make
speeches; they have administrative work. But I am a
scientist, a teacher."

"I'm afraid you can't very well avoid it," said the
General, still heartily, though he looked at Professor
Malzius. "Your induction will be quite a ceremony.
His Excellency himself will preside. And you will speak
on the new glories of our science. It will be a magnificent answer to the petty and jealous criticisms of our
neighbors. Oh, you needn't worry about the speech,"
he added quickly. "It will be prepared; you will only
have to read it. His Excellency thinks of everything."

"Very well," said Professor Malzius; "and then may
I go back to my work?"

"Oh, don't worry about that," said the General,
smiling. "I'm only a simple soldier; I don't know about
those things. But you'll have plenty of work."

"The more the better," said Malzius eagerly. "I still
have ten good years."

He opened his mouth to smile, and a shade of dis-
may crossed the General's face.

"Yes," he said, as if to himself. "The teeth must be
attended to. At once. And a rest, undoubtedly, before
the photographs are taken. Milk. You are feeling suffi-
ciently well, Professor Malzius?"

"I am very happy," said Professor Malzius. "I have
been very well treated and I come of peasant stock."

"Good," said the General. He paused for a moment, and spoke in a more official voice.

"Of course, it is understood, Professor Malzius——" he said.

"Yes?" said Professor Malzius. "I beg your pardon. I was thinking of something else."

"It is understood, Professor Malzius," repeated the General, "that your—er—rehabilitation in the service of the state is a permanent matter. Naturally, you will be under observation, but, even so, there must be no mistake."

"I am a scientist," said Professor Malzius impatiently. "What have I to do with politics? If you wish me to take oaths of loyalty, I will take as many as you wish."

"I am glad you take that attitude," said the General, though he looked at Professor Malzius curiously. "I may say that I regret the unpleasant side of our interviews. I trust you bear no ill will."

"Why should I be angry?" said Professor Malzius. "You were told to do one thing. Now you are told to do another. That is all."

"It is not quite so simple as that," said the General rather stiffly. He looked at Professor Malzius for a third time. "And I'd have sworn you were one of the stiff-necked ones," he said. "Well, well, every man has his breaking point, I suppose. In a few moments you will receive the final commands of His Excellency. Tonight you will go to the capitol and speak over the radio. You will have no difficulty there—the speech is written. But it will put a quietus on the activities of our friend Bonnard and the question that has been raised in the

British Parliament. Then a few weeks of rest by the sea and the dental work, and then, my dear president of the National Academy, you will be ready to undertake your new duties. I congratulate you and hope we shall meet often under pleasant auspices." He bowed from the waist to Malzius, the bow of a man of the world, though there was still something feline in his mustaches. Then he stood to attention, and Malzius, too, for the Dictator had come into the room.

"It is settled?" said the Dictator. "Good. Gregor Malzius, I welcome you to the service of the new state. You have cast your errors aside and are part of our destiny."

"Yes," said Professor Malzius, "I will be able to do my work now."

The Dictator frowned a little.

"You will not only be able to continue your invaluable researches," he said, "but you will also be able—and it will be part of your duty—to further our national ideals. Our reborn nation must rule the world for the world's good. There is a fire within us that is not in other stocks. Our civilization must be extended everywhere. The future wills it. It will furnish the subject of your first discourse as president of the Academy."

"But," said Professor Malzius, in a low voice, "I am not a soldier. I am a biochemist. I have no experience in these matters you speak of."

The Dictator nodded. "You are a distinguished man of science," he said. "You will prove that our women must bear soldiers, our men abandon this nonsense of republics and democracies for trust in those born to rule them. You will prove by scientific law that certain races—our race in particular—are destined to rule the world. You will prove they are destined to rule by the virtues of war, and that war is part of our heritage."

"But," said Professor Malzius, "it is not like that. I mean," he said, "one looks and watches in the laboratory. One waits for a long time. It is a long process, very long. And then, if the theory is not proved, one discards the theory. That is the way it is done. I probably do not explain it well. But I am a biochemist; I do not know how to look for the virtues of one race against another, and I can prove nothing about war, except that it kills. If I said anything else, the whole world would laugh at me."

"Not one in this nation would laugh at you," said the Dictator.

"But if they do not laugh at me when I am wrong, there is no science," said Professor Malzius, knotting his brows. He paused. "Do not misunderstand me," he said earnestly. "I have ten years of good work left; I want to get back to my laboratory. But, you see, there are the young men—if I am to teach the young men."

He paused again, seeing their faces before him. There were many. There was Williams, the Englishman, who had died in the war, and little Gregopolous with the fox-terrier eyes. There were all who had passed through his classrooms, from the stupidest to the best. They had shot little Gregopolous for treason, but that did not alter the case. From all over the world they had come—he remembered the Indian student and the Chinese. They wore cheap overcoats, they were hungry for knowledge, they ate the bad, starchy food of the poor restaurants, they had miserable little love affairs and played childish games of politics, instead of doing their work. Nevertheless, a few were promising—all must be given the truth. It did not matter if they died, but they must be given the truth. Otherwise there could be no continuity and no science.

He looked at the Dictator before him—yes, it was a hysteric face. He would know how to deal with it in his classroom—but such faces should not rule countries or young men. One was willing to go through a great many meaningless ceremonies in order to do one's work—wear a uniform or salute or be president of the Academy. That did not matter; it was part of the due to Caesar. But not to tell lies to young men on one's own subject. After all, they had called him The Bear and said he carried improper post cards in his brief case. They had given him their terrible confidence— not for love or kindness, but because they had found him honest. It was too late to change.

The Dictator looked sharply at the General. "I thought this had been explained to Professor Malzius," he said.

"Why, yes," said Professor Malzius. "I will sign any papers. I assure you I am not interested in politics— a man like myself, imagine! One state is as good as another. And I miss my tobacco—I have not smoked in five months. But, you see, one cannot be a scientist and tell lies."

He looked at the two men.

"What happens if I do not?" he said, in a low voice. But, looking at the Dictator, he had his answer. It was a fanatic face.

"Why, we shall resume our conversations, Professor Malzius," said the General, with a simper.

"Then I shall be beaten again," said Professor Malzius. He stated what he knew to be a fact.

"The process of rehabilitation is obviously not quite complete," said the General, "but perhaps, in time——"

"It will not be necessary," said Professor Malzius. "I cannot be beaten again." He stared wearily around the room. His shoulders straightened—it was so he had looked in the classroom when they had called him The Bear. "Call your other officers in," he said in a clear voice. "There are papers for me to sign. I should like them all to witness."

"Why——" said the General. "Why——" He looked doubtfully at the Dictator.

An expression of gratification appeared on the lean, semi-Napoleonic face. A white hand, curiously limp, touched the hand of Professor Malzius.

"You will feel so much better, Gregor," said the hoarse, tense voice. "I am so very glad you have given in."

"Why, of course, I give in," said Gregor Malzius. "Are you not the Dictator? And besides, if I do not, I shall be beaten again. And I cannot—you understand? —I cannot be beaten again."

He paused, breathing a little. But already the room was full of other faces. He knew them well, the hard faces of the new regime. But youthful some of them too.

The Dictator was saying something with regard to

receiving the distinguished scientist, Professor Gregor Malzius, into the service of the state.

"Take the pen," said the General in an undertone. "The inkwell is there, Professor Malzius. Now you may sign."

Professor Malzius stood, his fingers gripping the big, old-fashioned inkwell. It was full of ink—the servants of the Dictator were very efficient. They could shoot small people with the eyes of fox terriers for treason, but their trains arrived on time and their inkwells did not run dry.

"The state," he said, breathing. "Yes. But science does not know about states. And you are a little man— a little, unimportant man."

Then, before the General could stop him, he had picked up the inkwell and thrown it in the Dictator's face. The next moment the General's fist caught him on the side of the head and he fell behind the desk to the floor. But lying there, through his cracked glasses, he could still see the grotesque splashes of ink on the Dictator's face and uniform, and the small cut above his eye where the blood was gathering. They had not fired; he had thought he would be too close to the Dictator for them to fire in time.

"Take that man out and shoot him. At once," said the Dictator in a dry voice. He did not move to wipe the stains from his uniform—and for that Professor Malzius admired him. They rushed then, each anxious to be first. But Professor Malzius made no resistance.

As he was being hustled along the corridors, he fell now and then. On the second fall, his glasses were broken completely, but that did not matter to him. They were in a great hurry, he thought, but all the better—one did not have to think while one could not see.

Now and then he heard his voice make sounds of discomfort, but his voice was detached from himself. There was little Gregopolous—he could see him very plainly—and Williams, with his fresh English coloring —and all the men whom he had taught.

He had given them nothing but work and the truth; they had given him their terrible trust. If he had been beaten again, he might have betrayed them. But he had avoided that.

He felt a last weakness—a wish that someone might know. They would not, of course; he would have died of typhoid in the castle and there would be regretful notices in the newspapers. And then he would be forgotten, except for his work, and that was as it should be. He had never thought much of martyrs—hysterical people in the main. Though he'd like Bonnard to have known about the ink; it was in the coarse vein of humor that Bonnard could not appreciate. But then, he was a peasant; Bonnard had often told him so.

They were coming out into an open courtyard now; he felt the fresh air of outdoors. "Gently," he said. "A little gently. What's the haste?" But already they were tying him to the post. Someone struck him in the face and his eyes watered. "A schoolboy covered with ink," he muttered through his lost teeth. "A hysterical schoolboy too. But you cannot kill truth."

They were not good last words, and he knew that

they were not. He must try to think of better ones—
not shame Bonnard. But now they had a gag in his
mouth; just as well; it saved him the trouble.

His body ached, bound against the post, but his
sight and his mind were clearer. He could make out the
evening sky, gray with fog, the sky that belonged to no
country, but to all the world.

He could make out the gray high buttress of the
castle. They had made it a jail, but it would not always
be a jail. Perhaps in time it would not even exist. But
if a little bit of truth were gathered, that would always
exist, while there were men to remember and redis-
cover it. It was only the liars and the cruel who always
failed.

Sixty years ago, he had been a little boy, eating black
bread and thin cabbage soup in a poor house. It had
been a bitter life, but he could not complain of it. He
had had some good teachers and they had called him
The Bear.

The gag hurt his mouth—they were getting ready
now. There had been a girl called Anna once; he had
almost forgotten her. And his rooms had smelt a certain way and he had had a dog. It did not matter what
they did with the medals. He raised his head and
looked once more at the gray foggy sky. In a moment
there would be no thought, but, while there was
thought, one must remember and note. His pulse rate
was lower than he would have expected and his breathing oddly even, but those were not the important
things. The important thing was beyond, in the gray
sky that had no country, in the stones of the earth and

the feeble human spirit. The important thing was truth.

"Ready!" called the officer. "Aim! Fire!" But Professor Malzius did not hear the three commands of the officer. He was thinking about the young men.

THE KING OF THE CATS

"B UT, my *dear*," said Mrs. Culverin, with a tiny
gasp, "you can't actually mean—a *tail!*"

Mrs. Dingle nodded impressively. "Exactly. I've seen
him. Twice. Paris, of course, and then, a command
appearance at Rome—we were in the Royal box. He
conducted—my dear, you've never heard such effects
from an orchestra—and, my dear," she hesitated slightly,
"he conducted *with it.*"

"How perfectly, fascinatingly too horrid for words!"
said Mrs. Culverin in a dazed but greedy voice. "We
must have him to dinner as soon as he comes over—
he is coming over, isn't he?"

"The twelfth," said Mrs. Dingle with a gleam in her
eyes. "The New Symphony people have asked him to be
guest-conductor for three special concerts—I do hope
you can dine with *us* some night while he's here—he'll
be very busy, of course—but he's promised to give us
what time he can spare——"

"Oh, thank you, dear," said Mrs. Culverin, abstractedly, her last raid upon Mrs. Dingle's pet British novelist still fresh in her mind. "You're always so delight-
fully hospitable—but you mustn't wear yourself out—
the rest of us must do *our* part—I know Henry and
myself would be only too glad to——"

"That's very sweet of you, darling." Mrs. Dingle also

remembered the larceny of the British novelist. "But we're just going to give Monsieur Tibault—sweet name, isn't it! They say he's descended from the Tybalt in 'Romeo and Juliet' and that's why he doesn't like Shakespeare—we're just going to give Monsieur Tibault the simplest sort of time—a little reception after his first concert, perhaps. He hates," she looked around the table, "large, mixed parties. And then, of course, his— er—little idiosyncrasy——" she coughed delicately. "It makes him feel a trifle shy with strangers."

"But I don't understand yet, Aunt Emily," said Tommy Brooks, Mrs. Dingle's nephew. "Do you really mean this Tibault bozo has a tail? Like a monkey and everything?"

"Tommy dear," said Mrs. Culverin, crushingly, "in the first place Monsieur Tibault is not a bozo—he is a very distinguished musician—the finest conductor in Europe. And in the second place——"

"He has," Mrs. Dingle was firm. "He has a tail. He conducts with it."

"Oh, but honestly!" said Tommy, his ears pinkening. "I mean—of course, if you say so, Aunt Emily, I'm sure he has—but still, it sounds pretty steep, if you know what I mean! How about it, Professor Tatto?"

Professor Tatto cleared his throat. "Tck," he said, putting his fingertips together cautiously, "I shall be very anxious to see this Monsieur Tibault. For myself, I have never observed a genuine specimen of *homo caudatus,* so I should be inclined to doubt, and yet . . . In the Middle Ages, for instance, the belief in men— er—tailed or with caudal appendages of some sort, was both widespread and, as far as we can gather, well-

founded. As late as the Eighteenth Century, a Dutch
sea-captain with some character for veracity recounts
the discovery of a pair of such creatures in the island
of Formosa. They were in a low state of civilization, I
believe, but the appendages in question were quite distinct. And in 1860, Dr. Grimbrook, the English surgeon,
claims to have treated no less than three African natives
with short but evident tails—though his testimony rests
upon his unsupported word. After all, the thing is not
impossible, though doubtless unusual. Web feet—rudi-
mentary gills—these occur with some frequency. The
appendix we have with us always. The chain of our
descent from the ape-like form is by no means complete. For that matter," he beamed around the table,
"what can we call the last few vertebrae of the normal
spine but the beginnings of a concealed and rudimen-
tary tail? Oh, yes—yes—it's possible—quite—that in an
extraordinary case—a reversion to type—a survival—
though, of course——"

"I told you so," said Mrs. Dingle triumphantly.
"Isn't it fascinating? Isn't it, Princess?"

The Princess Vivrakanarda's eyes, blue as a field of
larkspur, fathomless as the centre of heaven, rested
lightly for a moment on Mrs. Dingle's excited counte-
nance.

"Ve-ry fascinating," she said, in a voice like stroked,
golden velvet. "I should like—I should like ve-ry much
to meet this Monsieur Tibault."

"Well, *I* hope he breaks his neck!" said Tommy
Brooks, under his breath—but nobody ever paid much
attention to Tommy.

Nevertheless as the time for Mr. Tibault's arrival

in these States drew nearer and nearer, people in gen·
eral began to wonder whether the Princess had spoken
quite truthfully—for there was no doubt of the fact
that, up till then, she had been the unique sensation
of the season—and you know what social lions and
lionesses are

It was, if you remember, a Siamese season, and genuine Siamese were at quite as much of a premium as
Russian accents had been in the quaint old days when
the Chauve-Souris was a novelty. The Siamese Art
Theatre, imported at terrific expense, was playing to
packed houses. "Gushuptzgu," an epic novel of Siamese
farm life, in nineteen closely-printed volumes, had just
been awarded the Nobel prize. Prominent pet-and-newt
dealers reported no cessation in the appalling demand
for Siamese cats. And upon the crest of this wave of
interest in things Siamese, the Princess Vivrakanarda
poised with the elegant nonchalance of a Hawaiian
water-baby upon its surfboard. She was indispensable.
She was incomparable. She was everywhere.

Youthful, enormously wealthy, allied on one hand
to the Royal Family of Siam and on the other to the
Cabots (and yet with the first eighteen of her twenty-
one years shrouded from speculation in a golden zone
of mystery), the mingling of races in her had produced
an exotic beauty as distinguished as it was strange. She
moved with a feline, effortless grace, and her skin was
as if it had been gently powdered with tiny grains of
the purest gold—yet the blueness of her eyes, set just
a trifle slantingly, was as pure and startling as the sea
on the rocks of Maine. Her brown hair fell to her
knees—she had been offered extraordinary sums by the

Master Barbers' Protective Association to have it shin-
gled. Straight as a waterfall tumbling over brown rocks,
it had a vague perfume of sandalwood and suave spices
and held tints of rust and the sun. She did not talk
very much—but then she did not have to—her voice
had an odd, small, melodious huskiness that haunted
the mind. She lived alone and was reputed to be very
lazy—at least it was known that she slept during most
of the day—but at night she bloomed like a moon-
flower and a depth came into her eyes.

It was no wonder that Tommy Brooks fell in love
with her. The wonder was that she let him. There
was nothing exotic or distinguished about Tommy—
he was just one of those pleasant, normal young men
who seem created to carry on the bond business by
reading the newspapers in the University Club during most of the day, and can always be relied upon at
night to fill an unexpected hole in a dinner-party. It
is true that the Princess could hardly be said to do more
than tolerate any of her suitors—no one had ever
seen those aloofly arrogant eyes enliven at the entrance
of any male. But she seemed to be able to tolerate
Tommy a little more than the rest—and that young
man's infatuated day-dreams were beginning to be beset
by smart solitaires and imaginary apartments on Park
Avenue, when the famous M. Tibault conducted his
first concert at Carnegie Hall.

Tommy Brooks sat beside the Princess. The eyes he
turned upon her were eyes of longing and love, but
her face was as impassive as a mask, and the only remark she made during the preliminary bustlings was

that there seemed to be a number of people in the audience. But Tommy was relieved, if anything, to find her even a little more aloof than usual, for, ever since Mrs. Culverin's dinner-party, a vague disquiet as to the possible impression which this Tibault creature might make upon her had been growing in his mind. It shows his devotion that he was present at all. To a man whose simple Princetonian nature found in "Just a Little Love, a Little Kiss," the quintessence of musical art, the average symphony was a positive torture, and he looked forward to the evening's programme itself with a grim, brave smile.

"Ssh!" said Mrs. Dingle, breathlessly. "He's coming!" It seemed to the startled Tommy as if he were suddenly back in the trenches under a heavy barrage, as M. Tibault made his entrance to a perfect bombardment of applause.

Then the enthusiastic noise was sliced off in the middle and a gasp took its place—a vast, windy sigh, as if every person in that multitude had suddenly said, "Ah." For the papers had not lied about him. The tail was there.

They called him theatric—but how well he understood the uses of theatricalism! Dressed in unrelieved black from head to foot (the black dress-shirt had been a special token of Mussolini's esteem), he did not walk on, he strolled, leisurely, easily, aloofly, the famous tail curled nonchalantly about one wrist—a suave, black panther lounging through a summer garden with that little mysterious weave of the head that panthers have when they pad behind bars—the glittering darkness of his eyes unmoved by any surprise or elation. He

nodded, twice, in regal acknowledgment, as the clap-
ping reached an apogee of frenzy. To Tommy there was
something dreadfully reminiscent of the Princess in the
way he nodded. Then he turned to his orchestra.

A second and louder gasp went up from the audience at this point, for, as he turned, the tip of that incredible tail twined with dainty carelessness into some
hidden pocket and produced a black baton. But Tommy
did not even notice. He was looking at the Princess
instead.

She had not even bothered to clap, at first, but now
—He had never seen her moved like this, never. She
was not applauding, her hands were clenched in her
lap, but her whole body was rigid, rigid as a steel bar,
and the blue flowers of her eyes were bent upon the
figure of M. Tibault in a terrible concentration. The
pose of her entire figure was so still and intense that
for an instant Tommy had the lunatic idea that any
moment she might leap from her seat beside him as
lightly as a moth, and land, with no sound, at M.
Tibault's side to—yes—to rub her proud head against
his coat in worship. Even Mrs. Dingle would notice in
a moment.

"Princess——" he said, in a horrified whisper,
"Princess——"

Slowly the tenseness of her body relaxed, her eyes
veiled again, she grew calm.

"Yes, Tommy?" she said, in her usual voice, but
there was still something about her . . .

"Nothing, only—oh, hang—he's starting!" said
Tommy, as M. Tibault, his hands loosely clasped before
him, turned and *faced* the audience. His eyes dropped,

his tail switched once impressively, then gave three little preliminary taps with his baton on the floor.

Seldom has Gluck's overture to "Iphigenie in Aulis" received such an ovation. But it was not until the Eighth Symphony that the hysteria of the audience reached its climax. Never before had the New Symphony played so superbly—and certainly never before had it been led with such genius. Three prominent conductors in the audience were sobbing with the despairing admiration of envious children toward the close, and one at least was heard to offer wildly ten thousand dollars to a well-known facial surgeon there present for a shred of evidence that tails of some variety could by any stretch of science be grafted upon a normally decaudate form. There was no doubt about it—no mortal hand and arm, be they ever so dexterous, could combine the delicate elan and powerful grace displayed in every gesture of M. Tibault's tail.

A sable staff, it dominated the brasses like a flicker of black lightning; an ebon, elusive whip, it drew the last exquisite breath of melody from the woodwinds and ruled the stormy strings like a magician's rod. M. Tibault bowed and bowed again—roar after roar of frenzied admiration shook the hall to its foundations—and when he finally staggered, exhausted, from the platform, the president of the Wednesday Sonata Club was only restrained by force from flinging her ninety-thousand-dollar string of pearls after him in an excess of aesthetic appreciation. New York had come and seen—and New York was conquered. Mrs. Dingle was immediately besieged by reporters, and Tommy Brooks looked forward to the "little party" at which he was to meet the new hero of the hour with feelings only a little less lugubrious than those that would have come to him just before taking his seat in the electric chair.

The meeting between his Princess and M. Tibault was worse and better than he expected. Better because, after all, they did not say much to each other—and worse because it seemed to him, somehow, that some curious kinship of mind between them made words unnecessary. They were certainly the most distinguished-looking couple in the room, as he bent over her hand. "So darlingly foreign, both of them, and yet so different," babbled Mrs. Dingle—but Tommy couldn't agree.

They were different, yes—the dark, lithe stranger with the bizarre appendage tucked carelessly in his pocket, and the blue-eyed, brown-haired girl. But that difference only accentuated what they had in common —something in the way they moved, in the suavity of their gestures, in the set of their eyes. Something deeper, even, than race. He tried to puzzle it out—then, looking around at the others, he had a flash of revelation. It was as if that couple were foreign, indeed—not only to New York but to all common humanity. As if they were polite guests from a different star.

Tommy did not have a very happy evening, on the whole. But his mind worked slowly, and it was not until much later that the mad suspicion came upon him in full force.

Perhaps he is not to be blamed for his lack of immediate comprehension. The next few weeks were weeks of bewildered misery for him. It was not that the Princess's attitude toward him had changed—she was just as tolerant of him as before, but M. Tibault was always there. He had a faculty of appearing as out of thin air —he walked, for all his height, as lightly as a butterfly—and Tommy grew to hate that faintest shuffle on the carpet that announced his presence.

And then, hang it all, the man was so smooth, so infernally, unrufflably smooth! He was never out of temper, never embarrassed. He treated Tommy with the extreme of urbanity, and yet his eyes mocked, deepdown, and Tommy could do nothing. And, gradually, the Princess became more and more drawn to this stranger, in a soundless communion that found little need for speech—and that, too, Tommy saw and hated, and that, too, he could not mend.

He began to be haunted not only by M. Tibault in the flesh, but by M. Tibault in the spirit. He slept badly, and when he slept, he dreamed—of M. Tibault, a man no longer, but a shadow, a spectre, the limber ghost of an animal whose words came purringly between sharp little pointed teeth. There was certainly something odd about the whole shape of the fellow— his fluid ease, the mould of his head, even the cut of his fingernails—but just what it was escaped Tommy's intensest cogitation. And when he did put his finger on it at length, at first he refused to believe.

A pair of petty incidents decided him, finally, against all reason. He had gone to Mrs. Dingle's, one winter afternoon, hoping to find the Princess. She was out with his aunt, but was expected back for tea, and he wandered idly into the library to wait. He was just about to switch on the lights, for the library was always dark even in summer, when he heard a sound of light breathing that seemed to come from the leather couch in the corner. He approached it cautiously and dimly made out the form of M. Tibault, curled up on the couch, peacefully asleep.

The sight annoyed Tommy so that he swore under his breath and was back near the door on his way out, when the feeling we all know and hate, the feeling that eyes we cannot see are watching us, arrested him. He turned back—M. Tibault had not moved a muscle of his body to all appearance—but his eyes were open now. And those eyes were black and human no longer. They were green—Tommy could have sworn it—and he could have sworn that they had no bottom and gleamed like little emeralds in the dark. It only lasted a moment, for Tommy pressed the light-button automatically—and there was M. Tibault, his normal self, yawning a little but urbanely apologetic, but it gave Tommy time to think. Nor did what happened a trifle later increase his peace of mind.

They had lit a fire and were talking in front of it— by now Tommy hated M. Tibault so thoroughly that he felt that odd yearning for his company that often occurs in such cases. M. Tibault was telling some anecdote and Tommy was hating him worse than ever for basking with such obvious enjoyment in the heat of the flames and the ripple of his own voice.

Then they heard the street-door open, and M. Tibault jumped up—and jumping, caught one sock on a sharp corner of the brass fire-rail and tore it open in a jagged flap. Tommy looked down mechanically at the tear—a second's glance, but enough—for M. Tibault, for the first time in Tommy's experience, lost his temper completely. He swore violently in some spitting, foreign tongue—his face distorted suddenly—he clapped his hand over his sock. Then, glaring furiously at Tommy, he fairly sprang from the room, and Tommy could hear him scaling the stairs in long, agile bounds.

Tommy sank into a chair, careless for once of the fact that he heard the Princess's light laugh in the hall. He didn't want to see the Princess. He didn't want to see anybody. There had been something revealed when M. Tibault had torn that hole in his sock—and it was not the skin of a man. Tommy had caught a glimpse of—black plush. Black velvet. And then had come M. Tibault's sudden explosion of fury. Good *Lord*—did the man wear black velvet stockings under his ordinary socks? Or could he—could he—but here Tommy held his fevered head in his hands.

He went to Professor Tatto that evening with a series of hypothetical questions, but as he did not dare confide his real suspicions to the Professor, the hypothetical answers he received served only to confuse him the more. Then he thought of Billy Strange. Billy was a good sort, and his mind had a turn for the bizarre. Billy might be able to help.

He couldn't get hold of Billy for three days and lived through the interval in a fever of impatience. But finally they had dinner together at Billy's apartment. where his queer books were, and Tommy was able to blurt out the whole disordered jumble of his suspicions.

Billy listened without interrupting until Tommy was quite through. Then he pulled at his pipe. "But, my dear *man*——" he said, protestingly.

"Oh, I know—I know——" said Tommy, and waved his hands, "I know I'm crazy—you needn't tell me that —but I tell you, the man's a cat all the same—no, I don't see how he could be, but he is—why, hang it, in the first place, everybody knows he's got a tail!"

"Even so," said Billy, puffing. "Oh, my dear Tommy, I don't doubt you saw, or think you saw, everything you say. But, even so——" He shook his head.

"But what about those other birds, werwolves and things?" said Tommy.

Billy looked dubious. "We-ll," he admitted, "you've got me there, of course. At least—a tailed man *is* possible. And the yarns about werwolves go back far enough, so that—well, I wouldn't say there aren't or haven't been werwolves—but then I'm willing to believe more things than most people. But a wer-cat— or a man that's a cat and a cat that's a man—honestly, Tommy——"

"If I don't get some real advice I'll go clean off my hinge. For Heaven's sake, tell me something to *do!*"

"Lemme think," said Billy. "First, you're pizen-sure this man is——"

"A cat. Yeah," and Tommy nodded violently.

"Check. And second—if it doesn't hurt your feelings, Tommy—you're afraid this girl you're in love with has—er—at least a streak of—felinity—in her— and so she's drawn to him?"

"Oh, Lord, Billy, if I only knew!"

"Well—er—suppose she really is, too, you know—would you still be keen on her?"

"I'd marry her if she turned into a dragon every Wednesday!" said Tommy, fervently.

Billy smiled. "H'm," he said, "then the obvious thing to do is to get rid of this M. Tibault. Lemme think."

He thought about two pipes full, while Tommy sat on pins and needles. Then, finally, he burst out laughing.

"What's so darn funny?" said Tommy, aggrievedly.

"Nothing, Tommy, only I've just thought of a stunt—something so blooming crazy—but if he is—h'm—what you think he is—it *might* work——" And, going to the bookcase, he took down a book.

"If you think you're going to quiet my nerves by reading me a bedtime story——"

"Shut up, Tommy, and listen to this—if you really want to get rid of your feline friend."

"What is it?"

"Book of Agnes Repplier's. About cats. Listen.

" 'There is also a Scandinavian version of the ever famous story which Sir Walter Scott told to Washington Irving, which Monk Lewis told to Shelley and which, in one form or another, we find embodied in the folklore of every land'—now, Tommy, pay attention—'the story of the traveller who saw within a ruined abbey, a procession of cats, lowering into a grave a little coffin with a crown upon it. Filled with horror, he hastened from the spot; but when he had reached his destination, he could not forbear relating to a friend the wonder he had seen. Scarcely had the tale been told when his friend's cat, who lay curled up tranquilly by the fire, sprang to its feet, cried out, "Then I am the King of the Cats!" and disappeared in a flash up the chimney.'

"Well?" said Billy, shutting the book.

"By gum!" said Tommy, staring. "By gum! Do you think there's a chance?"

"*I* think we're both in the booby-hatch. But if you want to try it——"

"Try it! I'll spring it on him the next time I see him. But—listen—I can't make it a ruined abbey——"

"Oh, use your imagination! Make it Central Park—anywhere. Tell it as if it happened to you—seeing the funeral procession and all that. You can lead into it somehow—let's see—some general line—oh, yes—'Strange, isn't it, how fact so often copies fiction. Why, only yesterday——' See?"

"Strange, isn't it, how fact so often copies fiction," repeated Tommy dutifully. "Why, only yesterday——"

"I happened to be strolling through Central Park when I saw something very odd."

"I happened to be strolling through—here, gimme that book!" said Tommy, "I want to learn the rest of it by heart!"

Mrs. Dingle's farewell dinner to the famous Monsieur Tibault, on the occasion of his departure for his Western tour, was looked forward to with the greatest expectations. Not only would everybody be there, including the Princess Vivrakanarda, but Mrs. Dingle, a hinter if there ever was one, had let it be known that at this dinner an announcement of very unusual interest to Society might be made. So everyone, for once, was almost on time, except for Tommy. He was at least fifteen minutes early, for he wanted to have speech with his aunt alone. Unfortunately, however, he had hardly taken off his overcoat when she was whispering some news in his ear so rapidly that he found it difficult to understand a word of it.

"And you mustn't breathe it to a soul!" she ended, beaming. "That is, not before the announcement—I think we'll have *that* with the salad—people never pay very much attention to salad———"

"Breathe what, Aunt Emily?" said Tommy, confused.

"The Princess, darling—the dear Princess and Monsieur Tibault—they just got engaged this afternoon, dear things! Isn't it *fascinating?*"

"Yeah," said Tommy, and started to walk blindly through the nearest door. His aunt restrained him.

"Not there, dear—not in the library. You can congratulate them later. They're just having a sweet little moment alone there now———" And she turned away to harry the butler, leaving Tommy stunned.

But his chin came up after a moment. He wasn't beaten yet.

"Strange, isn't it, how often fact copies fiction?" he repeated to himself in dull mnemonics, and, as he did so, he shook his fist at the library door.

Mrs. Dingle was wrong, as usual. The Princess and M. Tibault were not in the library—they were in the conservatory, as Tommy discovered when he wandered aimlessly past the glass doors.

He didn't mean to look, and after a second he turned away. But that second was enough.

Tibault was seated in a chair and she was crouched on a stool at his side, while his hand, softly, smoothly, stroked her brown hair. Black cat and Siamese kitten. Her face was hidden from Tommy, but he could see Tibault's face. And he could hear.

They were not talking, but there was a sound between them. A warm and contented sound like the murmur of giant bees in a hollow tree—a golden, musical rumble, deep-throated, that came from Tibault's lips and was answered by hers—a golden purr.

Tommy found himself back in the drawing-room, shaking hands with Mrs. Culverin, who said, frankly, that she had seldom seen him look so pale.

The first two courses of the dinner passed Tommy like dreams, but Mrs. Dingle's cellar was notable, and by the middle of the meat course, he began to come to himself. He had only one resolve now.

For the next few moments he tried desperately to break into the conversation, but Mrs. Dingle was talking, and even Gabriel will have a time interrupting Mrs. Dingle. At last, though, she paused for breath and Tommy saw his chance.

"Speaking of that," said Tommy, piercingly, without knowing in the least what he was referring to, "Speaking of that——"

"As I was saying," said Professor Tatto. But Tommy would not yield. The plates were being taken away. It was time for salad.

"Speaking of that," he said again, so loudly and strangely that Mrs. Culverin jumped and an awkward hush fell over the table. "Strange, isn't it, how often fact copies fiction?" There, he was started. His voice rose even higher. "Why, only to-day I was strolling through——" and, word for word, he repeated his lesson. He could see Tibault's eyes glowing at him, as he described the funeral. He could see the Princess, tense.

He could not have said what he had expected might happen when he came to the end; but it was not bored silence, everywhere, to be followed by Mrs. Dingle's acrid, "Well, Tommy, is that *quite* all?"

He slumped back in his chair, sick at heart. He was a fool and his last resource had failed. Dimly he heard his aunt's voice, saying, "Well, then——" and realized that she was about to make the fatal announcement.

But just then Monsieur Tibault spoke.

"One moment, Mrs. Dingle," he said, with extreme politeness, and she was silent. He turned to Tommy.

"You are—positive, I suppose, of what you saw this afternoon, Brooks?" he said, in tones of light mockery.

"Absolutely," said Tommy sullenly. "Do you think I'd——"

"Oh, no, no, no," Monsieur Tibault waved the implication aside, "but—such an interesting story—one likes to be sure of the details—and, of course, you *are* sure—*quite* sure—that the kind of crown you describe was on the coffin?"

"Of course," said Tommy, wondering, "but——"

"Then I'm the King of the Cats!" cried Monsieur Tibault in a voice of thunder, and, even as he cried it, the house-lights blinked—there was the soft thud of an explosion that seemed muffled in cotton-wool from the minstrel gallery—and the scene was lit for a second by an obliterating and painful burst of light that vanished in an instant and was succeeded by heavy, blinding clouds of white, pungent smoke.

"Oh, those *horrid* photographers," came Mrs. Dingle's voice in a melodious wail. "I *told* them not to take the flashlight picture till dinner was over, and now they've taken it *just* as I was nibbling lettuce!"

Someone tittered a little nervously. Someone coughed. Then, gradually the veils of smoke dislimned and the green-and-black spots in front of Tommy's eyes died away.

They were blinking at each other like people who have just come out of a cave into brilliant sun. Even yet their eyes stung with the fierceness of that abrupt illumination and Tommy found it hard to make out the faces across the table from him.

Mrs. Dingle took command of the half-blinded company with her accustomed poise. She rose, glass in hand. "And now, dear friends," she said in a clear voice, "I'm sure all of us are very happy to——" Then she stopped, open-mouthed, an expression of incredulous horror on her features. The lifted glass began to spill its contents on the tablecloth in a little stream of amber. As she spoke, she had turned directly to Monsieur Tibault's place at the table—and Monsieur Tibault was no longer there.

Some say there was a bursting flash of fire that disappeared up the chimney—some say it was a giant cat that leaped through the window at a bound, without breaking the glass. Professor Tatto puts it down to a mysterious chemical disturbance operating only over

M. Tibault's chair. The butler, who is pious, believes the devil in person flew away with him, and Mrs. Dingle hesitates between witchcraft and a malicious ectoplasm dematerializing on the wrong cosmic plane. But be that as it may, one thing is certain—in the instant of fictive darkness which followed the glare of the flashlight, Monsieur Tibault, the great conductor, disappeared forever from mortal sight, tail and all.

Mrs. Culverin swears he was an international burglar and that she was just about to unmask him, when he slipped away under cover of the flashlight smoke, but no one else who sat at that historic dinner-table believes her. No, there are no sound explanations, but Tommy thinks he knows, and he will never be able to pass a cat again without wondering.

Mrs. Tommy is quite of her husband's mind regarding cats—she was Gretchen Woolwine, of Chicago—for Tommy told her his whole story, and while she doesn't believe a great deal of it, there is no doubt in her heart that one person concerned in the affair was a *perfect* cat. Doubtless it would have been more romantic to relate how Tommy's daring finally won him his Princess—but, unfortunately, it would not be veracious. For the Princess Vivrakananda, also, is with us no longer. Her nerves, shattered by the spectacular denouement of Mrs. Dingle's dinner, required a sea-voyage, and from that voyage she has never returned to America.

Of course, there are the usual stories—one hears of her, a nun in a Siamese convent, or a masked dancer at Le Jardin de ma Soeur—one hears that she has been murdered in Patagonia or married in Trebizond—but, as far as can be ascertained, not one of these gaudy fables has the slightest basis of fact. I believe that Tommy, in his heart of hearts, is quite convinced that the sea-voyage was only a pretext, and that by some unheard-of means, she has managed to rejoin the formidable Monsieur Tibault, wherever in the world of the visible or the invisible he may be—in fact, that in some ruined city or subterranean palace they reign together now, King and Queen of all the mysterious Kingdom of Cats. But that, of course, is quite impossible.

A STORY BY ANGELA POE

I WAS a very young man in the publishing business at the time—even younger, I think, than most young men are nowadays, for this was before the war. Diana poised her bow at the sky above a Madison Square Garden that was actually on Madison Square—and some of the older men in our New York office still wore the paper sleeve-protectors and worn alpaca coats of an older day. There are young offices and old ones: brisk, shiny, bumptious new offices that positively buzz with expert inefficiency; and resigned, rather wistful little offices that have come to know they will never do well in the world. But the prevailing atmosphere of Thrushwood, Collins, and Co. was that of substantial tradition and solid worth. The faded carpet in the reception-room had been trodden by any number of famous feet—perhaps by not quite so many as I avouched to the young men of other publishers, but still the legends were there. Legends of Henry James and William Dean Howells and a young man from India named Kipling who was taken for a boy from the printer's and sent off with a flea in his ear. New authors were always greatly impressed by our atmosphere—until they looked over their contracts and discovered that even their Australian rights had, somehow or other, become the inalienable property of Thrushwood, Col-

lins, and Co. But then they had only to see Mr. Thrushwood to be convinced that their most successful works
were being published from a rigid sense of duty at a
distinct financial loss.

I had the desk that was farthest away from both
radiators and window, in the front office, so I broiled
in summer and froze in winter and was perfectly happy.
I was in New York, I was part of the making of books,
I saw celebrities, and every Sunday I wrote home about
it to my family. True, some of the celebrities were not
nearly so impressive in the flesh as in the print; but
that made me feel I was seeing Real Life at last. And
there was always Mr. Thrushwood, with his thin, worn,
cameo face and his white plume of hair, to restore my
faith in mankind. When he put his hand on my shoulder and said, "You're coming along nicely, Robbins,"
I felt an accolade. I did not discover until later that I
was doing three men's work, but, if I had known it,
then, I would not have cared. And when Randall Day,
of Harper's, irreverently alluded to us as "The Holy
Burglars," I flung the insinuation back in his teeth,
with an apt quotation about Philistines. For we talked
about Philistines, then.

As a matter of fact, we had an excellent list, on the
whole—for, though Mr. Thrushwood, like most successful publishers, hardly ever read a book, he had a
remarkable nose for the promising and the solid. On
the other hand, there were names which, as an idealist,
I boggled over—and the first and foremost of these was
Angela Poe. I could tolerate Caspar Breed and his lean-
jawed, stern-muscled cowboys with the hearts of little
children. I could stomach Jeremy Jason, the homespun

philosopher, whose small green ooze-leather booklets, "A Wayfarer's Creed," "A Wayfarer's Vow," "A Wayfarer's Hearthstone," produced much the same sensation in me as running a torn fingernail over heavy plush. Publishers must live, and other publishers had their Breeds and their Jasons. But Angela Poe was not merely an author—she was something like breakfast-food or chewing-gum, an American institution, untidy, inescapable, and vast. I could have forgiven her—and Thrushwood, Collins—if she had sold moderately well. But long ago, the New York Times had ceased to say anything about her except, "Another Angela Poe . . . sure to appeal to her huge audience . . ." before its painstaking resumé of the plot. I often wondered what unhappy reviewer wrote those resumés. For he must have had to read the books, from "Wanda of the Marshes" to "Ashes of Roses," and I did not see how that was possible for any one man.

The settings of the novels ranged from the fjords of Norway to the coasts of Tasmania, and every page betrayed that intimate knowledge of a foreign country which can only be acquired by a thorough study of the chattier sort of guide-books. But though the scene might shift, the puppets remained defiantly the same. Even in Tasmania, the wild roses in the heroine's cheeks remained quite unaffected by the climate and the malign but singularly unintelligent snares of the cynical villain in riding-clothes. The villains almost always wore riding-clothes, as I remember it, and were usually militant atheists, though of high social position. The heroines were petite, unworldly, and given to calling the native flora pet names. And over all, insipid, lingering, and sweet as the taste of a giant marshmallow, there brooded the inimitable style of Angela Poe. Occasionally, this style would goad some fledgling reviewer to fury and he would write the sort of scarifying review that only very young reviewers write. Then the girl at our reception desk would be warned and Mr. Thrushwood would put off all other appointments for the day. For Angela Poe read all her reviews with passion.

It was on such an occasion that I saw her for the first time. I was passing Mr. Thrushwood's private office, when Mr. Collins popped out of it with a worried look on his face. A dumpy little man who haunted the business department, he left all personal contacts with authors to Mr. Thrushwood, as a rule. But this time, Angela Poe had descended in Mr. Thrushwood's absence and caught him unprepared.

"Look here, Robbins," he said, with no more preface than a drowning man, "have we got any really magnificent reviews on the last Poe? You know the kind I mean—all honey and butter. The Washoe Gazette has just called her a purveyor of literary lollipops—and if I could get hold of her clipping-agency, there'd be blood on the moon."

"Why," I said, "I'm afraid I——" and then I remembered. Randall Day had the pestilent habit of sending me all the most fulsome reviews of Angela Poe that he could find—and one had arrived only that morning, with a neat border of hearts and flowers drawn around it.

"As a matter of fact, I have," I said, "but——"

"Thank God!" said Mr. Collins fervently and, taking me by the hand, he fairly ran me into the room.

But at first I could see no reason for the odd, tense look on his face—and on that of Mr. Catherwood, our art director, who was also there. The plump, demure, little old lady with the face of a faded pansy who sat in the big chair opposite them had nothing terrifying about her. She was Angela Poe, of course, though ten years older than her oldest publicity-pictures. And then she began to talk.

It was a sweet, tinkling voice, monotonous and constant. And as it went on, about Mr. Thrushwood and all her kind friends in Thrushwood, Collins, and then— I could not mark the transition—about how her flowers in her wee garden were also her friends, I began to realize the secret of the look on Mr. Collins' face. It was boredom, pure and simple, but boredom raised to a fine art. For when Angela Poe was angry she did not fly into a temper any more. She merely talked in her low, sweet voice—and, as she talked, she bored, relentlessly and persistently, like a drill boring into a shell.

It was no use trying to interrupt her or change the conversation—you cannot change a conversation that has no real subject to change. And yet, as she continued, and each moment seemed longer than the last until the brute flesh could hardly be restrained from breaking into a veritable whimper of tedium, I began to realize that she knew exactly what she was about. For somehow or other, we always came back to Angela Poe and the fact that she was waiting for Mr. Thrushwood. Till I began to feel, myself, that Mr. Thrushwood's absence was a grave calamity of nature and that, if he did not come soon, I, too, might burst into tears.

Fortunately, he arrived in time, and saved us, as only Mr. Thrushwood could. Fortunately or unfortunately, for he came while I was showing her the review that Day had sent me. It mollified her greatly, though she said, in a serious voice, that of course she never read reviews. They broke the wings of the butterfly. I didn't know what she meant by that, but I must have made some appropriate response. For Mr. Thrushwood, with one of his Napoleonic gestures, informed me at five o'clock that afternoon that henceforth my salary was raised ten dollars a month.

"And, by the way, Robbins," he said, "I don't want to put too much on you—but Miss Poe liked your looks today. Well, Miss Poe is just beginning a new novel—I think this one is to be about Iceland, or possibly Finland—not that it matters greatly——" and he gave me a smile of complicity. "But, as you know, we always get her reference books for her and send them out every week-end—and she will have them brought by some member of the staff. It's on the west shore of the Hudson—and I'm afraid she calls her house The Eyrie," he went on, with a chuckle. "But she's really a very sensible little woman—quite a head for business, yes, indeed, quite a head," and his face held unwilling respect. "So, if you wouldn't mind? Then that's all settled. How jolly of you, Robbins!" he said, with his boyish laugh.

I had meant to tell him I would do nothing of the sort, but, while you were with him you were under his spell. Nevertheless, it was with internal revolt that I got on the ferry that week-end, with my bag of books in my hand. And then, when I got to The Eyrie, I met a nice old lady who reminded me of my aunts. She put me at ease at once, she fed me enormously, she fussed over me with just the right amount of fussiness. The tea was solid and bountiful—I was sent to the station in a carriage and pair. To my despair, in the train going back, I discovered that I had enjoyed myself. And through my mind still ran the small, tinkling monotonous voice of Angela Poe—saying nothing, and yet, remembered. I tried very hard to place her; she was like any dozen ladies I knew in Central City, ladies with little gold watches pinned over their bosoms, who fussily but efficiently presided over strawberry festivals and sales at the Woman's Exchange. And she was not—there was something else about her, some quality I could not place. It had made her Angela Poe—and yet, what was it? Her servants, I had noticed, were perfectly trained and civil and the dog got up from the hearthrug when she told it to get up. And yet, instinctively, you gave her your arm, when she came down a staircase. I could not make it out, but I knew, rather shamefacedly, that I was looking forward to returning to The Eyrie. Young men are apt to be hungry—and the tea was superb.

And then, as I told Randall Day, The Eyrie alone was worth the price of admission. It was one of those big wooden houses with wide verandas that the Eighties built on the cliffs of the Hudson—houses that, somehow or other, remind you of grandiose cuckoo-clocks. There were the lawns and the shrubbery, the big, cupolaed

stable and the graveled drive; the hardwood floors and
the heavily framed oil-paintings. It might all have come
out of an Angela Poe novel—she had done it perfectly,
down to the last gas-bracket. And through it all wandered Mr. Everard De Lacey, the man one must never
address as Mr. Angela Poe.

It was my first experience with the husband of a
celebrated authoress, and he still remains unique in
my memory. You do not meet them now as often as
you did—those men with the large, mobile mouths,
the Hamlet eyes, and the skin that has known the
grease-paint of a thousand small-town dressing-rooms.
The new actors are another breed. Mr. De Lacey was
not merely an actor, he was a Thespian—and it makes
a difference. He must have been very handsome in his
youth—handsome in the old barnstorming tradition of
black, flashing eyes and Hyacinthine curls—and his
voice still had the rich, portentous boom of Michael
Strogoff, the Courier of the Czar. When he fixed me
with his Hamlet eyes and quoted—it was The Bard—
I felt ashamed of myself for not being a larger audience.
But he was really very considerate about it, and I liked
the way he treated Miss Poe.

For they were obviously and deeply attached to each
other, those two aging people, and one sensed the bond
the moment one saw them together. They deferred to
each other ceremoniously, with a Victorian civility
that I found rather touching. And Everard was by no
means the harmless, necessary husband such husbands
often are. It was agreed that he was "resting" from a
modern and sin-struck stage unworthy of his talents.

but it was also agreed that, at any moment, he might return to the boards, amid the plaudits of welcoming multitudes. Later on I discovered that he had been "resting" for almost thirty years, or since Angela Poe first started to sell by the carload. But that made no difference to either of them.

"I could never have done what I have done without Mr. De Lacey," she would say in her sweet, tinkling voice and Everard would boom in return, "My dear, it was but given me to water and tend the rose. The flowers are all your own." Such things, if said, are oftener said than meant. But you felt that the Poes, I mean the De Laceys, meant them. Then a look would pass between them, the look of two souls who are linked by a deeper tie than the crass world knows.

I seem to be writing a little like Angela Poe myself in describing them. But it was difficult, in that setting, not to become infected with Poe-ishness. If a beautiful girl in a simple muslin frock had met me accidentally in the garden and flitted away with flushed cheeks and a startled cry, I would have been embarrassed but not in the least surprised. And there were times when I fully expected to meet a little lame boy, his pale, courageous face radiant for once with the sunset glow, at almost any corner of the drive. But the De Laceys had no children, though they were extremely kind to the innumerable offspring of Mr. De Lacey's relatives. And that seemed to me rather a shame.

I had come to scoff, you see. But I remained, if not to pray, well, to be rather fascinated. They fed me well, they treated me with ceremonious politeness, they were sentimental, but generous as well. I had to listen a good deal to the tinkling, incessant flow of Angela Poe's words—but, as time wore on, I even became used to that. It was as Mr. Thrushwood had said; she could be extremely sensible, even pungent, when she wished. And she could take criticism, too, which surprised me. At least she could take it from Everard De Lacey. Now and then he would say, in his rich boom, as she sketched a scene or a character for us, "No, my dear, that will not do."

"But, Everard, how is Zepha to escape from the insane asylum, then?"

"That, my dear, I have to leave to your genius. But this passage will not do. I sense it. I feel it. It is not Angela Poe."

"Very well, my dear," she would say submissively, and turn to me with, "Mr. De Lacey is always right, you know." And he would say, at the same moment, "Young Man, I am not always right. But such poor gifts as I possess are always at Mrs. De Lacey's service——"

"The fruits of a richly stored mind, Everard——"

"Well, my dear, perhaps some slight acquaintance with the classics of our tongue—some trifling practical experience in interpreting The Bard——"

Then each would make the other a little bob, and again I would be irresistibly reminded, not of a cuckoo-clock but of one of those wooden weather-prophets where an old woman comes out for fine weather, an old man for rain. Only, here, the old man and the old woman were coming out at the same time.

I hope I have given the impression that they gave

me—that of two aging people, a trifle quaint, more than
a trifle ridiculous, but, beyond all that, essential to
each other. For that is an important thing for a young
man to see, now and then; it restores his faith in the
cosmos, though he may not realize it at the time. The
first taste of real life, for the young, has its frightening
moments: one suddenly discovers that actual people,
not in books, commit suicide in gas-filled bedrooms because they would rather die than live; one discovers
that others really enjoy being vicious and make a success of it. Then, instinctively, one clings to the first
security at hand, like a swimmer to an overturned boat.
I wouldn't have thought it possible when I first met
them, but one of the things I clung to was the De
Laceys.

And as I became more and more drawn into the endless spider-web of the work of Angela Poe, I began to
realize how much she owed to her husband. Oh, he
could never have written anything—be sure of that.
But he knew the well-worn paths of stock-melodrama
in all their spurious vitality, he knew when a thing
would "go." I know because, inevitably, I followed one
book of Angela Poe's from conception to delivery. It
was not any better, speaking from the point of view of
letters, for his suggestions; for it was perfectly terrible.
But it worked; it was Angela Poe; the sun rose over the
cardboard mountains at precisely the right instant. And
every one of his criticisms helped it on.

Then one day, when I came to The Eyrie, she had
a touch of influenza and was in bed. He was obviously
worried about her, but insisted on my staying to tea
because I always had. I had my own worries at the

moment and was glad for a breath of serenity. All his courtliness came into play and he told me a couple of mild theatrical jokes, but you could feel his eyes wandering, his ears listening for any sound from upstairs. If he had not been worried, I wonder—but worry makes people confidential. I thought it a good chance to congratulate him on his part in her work. He listened abstractedly, but I could see he was pleased.

"Glad you think so, my dear fellow, glad you think so," he said. "Often I have said to myself, 'No! This time, old boy, let genius burn unhampered! Who are you to profane the—um—the sacred flame?' But genius —even genius—must have its trammels to bring it down to the level of us workaday folk. And, as the— er—appreciative trammel, perhaps I have played my part. I hope so," he said, quite simply. "She means a great deal to me."

"I know that, sir," I said, but he wasn't listening.

"Yes," he said, "we mean a great deal to each other. I hope she's taking those drops; you know, she hates drops. Yes, indeed, my dear fellow. Our first meeting was like a flash of lightning." He stared at me solemnly. "I wish that Mr. Wedge, her first husband, could have understood it better. But he was an earth-bound soul. He could not comprehend a marriage of true minds."

"Mrs. De Lacey was married before?" I said, and I could not keep the shrillness of surprise from my voice.

"My dear boy," said Mr. De Lacey, looking surprised in his turn, "I forgot that you did not know. She was Mrs. Marvin Wedge when we first met," he said, reflectively, "and beautiful as a just-unfolding rose."

A thousand unphrasable questions rose to my lips and died there. For Mr. De Lacey continued.

"I used to call her the Rose of Goshen," he said. "Goshen, Indiana, dear boy—I was—er—resting there at the time, after my tour with Barrett. I played both grave-diggers and Charles, the wrestler. Charles, the wrestler, is not a large part, but one can make it tell. It was hard to return to Goshen, after that, but there are financial necessities. But as soon as I met Angela, I knew that I had been led. Wedge was—um—proprietor of our hay-and-feed store—rather older than I am; he used to chase me and call me Slats when I was a boy. But I had not known Angela before. She came from Zook Springs."

He paused and stared at me with his Hamlet eyes. I could see the whole scene so plainly—the dusty streets of the small town and the young, down-at-heels actor, back home discouraged, after his trial flight. I could see Angela Poe, forty years ago, in the simple gingham dress of one of her heroines. It must have all been so innocent and high-minded—innocent and unreal as a stage melodrama, even to the cynical figure of the burly hay-and-feed merchant. I could see him, somehow, in his shirt sleeves, roaring with laughter at the timid respectful speeches of—but the boy could not have been called Everard De Lacey, then. And yet, Romance had triumphed in Goshen. I wondered how.

"So Miss Poe was divorced—divorced Mr. Wedge, I mean," I said.

My companion looked curiously shocked. "Dear boy," he said, with dignity, "never once, in any of her books, has Angela Poe drawn a divorced woman."

"I know," I said feebly, though I didn't. "But in real life—"

"The books of Angela Poe are real life," said Mr. De Lacey, crushingly. Then he relented. "No," he said, "Mr. Wedge is not living. He passed over."

"Passed over?"

"Within a year of my return to Goshen. As a matter of fact, he was murdered," he said, with his Hamlet eyes fixed upon me so sternly that, for an instant, I had the horrific idea that I was about to listen to an incredible confession. But I was not. "By a tramp," he said at last. "In his feed store. For purposes of robbery. It was very upsetting for Angela."

I opened and shut my mouth, but no words came forth.

"Yes, really very upsetting. I was glad I could be with her," he said, naïvely. "Though, naturally, we were not married till later. She was married in a tailored dress, but she held a bouquet of orange-blossoms and lilies-of-the-valley. I insisted upon that," he said, with some pride.

"And the tramp?" I said with youth's delight in horrors. "Was he—"

"Oh, he was never found," boomed Mr. De Lacey abstractedly, as a small sound came from upstairs, "but Angela bore up wonderfully. She is a wonderful woman." He rose. "If you'll just excuse me one moment, my dear fellow—"

"I must catch my train," I said. "But thank you, Mr. De Lacey. And be assured I shall respect your confidence," I said, trying to equal his manner.

He nodded seriously. "Yes, yes," he said. "Perhaps

I should have said nothing—but, well, my dear boy, we have grown to know you and value you, in your visits to The Eyrie. And they must not cease with this book—my dear fellow, no. Only, I would not bring up the matter in talking with Miss Poe. She does not like to dwell upon those days; they were not happy ones for her. Mr. Wedge was really—" Words failed him. "Mr. Wedge was really not a very sensitive man," he said.

I assured him of my entire understanding and took my leave. But, all the way home, certain thoughts kept revolving in my mind. I was not surprised that Providence, in the shape of a burglarious tramp, had seen fit to remove the insensitive Mr. Wedge. That was just the sort of thing that happened to Angela Poes. But why had she ever married him, in the first place, and how, having touched real life in her own person, had she been able to forget it so completely in her books? But those were the sorts of questions one could not ask.

And yet in the end I asked them, with youth's temerity. I asked them because I had come to like her— to like them both. And when you like people, you are apt to be more honest with them—that is the trouble.

We had planned to have a little celebration—the three of us—when the book was actually published. But it was not I who put the first copy in her hands. I brought out the dummy and the jacket. That particular Saturday Mr. De Lacey had made one of his rare excursions to New York. I was glad to find her alone, as a matter of fact, for I thought I had noticed a slight constraint between us since my conversation with him. At least, I was conscious that I knew a secret—and kept wondering if she knew that I knew. And I meant to tell her, in all honesty, how much the security and peace of The Eyrie had meant to me through the year. I was only waiting a good opening. But, naturally, we started by talking publishing. Her comments were shrewd and I enjoyed them—though the influenza had left its mark, and she looked frailer than before. And then suddenly she startled me by asking what I really thought of her work.

Six months before, I would merely have buttered her, buttered her with a trowel, for the good of Thrushwood, Collins, and let it go at that. But now I had come to like her—and, after all, one has one's convictions. It wasn't the best butter, and she knew it. And monotonously, relentlessly, in her small, gracious voice, she kept pressing the point. That should have warned me, but it didn't. If authors were not megalomaniacs, no books would ever get written. But I forgot that first rule of publishing and floundered on.

"And yet, Mr. Robbins, I can feel that you don't really believe in me—you don't really believe in Angela Poe," she would say, gently and maddeningly, till at last with the rashness of youth I took my courage in both hands.

"It isn't that, Miss Poe," I stammered, "but if you'd only once—why don't you? It mightn't please your audience, but a woman of your experiences—of your life—"

"My life?" she said, with dignity. "And what do you know of my life, young man?"

"Oh, nothing," I said, blundering from bad to worse, "but Mr. De Lacey said you both came from small towns—well, now, a *real* novel about an American small town—"

"So Everard has been telling tales—naughty boy! I must scold him," said Angela Poe brightly. But the brightness was all in the voice. I suddenly had the impression that she thought me a tedious young fool and wished me away. I began to long for Mr. De Lacey's return. But though I strained my ears I heard no echo of his rich boom from any corner of the house.

"Oh," I said, "please don't. They were *such* delightful stories. He—he told me you were married in a traveling dress."

"Dear Everard!" said Angela Poe. "He remembers everything. A dove-gray silk, with white collar and cuffs. I looked very pretty in it. And you think I might make a story of that, Mr. Robbins?"

"We have always hoped—your memoirs—the readers of Angela Poe—" I said.

She shook her head, decisively. "I shall never write my memoirs," she said. "Authors' memoirs never sell, you know—not really. The publishers think they are going to, but they don't. And then, it would lift the veil. Do you know who I am, young man? Do you know that people write me from all over the country, every day? They write me asking me what to do with their lives. And I tell them," she said, sitting up very straight. "I tell them. Very often they do it, too. Because I'm Angela Poe—and they know my picture and my books. So they can write as they might to Another," and she bowed her head for an instant. "And that **is** not bad for a woman who writes what you think trash, Mr. Robbins. But I always knew I could do it," she ended, unexpectedly. "I always knew I could do it. But things were put in my way."

I could not leave, for it was not my train-time yet, but I began to feel more and more uncomfortable. There was something odd in the sweet, tinkling voice—the note of a fanatic egoism almost religious in its sincerity. I was used to the egoism of authors, but this was in another key.

She passed a handkerchief across her lips for a moment. "Dear, dear, I forget so many things since my illness," she said. "What were we talking about? Oh, yes, you were suggesting an idea to me—a story about an American small town. Do you know them, Mr. Robbins?"

She asked the question so suddenly and fiercely that I almost said no instead of yes. Then she relaxed.

"But of course," she said, a trifle primly, "you do know them. You know how cramped one's cultural opportunities are. And how one is mocked, perhaps, for striving after them? Or perhaps you do not know that?"

It was a rhetorical question, obviously. So I nodded, hoping against hope for the sound of Mr. De Lacey's footfall in the hall.

"Even so," she said sweetly, "you are not a member of the female sex. And they are more easily wounded than gentlemen think. Even Everard has wounded me now and then—oh, not intentionally and I soon forgave him," she said, with a regal gesture. "Still, he has wounded." She was, evidently, talking more to herself than to me, now, but the fact did not increase my comfort.

"I could have forgiven Marvin everything else," she said, "his drinking, his unbridled passions, his coarse jests. That is woman's mission—to submit and forgive. He made jokes about my housekeeping, too. And it would have cost him only eighty dollars to publish my poems. I had the sweetest wreath of field daisies for the cover. I thought he would be a way to higher things; after all, one has so little opportunity in a small town and the feed store was quite successful, financially. But I was mistaken," and she sighed, gently. I was now past wishing for Mr. De Lacey's appearance; I only wished for my train to roar into the room and bear me away. But such things do not happen, unfortunately.

"But I never thought of divorce," the mild, tinkling voice went on. "Never. It crossed my mind, once or twice, but I firmly put it aside. I have always been glad of that. I don't think he really *cared,*" she said, opening her pansy eyes widely. "But he might have hurt Everard badly—he was such a very strong man. Sometimes, in the early days of our marriage, he used to carry me around the room on one arm. It frightened me, rather, but I always submitted and forgave. It was always so dusty in the store, too. It used to make me sneeze and then he would laugh. He laughed when Everard read Shakespeare to me. I sneezed that evening, as I was wiping the handle of the hatchet, but no one heard me."

"As you were what?" I said, and my voice was thin and high.

"I suppose it wasn't necessary," she said thoughtfully. "It would be, now, with the fingerprints, but they were quite stupid people and we knew little of fingerprints then. But it seemed tidier—I'd let it fall on the floor and the floor was dirty. They never really swept the store. He was sitting with his back to me, reading my poems and laughing. I'd hidden the new ones, but he'd found them and broken open the drawer. The hatchet was an old one—they used to cut the wire on the feed bales with it. You know, he didn't say anything at all. He was still laughing and trying to get out of the chair. But he wasn't quick enough. I burned the money in the stove and nobody even asked me about the dress. They say salts of lemon will take out blood stains *immediately,*" she murmured. "But it seemed better not to try though it was quite a nice dress."

"But weren't you ever—didn't they ever—" I babbled.

"Why, Mr. Robbins, of course," she said, with perfect placidity, "you have no *idea* of the petty malice and gossip of a small town. But I was in bed, you know, when they came to tell me—in bed with a bad cold. Any emotional strain always gives me a very bad cold— I had quite a bad one the day Everard and I were married. And everybody knew he used to sit up in the feed store till all hours, drinking and reading vile atheist books like that horrid Colonel Ingersoll's. The old cats said it was because he was afraid to go home. Afraid of me!" she said with perfect ingenuousness. "There's no limit to what people will say. Why, they even talked about Everard, though everybody knew he was driving a load of vegetables to market with his father. I thought of that before I went to the store."

"And yet," I said, "you lived in Goshen—you didn't marry Mr. De Lacey till a year later—"

"A year and a day," she corrected. "That seemed

more fitting. But I went into half mourning at the end of six months. It's rather soon, I know, but I thought I might. As long as I was to be engaged to Everard," and a faint blush colored her cheeks. "I told him I could discuss nothing of the sort while I was still in full mourning and he appreciated my wishes—Everard has always been so considerate. At first, I thought the time would hang very heavy on my hands. But, as a matter of fact, it passed quite quickly. I was writing my first novel," she said, in a hushed voice.

I do not know yet how I got out of the house—I hope with decency. But I had left The Eyrie behind and was well along on my two-mile tramp to the station before I really came to myself. It was her last words— and the picture they gave me—that sent the cold, authentic shudder down my spine. I kept wondering wildly how many successful authors were murderers or murderesses and why the police did not arrest them all. For I could see the whole story and fill in every detail. It was fatally plausible, even to Angela Poe's primness. I could even believe that if the unfortunate Mr. Wedge had paid a printer eighty dollars, he might have lived. For there are egoisms which it is not safe to mock or dam up—if you do, you are tempting the explosion of primal forces.

And then, when I had almost reached the station, I suddenly began to laugh—the healing laughter of sanity. For the whole thing was ridiculous and Angela Poe had taken an impeccable revenge. I had told her what I thought of her work—and subtly, tinklingly, convincingly, she had made me swallow the most preposterous farrago of nonsense she could think of; swallow it whole. And, in doing so, she had proved her powers as a story-teller past cavil. But, once away from the monotonous spell of her voice, it was merely impossible to think of her as a murderess, and yet more impossible to think of Everard De Lacey as an accomplice. For accomplice he must have been—after the fact if not before it. Or else, she had hidden the truth from him all these years—and that was impossible, too.

For a second, I even thought of turning back to The Eyrie and humbly admitting to its mistress my folly and my defeat. But my train, after all, was due in fifteen minutes, and I had a dinner engagement in New York. I would write her a letter instead—she would like a letter. I walked up and down the station platform, composing orotund phrases in my mind.

The late afternoon train from New York arrived some six minutes before my own, and I was pleased to see it disgorge the statuesque form of Everard De Lacey. He shook hands with me and boomed apologies for missing my visit. "And how did you leave Miss Poe?" he said, anxiously. "I have been away since early morning."

"Oh, she was perfectly splendid—I never saw her looking better," I said, warmed by a glow of secret laughter. "We talked for hours—she'll tell you."

"That's good—that's good, my dear fellow—you relieve me greatly," he said, while his eyes roved for the carriage that had not yet arrived. "Jenks is tardy, today," he said. Then he gave me a quick look. "You didn't happen to mention what you told me in our little chat when she was so ill?" he said.

"Mention it?" I said with a broad grin. "Oh, yes, indeed."

He seemed curiously relieved. "I am much indebted," he said. "Then you really do feel—and it means something coming from you—that I am of some genuine help to her? To her books, I mean—her career?"

"I do, indeed," I said, though I was now puzzled.

"Excellent," he boomed. "Excellent." He took me by the lapel with the old actor's gesture. "You see," he said, "oh, it's foolish of me, I know—and we are old now, of course. But every now and then I have the feeling that I may not really be indispensable to her. And it worries me greatly."

For the instant, as he said it, I saw fear look out of his eyes. It was not an ignoble fear, but he must have lived with it a long time.

I did not go back to The Eyrie; indeed, I did not go back to Thrushwood, Collins. To do the latter without doing the former would have required explanations and I did not feel like giving them. Instead, I changed my boarding-house, and went to work as a salesman of aluminum-ware. And, after six months of that, I went back to Central City and the place in my father's cement business that had been waiting for me. For I had come to the decision that I was not made for New York, nor the life of letters; I did not have the self-confidence of Angela Poe.

Once, during the six months, I thought I saw Mr. De Lacey on the street, but he did not see me and I fled him. And, naturally, though I tried to escape them,

I saw advertisements of the last completed novel of Angela Poe. She died when I had been three months in Central City, and when I read that she was survived by her husband, the actor, Everard De Lacey, I felt as if a weight had been lifted from my breast. But he only survived her a few months. He missed her too much, I suppose, and some ties are enduring. I should like to have asked him one question, only one, and now I shall never know. He certainly played Shakespearian rôles— and there must have been quite a period, after they left Goshen, when he was playing. In fact the obituary mentions Othello and Hamlet. But there is another rôle—and I wonder if he ever played it and what he made of it. I think you know the one I mean.

THE TREASURE OF VASCO GOMEZ

THE brig was already a white-sailed toy on blue waters. Soon enough she would be hull down on the horizon, then nothing at all. No man among her crew would ever set foot again willingly on the island where that crew had marooned its captain. And Vasco Gomez, lost and alone on a pin-point of earth set down among waves that seemed to come from the other end of the world, stretched out his arms and laughed loudly for the first time since they had set him ashore.

He was known as a clever man and a lucky captain in every waterside tavern where the freebooters gathered. But this marooning of himself on a lost and uncharted island was the cleverest and luckiest exploit in a career that had held little mercy and no noteworthy failures.

It had not been an easy task. No, even for Vasco Gomez, it had not been easy. His own name for good fortune had worked against him, as had the quite justifiable fear his reputation inspired in the most hardbitten of free companions. It had taken untiring craft and skill to bring even a crew of wolves to the point of mutiny against Vasco Gomez. And even greater art to see to it that these wolves, once roused, should maroon a living man where he wished to be, and not merely cast a hacked body overside.

But it had been done, and well done—his luck had held. He was alive—he was here. He had taken the first huge step toward his kingdom. And it was time, for, though he was still as strong in body as any three men of the crew that had deserted him, he knew by certain warnings that he had entered middle age.

Middle age. The drying up of the life in a man, the gradual slowing of the heart. And yet, a man stronger and more cunning than the run of men might still manage to have his cake and eat it too—to get off scotfree and whistling—even to grow old. A man like him, for example.

And more than scot-free—rich—if he knew a secret. Rich. His eyes gleamed as he rolled the word on his tongue. He stared around him, measuring the extent of his riches.

They had left him without fresh water, but not a hundred paces inland were a spring and a stream. They had left him without victual, but he knew this island of old. There was provision for the crew of a frigate on the island; the unceasing provision of nature.

They had left him without tools or weapons, except for the sheath-knife hidden in his boot. But he had flint and steel, and the axes in the second cache should not have rusted by now, for they lay in dry soil. For that matter, if worst came to worst, he could hollow a boat by burning out a tree-bole. It might take time—but what was time to him, now? There was no time in this solitude—the measurements of time had ceased. There was only one long hour, his hour, the hour of his kingdom. He felt the first wave of it wash over him, peacefully, slowly. His heart rose in his body to meet it, his lips drank it in.

"A long time on the way—you've been a long time on the way here, Vasco Gomez," he thought to himself. But it was over now. Pedro's treasure lay buried where it had always lain, not ten feet down, between the rock and the palm. He had not yet seen it with his eyes, but he knew that it was still there. For seven years he had carried the secret, locked under his ribs, closer to him than his heart.

He exhaled a long breath, staring back through the years. He was the only man alive who knew.

There had been others who had an inkling. He had made it his business to find them and see that they got no further. There was a legend still, but a legend that few believed. And for a while, of course, there had been Pedro.

He saw the dark cruelty of that insatiable face swim up at him, in memory, like something seen through a wraith of sea fog. He smiled. Pedro was long since turned into leather at Execution Dock. He had not been able to come back, though he'd tried. But Vasco Gomez had come back. And, from the moment that he had landed on the island this noon, the treasure had been Pedro's no longer, but his treasure—the treasure of Vasco Gomez.

The men who had actually buried the spoil were safe enough. Their bones lay in the second cache with the tools of their labor. They would not disturb him. The one thing that did disturb him was the thought that the bags and chests that held the treasure might have rotted. In that case he would have to make new ones, somehow—one could not put to sea with half a boat-load of naked gold.

Half a boat-load at the least; there might be more. It would be interesting to see the full extent of the loot. He had only caught hasty glimpses of it by the bad light of the lanterns, on that night that was burned in his memory. But there would be enough for his wants— enough at the least to buy fat days and fine feathers— or even God's pardon, perhaps, weighed out in masses and candles. Enough to buy love and hate—and age for Gomez.

And all that remained to be done was so simple. A week, two, to lift the treasure. Two months, three months, to make a boat and provision it. Longer, perhaps, for he would not attempt the sea journey in the stormy season, but what was time, now he had all time to spend? Then a sixty-mile sail in an open boat to that other island, a daring exploit enough for landsmen, but child's play for Vasco Gomez. There were tamed Indians on that other island; he knew them, he had been careful to make them his friends. Then a little policy—a little murder, perhaps—another ship—a little intrigue with the mainland—he knew the fellow who had the Governor's ear and how to use him. And after that, anything: a king's coat to wear, a king's commission to carry—"Our well-beloved Vasco Gomez"—a decent estate at home, a little respectability, a little repentance, an altar of rose marble in an old cathedral to hold God strictly to the bargain,—and not only this world but the next one flung open for the penitent buccaneer.

All for gold—all there to be bought by gold. Nothing existed that could not be bought by gold.

He came out of his muse and stared seaward again, eagerly. The brig was only a speck, now; soon the abrupt night would come down. He must gather wood, make a fire, knock over a crab or two, find water, devise a bed. Tomorrow he would start building a hut for himself. Perhaps he might even finish his boat before he lifted the treasure. The treasure could wait—it would not run away. There was no time on earth that could take him from his treasure now.

It was one morning, when Vasco Gomez was busily at work upon his almost completed boat, that he first felt himself definitely alone.

To him it was a strange sensation. So strange, in fact, that when he received the first impact of it, the knife which he was using dropped from his hand as if something had struck him on the wrist. Then, after a moment, he picked up the knife again. But the feeling persisted.

His life, to say the least of it, had been an active and a crowded one. He had dealt with men and women and they had dealt with him, but never without physical impact. If he were to gaze back through the last score of years, he would hardly be able to find a single waking moment, even in shipwreck, when he had been entirely alone, divided from the world. He was alone now.

He was alone, and with that knowledge came

thought. He was not used to thinking—Vasco Gomez—
least of all to thinking about himself.

The work he was doing took up some of his thought
but not all of it—not enough. Before, in the pauses of
action, there had always been the treasure to think
about, to plan for. Now the treasure was here. That
space in his mind was suddenly filled by other, unac-
customed thoughts.

"Who is this fellow, Vasco Gomez?" he found himself thinking after a while, beset with a queer fear.

"Vasco Gomez? Why, that's you—that's me—you're
here, man—you're making a boat!" He said the words
aloud; they comforted him. But after a while he began
to think again.

Vasco Gomez—he certainly knew who Vasco Gomez
was! He saw him fighting, drinking, kissing a wench's
shoulder, climbing a ship's red side with a long knife
bitten in his teeth. A big, scarred bull of a man, solid
and awe inspiring.

But that wasn't Vasco Gomez any more. Vasco
Gomez was here. Vasco Gomez was here—and entirely
alone.

He felt himself diminish as he thought the words—
diminish as the brig had diminished. The brig, too, had
been solid and bulky at first—then smaller—then a
puppet—a speck on the sea. So now with him. He saw
a little man on a toy island—an ant-size figure set down
on a spoonful of land in the midst of blue immensities.

His face dripped with sweat, though he had not
been working hard. The rasp of his knife on the wood
made an acute and lonely sound. It seemed to him that
he could hear that small sound go out and out, through

infinities of water and air, and still meet no other sound that could be its fellow—and still—meet—no—other —sound.

His mind righted itself with a jerk. No, he had the clue to his thinking. He had been on the island for very nearly five months, as he reckoned. Well, he knew what happened sometimes to men so marooned, the look they got in their eyes, the voices they thought they heard.

He had not expected this to happen to him; he was too strong, too clever. But if it were so, so be it—he now knew where the danger lay and could guard against it. As soon as he had settled this in his mind, he felt restored. The sky and sea shrank back to their proper proportions.

He had hardly expected to finish the boat in less than ten days, but a fury of work took hold of him. While he toiled, he could not diminish—the sky and sea held their places. He found himself now and then trying over sentences in the jargon the Indians spoke. He caught himself listening thirstily as the sentences fell from his mouth. Only they lacked something—they lacked the note of a voice that was not his own.

In four days the boat was finished and afloat in the cove.

He had been gathering provisions during the last months. He had even made a keg for his water. It took no time at all to put these aboard or to rig his improvised sail. He wondered at himself, while he labored, that he labored so feverishly. Surely it did not matter if he set sail in a week or a month, now the season of storms was past. But, in these last days, time was no longer the one long hour that belonged to him and his treasure. It had become again a sifting of hasty grains through the blue hour-glass of the sky—and each grain that fell seemed to steal a little strength from his heart.

He stood up at last, hot and sweating. Night had fallen. All was ready now, except for the actual lifting of the treasure—and it was not sensible to begin that work at night. But he woke before the dawn.

When he had wakened, he lay there a moment without moving; entirely happy. He had known many women in his life, but today was the day of his true nuptials.

The sun was sinking when he uncovered the final chest. He struck a great blow with his axe at a rusty lock and stared. It was the bridal. The gold seemed to leap up at him, from the ground.

Next moment he was down among it, both fists were full. He felt as if he had been running, his breath came and went in the runner's gasp. How good it was to touch, how thick and heavy and smooth—better than any woman's shoulder—better than bread!

Slowly, luxuriously, he broke open the other chests. It was all there—idol and pyx—blood-ruby and rough cut emerald—the grandee's studded scabbard—the soft masks of virgin gold that the heathen priests had worn. He had dreamed of it as a king's ransom—he smiled at the poverty of his dreams.

The abrupt night came, shut down, but he did not stir. He did not light a fire, he did not go back to his hut. Time had resumed its long hour—time was not. He lay all night in the pit, he was perfectly happy.

The dawn came and he rose, but not as he had

risen twenty-four hours ago. That morning, when he got up, he was still poor and an adventurer; this morning he got up rich, with the cares of riches.

He laughed when he thought of his furious labor of the last few days. Time was his friend, not his enemy, there was no need to fight it. The boat was ready—put the gold aboard—cast off—and everything else would follow, as the ship's wake follows the ship.

The business of the Indians first. They were his friends, but even so they would not do all he wanted without reward. Well, there he could get off cheaply—they hardly knew the uses of the yellow metal. But then there was the Governor's friend and the Governor himself—and he frowned. Everything could be bought with a price, no doubt, but, even for the rich, certain things came high.

He knew, none better, what palms would have to be greased.

If it had but matched with the poverty of his dreams—even then, he saw the difficulty. But this king's ransom—why even the king himself might want a finger in the pie!

Yesterday, he would gladly have given half the treasure to get off safe with the other half. But now he had seen it and touched it.

A dull anger began to rise in him. What business had all these strangers, meddling with his treasure? They hadn't schemed for it or found it.

Now he saw them, one and all, roosted around the edge of the pit like vultures—the Indians, the Governors, the lawyers and courtiers, the women with thirsty eyes, a bishop even, a red-hatted cardinal. Yes, even the

Church itself, even God Himself exacted a portion of the treasure! They came closer, they stretched out their hands, bit by bit, drop by drop, then bled him of his precious gold. They gave him empty, useless things in return—a kiss—a patent of nobility—an altar of rose-marble—but the bleeding never ceased. At last, an old man crouched over the pitiful remnant of a king's ransom—and even then there were creatures coming to bleed him anew. He waved his arm in the air to drive off the vision.

Decidedly, he would have to revise his plans. He hurriedly tried to think of the least—the very least—he must spend to be safe. He pared his bribes down and down—and yet the total appalled him.

Then the mere passage of time brought with it a certain balm. After all, he did not have to set sail till he wished. He would eat and drink and sleep and play with his treasure—and in time some perfect plan might come to him.

The hours slipped into days, the days into weeks. One evening, notching his calendar-stick, he realized with a start that it was nearly two months since he had first uncovered the treasure. It seemed impossible, but it was true. Well, Vasco Gomez, he thought with an odd lethargy, it is time you were setting off, my friend— tomorrow we will begin.

The morrow came, the sea seemed calm as a mill pond. And yet, far down to the south—was not that the edge of a cloud? He shook himself impatiently—was he losing his mind?—a sailor and afraid of a speck of white? With dragging steps, he turned toward his boat.

Then a rescuing thought came to him—the bags for the treasure. The old bags were rotten—he would have to devise new bags, new chests. He felt at peace again immediately; he spent the morning happily, selecting the wood for his chests.

They were finished at last, but not before the stormy season. Vasco Gomez was no madman—he would not put out with such a cargo till the storms were done.

Meanwhile, with his treasure about him, Vasco Gomez lived many lives. Up till now, his life had left him little time for imagination beyond the needs of the day, but now his imagination flowered like a great poppy—his dreams spread a scarlet cloth for his bare feet to tread.

At first they were the simple visions and Elysiums of any sailor—enough food and drink, the easy girls of the ports—but as time went on they grew more elaborate, more refined, more clearly intense. He feasted delicately; music played while he feasted; the wines, poured for him, were the rarest of their kind. He did not gorge or lie drunken. When he went to take the air, outriders went before him; the king called him cousin and kissed him on the cheek. And when he returned to his palace, it was no girl of the ports whose lips were turned to him, but a king's daughter, a mermaid, a creature of light and foam. Sometimes she was dark as the soft nights, sometimes golden as the first spear of morning. It did not matter—she was whatever he wished, she was all women he had known, yet she was always new.

Then his power broadened, his shadow increased. He made wars and calmed them, raised one nation and put down another, appeased famine, tamed the seas.

The king no longer called him cousin,—he threw the king bones from his table and the king was grateful. Men whispered among themselves that only the protected of heaven could cast such a shade. And, indeed, to this man came messengers not wholly of this world.

Gomez, walking one morning when the season of storms had passed, came suddenly upon a boat, beached high and dry, protected by a rude shelter. For a moment he stared at it without recognition. Then he remembered—it was his boat, and he would never find better weather for his journey.

He looked the boat over carefully. The storms had not touched her—she was seaworthy still. He launched her in the cove again. Then he went slowly to the place where his chests were kept, and loaded them aboard. Only one thing remained, to fill the chests with the treasure. He dropped a rose-noble in one chest—it made a queer sound on the wood. Then he started for the rest of the treasure.

Two hours later, he sat in the boat, with his head in his hands. He had built his boat too small for the weight she was to carry.

Well, he must build another boat, that was all. But, as he thought this, he knew that even if he could build a boat big enough to bear that weight of gold, the boat would take more than one man to handle.

He could ferry what he now had aboard to the other island, bury it, come back for more. That meant a thousand risks with every voyage. He had lived with his treasure too long. He could not bear to bury a part of it elsewhere and leave it.

Well then, he would put it back in Pedro's old cache, taking only enough away with him to make a fresh start. Hire a ship—come back—to let other men into his secret—to go shares from the very first in what was his alone.

He thought for a long time, wearily revolving plans in his head. He knew that he could follow none of them. There must be another plan. All things were to be bought, if one had gold enough.

He lay all night in the boat, thinking. Morning came at length, and his riddle was still unsolved, but for a while he had ceased to think of it.

He had gone back, for a moment, to one of his many dreams. It was quite a simple dream and made but a poor show among his more ornate visions, yet he liked to dream it, at times.

He saw a tumbledown wine-shop with a dried bush over the door, on the crest of a hill road in Portugal. There was a girl in the wine-shop, a girl with fresh lips and hair as black as her comb.

She had a soldier for a lover, and a proud heart. Gomez was poor and a thief—it was in the days before he went to sea. They drove him away from the wine-shop often enough, but he came back to it. Once the soldier beat him, he took the beating with shut lips. The girl looked on, smiling. When at last Gomez saw that it was useless, he left the soldier in a mountain gully with a knife in his back and ran away before they caught him. Then his real life began.

In Gomez' dream, however, there was no soldier. There was only the girl, and himself as he had been at that time. But she was no longer scornful and they smiled at each other between the kisses.

The dream seemed very real to him, this time. He leaned over the side of the boat and stared at the water idly.

There was a face, reflected in the water. He observed it as he might the face of a stranger at first.

His own face was the face of the boy in his dream—a young, sharp face, ready for good or evil, but as yet not deeply marked with either—the face of youth. This was the withered face of an old man.

Slowly and wonderingly, he passed his hands over his body, regarded his legs, his arms. He had not looked at himself for a long time. But this scarecrow was he. "You've come a long way, Gomez," he muttered.

A new picture came to him, out of his other dreams. The splendid Vasco Gomez, the lord of the treasure, in his fine bed alone. The breath came faintly from the lips of the dying man. On one side of the bed was seated a priest, on the other a lawyer, but the dying eyes saw neither crucifix nor testament. They were staring ahead into darkness, trying to see something they could not fix upon. Outside the door, a servant kept back a silent throng—the throng of the claimants, the inheritors. A black-gloved personage waited in a corner, without impatience. Every man's end.

If some miracle—some incredible bribing of God—could set him ashore on the mainland, with his treasure! Even so, there were only so many lives in the world to live. And, already, he had lived those lives. If not in the body, yet very completely, very thoroughly. The body could do no more for him, the treasure could do no more. All but the one picture of the girl and the wine-shop—and that no treasure could repurchase, for it belonged to a past year.

Vasco Gomez braced one hand in the other hand till the muscles in his back stood out. He had always been a strong man, a clever and wary fighter. Now he must fight again, without ruth or scruple or weakness, as in the old days. But this time the adversary was invisible.

The next morning found him walking the beach, still fighting. Now and then he looked out to sea. It was very calm and clear. Then he realized that even the sea was a servant of his adversary, and turned his eyes away.

He sat down in the sand at last, arms lax, heart and body worn out. He was very tired but he would not give up the fight while breath was in him.

Everything to be bought with gold, he repeated to himself doggedly. One cannot fail with money—everything with a price in money—men—governors—kings —old age—God Himself, at the last. . . .

The wave came from afar—he could hear it coming. He braced himself to meet it, but it was too late. It was no wave of the sea, the sea was quiet enough. This wave gathered—rose—burst over him. He felt the shock, and trembled. He was beaten now.

Everything to be bought with gold, up to God Himself. Not without exception. You could buy much. You could buy candles and masses. But God, at the last, was not to be bought. That was the truth.

Slowly, without revulsion or outcry, for he was beaten, he lay on the sand and felt the cells of his body drink in this truth. After a long while a little stirring of peace began to move in his breast.

He rose at last. He felt weak when he had risen, and when he moved, his steps were the steps of an old man. But he would have strength enough for the work that remained.

He went back to the little cove where his boat was moored, and stood for a moment gazing at the water. Yes, that was the place. He had swum there often but never yet found bottom. The bottom must be very deep.

He took the piece of his treasure nearest to hand— it was one of the golden masks—and let it fall from his hand into the water. It shimmered as it went down, then that too was lost. He gave a sharp sigh, stooped stiffly and picked up the grandee's sword.

At last only one rose-noble was left. He weighed it in his hand a moment, as curiously as if it had been a sea-shell. It had a man's face on one side—the man had a nose like Pedro's. Strange, to put a man's face on a thing like that! He let it fall—it shone through green glooms and was gone.

Up till now, each piece that he had let fall had seemed to carry a small portion of his soul with it as it sank. But now, when there was no more treasure to drown, he felt otherwise. His soul could be divided no longer. It was either here in his body or down under the water with the treasure—but it did not matter, for, wherever it was, it was not in morsels.

He stared at the water anew with mild curiosity. A fish was swimming where the rose-noble had shimmered.

After a while, he wandered back to the beach and sat looking out toward the sea. For a moment he thought of his lost battle, but not with pain or shame. He had fought well and long. Now the fight was over. He would not fight again. There had been only one battle after all—it had lasted all his life—but he was done with it now.

He could not have eaten food for a long time. A day, perhaps more than a day? He could not remember. But when he thought of food, the thought revolted him. He was hungry now, but he was not hungry for bread.

The night fell and found him still on the beach. He thought of going back to his hut, but did not do so. Instead he moved farther up the beach and ensconced himself in a sort of niche, where one boulder overhung another. The bottom boulder was raised—it was out of the way of the landcrabs—the top one was almost a roof. He sat there, with his back propped by the rear of the niche, his hands on his knees. The night air was cool and pleasant, the stars had come out. He looked out over the sea and felt the cool air on his face. There was a horizon there, hidden away in that gulf of starry darkness, but he was not seeking that horizon.

After some hours, he moved a little and spoke. "You've come a long way, Vasco Gomez," he said anew, with a certain touch of affirmation. Nothing replied to the words.

Some eight months later, H.M.S. *Vixen,* sloop-of-war, blown out of her course by contrary gales, sent a boat ashore to the island in the hope of finding fresh water and fruit for a crew already in danger of scurvy.

The lieutenant in charge of the landing-party proceeded with all due precaution at first. But when the water-casks had been filled, and it was evident that the island was uninhabited, he allowed his men some liberty, and himself strolled down the beach.

It was a pretty beach and seemed to encircle the island completely. He had got this far in his musings when a shout from one of the men farther down the beach made him clap his hand to his cutlass. Then he saw that the man was standing up and waving his arms. He walked hurriedly.

The buzzing group of sailors fell back before him. He found himself abruptly face to face with a stranger. The man was seated in a species of natural niche made by two boulders, his hands on his knees, in an attitude of contemplation, his eyes staring out to sea. Some rags of clothing still clung to him and the crabs had not even touched him, but his whole body was the color and texture of leather. He must have been dead for a number of months—what remained was a mummy that the sun and the wind had embalmed between them. Yet the features were quite recognizable—there was even an expression upon them—an expression that the lieutenant had seen before. He touched his lips with his handkerchief, remembering the last time he had seen it. No, even the work of sun and wind could not account entirely for that emaciation.

A sailor was at his elbow, pulling a forelock.

"Do you know who that is, sir?" he said, in an eager voice. "It's Gomez, the bloody pirate, sir—I seen him before and so has Tom—and serve him right, the Portugee devil, that's what I say!"

"Yes," said the lieutenant, hardly listening, "it may well be he. We heard he had been marooned and—"

"Marooned is right, sir," said the sailor, "the bloody villain! Even his own crew got sick of him at the last and—" He leaned forward as if to spit upon the leathered image.

"Keep your wits about you, my man!" said the lieutenant, sternly, and the sailor retired. Now he and his fellows were reciting the dead man's crimes, but the lieutenant did not hear them.

He was looking at Vasco Gomez. He must be right— you could not mistake that expression, once you had seen it. And yet he could not understand.

His eye traveled down the beach to the land-crabs scuttling busily—yes, there were turtles, beyond there— fruit inland, fish in the sea. A small island, but provision enough to feed a whole ship's crew.

"And yet I could swear that the man died of hunger," muttered the lieutenant to himself. "It is strange."

III

THE CURFEW TOLLS

"It is not enough to be the possessor of genius—the time and the man must conjoin. An Alexander the Great, born into an age of profound peace, might scarce have troubled the world—a Newton, grown up in a thieves' den, might have devised little but a new and ingenious picklock. . . ."

Diversions of Historical Thought by
John Cleveland Cotton.

(The following extracts have been made from the letters of General Sir Charles William Geoffrey Estcourt, C.B., to his sister Harriet, Countess of Stokely, by permission of the Stokely family. Omissions are indicated by triple dots, thus . . .)

St. Philippe-des-Bains, September 3d, 1788.

MY DEAR SISTER: . . . I could wish that my excellent Paris physician had selected some other spot for my convalescence. But he swears by the waters of St. Philip and I swear by him, so I must resign myself to a couple of yawning months ere my constitution mends. Nevertheless, you will get long letters from me, though I fear they may be dull ones. I cannot bring you the gossip of Baden or Aix—except for its baths, St. Philip is but one of a dozen small white towns on this agreeable coast. It has its good inn and its bad inn, its dusty, little square with its dusty, fleabitten beggar, its posting-station and its promenade of scrubby lindens and palms. From the heights one may see Corsica on a clear day, and the Mediterranean is of an unexampled blue. To tell the truth, it is all agreeable enough, and an old Indian campaigner, like myself, should not complain. I am well treated at the Cheval Blanc—am I not an English milord?—and my excellent Gaston looks after me devotedly. But there is a bluebottle drowsiness about small watering places out of season, and our gallant enemies, the French, know how to bore themselves more exquisitely in their provinces than any nation on earth. Would you think that the daily arrival of the diligence from Toulon would be an excitement? Yet it is to me, I assure you, and to all St. Philip. I walk, I take the waters, I read Ossian, I play piquet with Gaston, and yet I seem to myself but half-alive. . . .

. . . You will smile and say to me, "Dear brother, you have always plumed yourself on being a student of human nature. Is there no society, no character for you to study, even in St. Philippe-des-Bains?" My dear sister, I bend myself earnestly to that end, yet so far with little result. I have talked to my doctor—a good man but unpolished; I have talked to the curé—a good man but dull. I have even attempted the society of the baths, beginning with Monsieur le Marquis de la Percedragon, who has ninety-six quarterings, soiled wristbands, and a gloomy interest in my liver, and ending with Mrs. Macgregor Jenkins, a worthy and red-faced lady whose conversation positively cannonades with dukes and duchesses. But, frankly, I prefer my chair in the garden and my Ossian to any of them, even at the risk of being considered a bear. A witty scoundrel would be the veriest godsend to me, but do such exist in St. Philip? I trow not. As it is, in my weakened condition, I am positively agog when Gaston comes in every morning with his budget of village scandal. A pretty pass to come to, you will say, for a man who has served with Eyre Coote and but for the mutabilities of fortune, not to speak of a most damnable cabal . . . (A long passage dealing with General Estcourt's East Indian services and his personal and unfavorable opinion of Warren Hastings is here omitted from the manuscript.) . . . But, at fifty, a man is either a fool or a philosopher. Nevertheless, unless Gaston provides me with a character to try my wits on, shortly, I shall begin to believe that they too have deteriorated with Indian suns. . . .

September 21st, 1788.

My Dear Sister: . . . Believe me, there is little soundness in the views of your friend, Lord Martindale. The French monarchy is not to be compared with our own, but King Louis is an excellent and well-beloved prince, and the proposed summoning of the States-General cannot but have the most salutary effect. . . . (Three pages upon French politics and the possibility of cultivating sugar-cane in Southern France are here omitted.) . . . As for news of myself, I continue my yawning course, and feel a decided improvement from the waters. . . . So I shall continue them though the process is slow. . . .

You ask me, I fear a trifle mockingly, how my studies in human nature proceed?

Not so ill, my dear sister—I have, at least, scraped

acquaintance with one odd fish, and that, in St. Philip, is a triumph. For some time, from my chair in the promenade, I have observed a pursy little fellow, of my age or thereabouts, stalking up and down between the lindens. His company seems avoided by such notables of the place as Mrs. Macgregor Jenkins and at first I put him down as a retired actor, for there is something a little theatrical in his dress and walk. He wears a wide-brimmed hat of straw, loose nankeen trousers and a quasi-military coat, and takes his waters with as much ceremony as Monsieur le Marquis, though not quite with the same *ton*. I should put him down as a Meridional, for he has the quick, dark eye, the sallow skin, the corpulence and the rodomontish airs that mark your true son of the Midi, once he has passed his lean and hungry youth.

And yet, there is some sort of unsuccessful oddity about him, which sets him off from your successful bourgeois. I cannot put my finger on it yet, but it interests me.

At any rate, I was sitting in my accustomed chair, reading Ossian, this morning, as he made his solitary rounds of the promenade. Doubtless I was more than usually absorbed in my author, for I must have pronounced some lines aloud as he passed. He gave me a quick glance at the time, but nothing more. But on his next round, as he was about to pass me, he hesitated for a moment, stopped, and then, removing his straw hat, saluted me very civilly.

"Monsieur will pardon me," he said, with a dumpy hauteur, "but surely monsieur is English? And surely the lines that monsieur just repeated are from the great poet, Ossian?"

I admitted both charges, with a smile, and he bowed again.

"Monsieur will excuse the interruption," he said, "but I myself have long admired the poetry of Ossian" —and with that he continued my quotation to the end of the passage, in very fair English, too, though with a strong accent. I complimented him, of course, effusively —after all, it is not every day that one runs across a fellow-admirer of Ossian on the promenade of a small French watering place—and after that, he sat down in the chair beside me and we fell into talk. He seems, astonishingly for a Frenchman, to have an excellent acquaintance with our English poets—perhaps he has been a tutor in some English family. I did not press him with questions on this first encounter, though I noted that he spoke French with a slight accent also, which seems odd.

There is something a little rascally about him, to tell you the truth, though his conversation with me was both forceful and elevated. An ill man, too, and a disappointed one, or I miss my mark, yet his eyes, when he talks, are strangely animating. I fancy I would not care to meet him in a *guet-apens,* and yet, he may be the most harmless of broken pedagogues. We took a glass of waters together, to the great disgust of Mrs. Macgregor Jenkins, who ostentatiously drew her skirts aside. She let me know, afterward, in so many words, that my acquaintance was a noted bandit, though, when pressed, she could give no better reason than that he lives a little removed from the town, that "nobody knows where he comes from" and that his wife is "no better than she should be," whatever that portentous phrase entails. Well, one would hardly call him a gentleman, even by Mrs. Macgregor's somewhat easy standards, but he has given me better conversation than I have had in a month—and if he is a bandit, we might discuss thuggee together. But I hope for nothing so stimulating, though I must question Gaston about him. . . .

October 11th.

. . . But Gaston could tell me little, except that my acquaintance comes from Sardinia or some such island originally, has served in the French army and is popularly supposed to possess the evil eye. About Madame he hinted that he could tell me a great deal, but I did not labor the point. After all, if my friend has been c-ck-ld-d—do not blush, my dear sister!—that, too, is the portion of a philosopher, and I find his wide range of conversation much more palatable than Mrs. Macgregor Jenkins' rewarmed London gossip. Nor has he tried to borrow money from me yet, something which, I am frank to say, I expected and was prepared to refuse. . . .

November 20th.

. . . Triumph! My character is found—and a character of the first water, I assure you! I have dined with him in his house, and a very bad dinner it was. Madame is not a good housekeeper, whatever else she may be. And what she has been, one can see at a glance—she has all the little faded coquetries of the garrison coquette. Good-tempered, of course, as such women often are, and must have been pretty in her best days, though with shocking bad teeth. I suspect her of a touch of the tarbrush, though there I may be wrong. No doubt she caught my friend young—I have seen the same thing happen in India often enough—the experienced woman and the youngster fresh from England. Well, 'tis an old story—an old one with him, too—and no doubt Madame has her charms, though she is obviously one reason why he has not risen.

After dinner, Madame departed, not very willingly, and he took me into his study for a chat. He had even procured a bottle of port, saying he knew the Englishman's taste for it, and while it was hardly the right Cockburn, I felt touched by the attention. The man is desperately lonely—one reads that in his big eyes. He is also desperately proud, with the quick, touchy sensitiveness of the failure, and I quite exerted myself to draw him out.

And indeed, the effort repaid me. His own story is simple enough. He is neither bandit nor pedagogue, but, like myself, a broken soldier—a major of the French Royal Artillery, retired on half pay for some years. I think it creditable of him to have reached so respectable a rank, for he is of foreign birth—Sardinian, I think I told you—and the French service is by no means as partial to foreigners as they were in the days of the first Irish Brigade. Moreover, one simply does not rise in that service, unless one is a gentleman of quarterings, and that he could hardly claim. But the passion of his life has been India, and that is what interests me. And, 'pon my honor, he was rather astonishing about it.

As soon as, by a lucky chance, I hit upon the subject, his eyes lit up and his sickness dropped away.

Pretty soon he began to take maps from a cabinet in the wall and ply me with questions about my own small experiences. And very soon indeed, I am abashed to state, I found myself stumbling in my answers. It was all book knowledge on his part, of course, but where the devil he could have got some of it, I do not know. Indeed, he would even correct me, now and then, as cool as you please. "Eight twelve pounders, I think, on the north wall of the old fortifications of Madras——" and the deuce of it is, he would be right. Finally, I could contain myself no longer.

"But, major, this is incredible," I said. "I have served twenty years with John Company and thought that I had some knowledge. But one would say you had fought over every inch of Bengal!"

He gave me a quick look, almost of anger, and began to roll up his maps.

"So I have, in my mind," he said, shortly, "but, as my superiors have often informed me, my hobby is a tedious one."

"It is not tedious to me," I said boldly. "Indeed, I have often marveled at your government's neglect of their opportunities in India. True, the issue is settled now——"

"It is by no means settled," he said, interrupting me rudely. I stared at him.

"It was settled, I believe, by Baron Clive, at a spot named Plassey," I said frigidly. "And afterward, by my own old general, Eyre Coote, at another spot named Wandewash."

"Oh, yes—yes—yes," he said impatiently, "I grant you Clive—Clive was a genius and met the fate of geniuses. He steals an empire for you, and your virtuous English Parliament holds up its hands in horror because he steals a few lakhs of rupees for himself as well. So he blows out his brains in disgrace—you inexplicable English!—and you lose your genius. A great pity. I would not have treated Clive so. But then, if I had been Milord Clive, I would not have blown out my brains."

"And what would you have done, had you been Clive?" I said, for the man's calm, staring conceit amused me.

His eyes were dangerous for a moment and I saw why the worthy Mrs. Macgregor Jenkins had called him a bandit.

"Oh," he said coolly, "I would have sent a file of grenadiers to your English Parliament and told it to hold its tongue. As Cromwell did. Now there was a man. But your Clive—faugh!—he had the ball at his feet and he refused to kick it. I withdraw the word genius. He was a nincompoop. At the least, he might have made himself a rajah."

This was a little too much, as you may imagine. "General Clive had his faults," I said icily, "but he was a true Briton and a patriot."

"He was a fool," said my puffy little major, flatly, his lower lip stuck out. "As big a fool as Dupleix, and that is saying much. Oh, some military skill, some talent for organization, yes. But a genius would have brushed him into the sea! It was possible to hold Arcot, it was possible to win Plassey—look!" and, with that, he ripped another map from his cabinet and began to expound to me eagerly exactly what he would have done in command of the French forces in India, in 1757, when he must have been but a lad in his twenties. He thumped the paper, he strewed corks along the table for his troops—corks taken from a supply in a tin box, so it must be an old game with him. And, as I listened, my irritation faded, for the man's monomania was obvious. Nor was it, to tell the truth, an ill-designed plan of campaign, for corks on a map. Of course these things are different, in the field.

I could say, with honesty, that his plan had features of novelty, and he gulped the words down hungrily—he has a great appetite for flattery.

"Yes, yes," he said. "That is how it should be done—the thickest skull can see it. And, ill as I am, with a fleet and ten thousand picked men——" He dreamed, obviously, the sweat of his exertions on his waxy face—it was absurd and yet touching to see him dream.

"You would find a certain amount of opposition," I said, in an amused voice.

"Oh, yes, yes," he said quickly, "I do not underrate the English. Excellent horse, solid foot. But no true knowledge of cannon, and I am a gunner——"

I hated to bring him down to earth and yet I felt that I must.

"Of course, major," I said, "you have had great experience in the field."

He looked at me for a moment, his arrogance quite unshaken.

"I have had very little," he said, quietly, "but one knows how the thing should be done or one does not know. And that is enough."

He stared at me for an instant with his big eyes. A

little mad, of course. And yet I found myself saying, "But surely, major—what happened?"

"Why," he said, still quietly, "what happens to folk who have naught but their brains to sell? I staked my all on India when I was young—I thought that my star shone over it. I ate dirty puddings—*corpo di Baccho!*— to get there—I was no De Rohan or Soubise to win the king's favor! And I reached there indeed, in my youth, just in time to be included in the surrender of Pondicherry." He laughed, rather terribly, and sipped at his glass.

"You English were very courteous captors," he said. "But I was not released till the Seven Years War had ended—that was in '63. Who asks for the special exchange of an unknown artillery lieutenant? And then ten years odd of garrison duty at Mauritius. It was there that I met Madame—she is a Creole. A pleasant spot, Mauritius. We used to fire the cannon at the sea birds when we had enough ammunition for target practice," and he chuckled drearily. "By then I was thirty-seven. They had to make me a captain—they even brought me back to France. To garrison duty. I have been on garrison duty, at Toulon, at Brest, at——" He ticked off the names on his fingers but I did not like his voice.

"But surely," I said, "the American war, though a small affair—there were opportunities——"

"And who did they send?" he said quickly. "Lafayette—Rochambeau—De Grasse—the sprigs of the nobility. Oh, at Lafayette's age, I would have volunteered like Lafayette. But one should be successful in youth—after that, the spring is broken. And when one is over forty, one has responsibilities. I have a large family, you see, though not of my own begetting," and he chuckled as if at a secret joke. "Oh, I wrote the Continental Congress," he said reflectively, "but they preferred a dolt like Von Steuben. A good dolt, an honest dolt, but there you have it. I also wrote your British War Office," he said in an even voice. "I must show you that plan of campaign—sometime—they could have crushed General Washington with it in three weeks."

I stared at him, a little appalled.

"For an officer who has taken his king's shilling to send to an enemy nation a plan for crushing his own country's ally," I said, stiffly—"well, in England, we would call that treason."

"And what is treason?" he said lightly. "If we call it unsuccessful ambition we shall be nearer the truth." He looked at me, keenly. "You are shocked, General Estcourt," he said. "I am sorry for that. But have you never known the curse"—and his voice vibrated—"the curse of not being employed when you should be employed? The curse of being a hammer with no nail to drive? The curse—the curse of sitting in a dusty garrison town with dreams that would split the brain of a Caesar, and no room on earth for those dreams?"

"Yes," I said, unwillingly, for there was something in him that demanded the truth, "I have known that."

"Then you know hells undreamed of by the Christian," he said, with a sigh, "and if I committed treason —well, I have been punished for it. I might have been a brigadier, otherwise—I had Choiseul's ear for a few weeks, after great labor. As it is, I am here on half pay and there will not be another war in my time. More over, M. de Ségur has proclaimed that all officers now must show sixteen quarterings. Well, I wish them joy of those officers, in the next conflict. Meanwhile, I have my corks, my maps and my family ailment." He smiled and tapped his side. "It killed my father at thirty-nine —it has not treated me quite so ill, but it will come for me soon enough."

And indeed, when I looked at him, I could well believe it, for the light had gone from his eyes and his cheeks were flabby. We chatted a little on indifferent subjects after that, then I left him, wondering whether to pursue the acquaintance. He is indubitably a character, but some of his speeches leave a taste in my mouth. Yet he can be greatly attractive—even now, with his mountainous failure like a cloak upon him. And yet why should I call it mountainous? His conceit is mountainous enough, but what else could he have expected of his career? Yet I wish I could forget his eyes. . . To tell the truth, he puzzles me and I mean to get to the bottom of him. . . .

February 12th, 1789.

. . . I have another sidelight on the character of my friend, the major. As I told you, I was half of a mind to break off the acquaintance entirely, but he came up to me so civilly, the following day, that I could find no excuse. And since then, he has made me no embarrassingly treasonable confidences, though whenever we discuss the art of war, his arrogance is unbelievable. He even informed me, the other day, that while Frederick of Prussia was a fair general, his tactics might have been improved upon. I merely laughed and turned the question. Now and then I play a war

game with him, with his corks and maps, and when I
let him win, he is as pleased as a child. . . . His illness
increases visibly, despite the waters, and he shows an
eagerness for my company which I cannot but find
touching. . . . After all, he is a man of intelligence, and
the company he has had to keep must have galled him
at times. . . .

Now and then I amuse myself by speculating what
might have happened to him, had he chosen some other
profession than that of arms. He has, as I have told you,
certain gifts of the actor, yet his stature and figure must
have debarred him from tragic parts, while he certainly does not possess the humors of the comedian.
Perhaps his best choice would have been the Romish
church, for there, the veriest fisherman may hope, at
least, to succeed to the keys of St. Peter. . . . And yet,
Heaven knows, he would have made a very bad
priest! . . .

But, to my tale. I had missed him from our accustomed walks for some days and went to his house—
St. Helen's it is called; we live in a pother of saints'
names hereabouts—one evening to inquire. I did not
hear the quarreling voices till the tousle-haired servant
had admitted me and then it was too late to retreat.
Then my friend bounced down the corridor, his sallow
face bored and angry.

"Ah, General Estcourt!" he said, with a complete
change of expression as soon as he saw me. "What fortune! I was hoping you would pay us a call—I wish to
introduce you to my family!"

He had told me previously of his pair of stepchil-
dren by Madame's first marriage, and I must confess

I felt curious to see them. But it was not of them he
spoke, as I soon gathered.

"Yes," he said. "My brothers and sisters, or most of
them, are here for a family council. You come in the
nick of time!" He pinched my arm and his face glowed
with the malicious naïveté of a child. "They do not
believe that I really know an English general—it will
be a great blow to them!" he whispered as we passed
down the corridor. "Ah, if you had only worn your
uniform and your Garters! But one cannot have everything in life!"

Well, my dear sister, what a group, when we entered
the salon! It is a small room, tawdrily furnished in the
worst French taste, with a jumble of Madame's feminin-
ities and souvenirs from the Island of Mauritius, and
they were all sitting about in the French after-dinner
fashion, drinking tisane and quarreling. And, indeed,
had the room been as long as the nave of St. Peter's,
it would yet have seemed too small for such a crew!
An old mother, straight as a ramrod and as forbidding,
with the burning eyes and the bitter dignity one sees
on the faces of certain Italian peasants—you could see
that they were all a little afraid of her except my friend,
and he, I must say, treated her with a filial courtesy
that was greatly to his credit. Two sisters, one fattish,
swarthy and spiteful, the other with the wreck of great
beauty and the evident marks of a certain profession
on her shabby-fine *toilette* and her pinkened cheeks.
An innkeeper brother-in-law called Buras or Durat,
with a jowlish, heavily handsome face and the manners
of a cavalry sergeant—he is married to the spiteful sis-

ter. And two brothers, one sheep-like, one fox-like, yet
both bearing a certain resemblance to my friend.

The sheep-like brother is at least respectable, I gathered—a provincial lawyer in a small way of business
whose great pride is that he has actually appeared before the Court of Appeals at Marseilles. The other, the
fox-like one, makes his living more dubiously—he seems
the sort of fellow who orates windily in taprooms about
the Rights of Man, and other nonsense of M. Rous-
seau's. I would certainly not trust him with my watch,
though he is trying to get himself elected to the States-
General. And, as regards family concord, it was obvious at first glance that not one of them trusted the
others. And yet, that is not all of the tribe. There are,
if you will believe me, two other brothers living, and
this family council was called to deal with the affairs
of the next-to-youngest, who seems, even in this mé-
lange, to be a black sheep.

I can assure you, my head swam, and when my
friend introduced me, proudly, as a Knight of the Garters, I did not even bother to contradict him. For they
admitted me to their intimate circle at once—there
was no doubt about that. Only the old lady remained
aloof, saying little and sipping her camomile tea as if
it were the blood of her enemies. But, one by one, the
others related to me, with an unasked-for frankness, the
most intimate and scandalous details of their brothers'
and sisters' lives. They seemed united only on two
points, jealousy of my friend, the major, because he is
his mother's favorite, and dislike of Madame Josephine
because she gives herself airs. Except for the haggard
beauty—I must say, that, while her remarks anent her

sister-in-law were not such as I would care to repeat, she seemed genuinely fond of her brother, the major, and expounded his virtues to me through an overpowering cloud of scent.

It was like being in a nest of Italian smugglers, or a den of quarrelsome foxes, for they all talked, or rather barked at once, even the brother-in-law, and only Madame Mère could bring silence among them. And yet, my friend enjoyed it. It was obvious he showed them off before me as he might have displayed the tricks of a set of performing animals. And yet with a certain fondness, too—that is the inexplicable part of it. I do not know which sentiment was upmost in my mind—respect for this family feeling or pity for his being burdened with such a clan.

For though not the eldest, he is the strongest among them, and they know it. They rebel, but he rules their family conclaves like a petty despot. I could have laughed at the farce of it, and yet, it was nearer tears. For here, at least, my friend was a personage.

I got away as soon as I could, despite some pressing looks from the haggard beauty. My friend accompanied me to the door.

"Well, well," he said, chuckling and rubbing his hands, "I am infinitely obliged to you, general. They will not forget this in a hurry. Before you entered, Joseph"—Joseph is the sheep-like one—"was boasting about his acquaintance with a *sous-intendant,* but an English general, bah! Joseph will have green eyes for a fortnight!" And he rubbed his hands again in a perfect paroxysm of delight.

It was too childlike to make me angry. "I am glad, of course, to have been of any service," I said.

"Oh, you have been a great service," he said. "They will not plague my poor Josie for at least half an hour. Ah, this is a bad business of Louis'—a bad business!"— Louis is the black sheep—"but we will patch it up somehow. Hortense is worth three of him—he must go back to Hortense!"

"You have a numerous family, major," I said, for want of something better to say.

"Oh, yes," he said, cheerfully. "Pretty numerous— I am sorry you could not meet the others. Though Louis is a fool—I pampered him in his youth. Well! He was a baby—and Jerome a mule. Still, we haven't done so badly for ourselves; not badly. Joseph makes a go of his law practice—there are fools enough in the world to be impressed by Joseph—and if Lucien gets to the States-General, you may trust Lucien to feather his nest! And there are the grandchildren, and a little money—not much," he said, quickly. "They mustn't expect that from me. But it's a step up from where we started—if papa had lived, he wouldn't have been so ill-pleased. Poor Elisa's gone, but the rest of us have stuck together, and, while we may seem a little rough, to strangers, our hearts are in the right place. When I was a boy," and he chuckled again, "I had other ambitions for them. I thought, with luck on my side, I could make them all kings and queens. Funny, isn't it, to think of a numskull like Joseph as a king! Well, that was the boy of it. But, even so, they'd all be eating chestnuts back on the island without me, and that's something."

He said it rather defiantly, and I did not know which to marvel at most—his preposterous pride in the group or his cool contempt of them. So I said nothing but shook his hand instead. I could not help doing the latter. For surely, if anyone started in life with a millstone about his neck . . . and yet they are none of them ordinary people. . . .

March 13th, 1789.

. . . My friend's complaint has taken a turn for the worse and it is I who pay him visits now. It is the act of a Christian to do so and, to tell the truth, I have become oddly attached to him, though I can give no just reason for the attachment. He makes a bad patient, by the way, and is often abominably rude to both myself and Madame, who nurses him devotedly though unskillfully. I told him yesterday that I could have no more of it and he looked at me with his strangely luminous eyes. "So," he said, "even the English desert the dying." . . . Well, I stayed; after that, what else might a gentleman do? . . . Yet I cannot feel that he bears me any real affection—he exerts himself to charm, on occasion, but one feels he is playing a game . . . yes, even upon his deathbed, he plays a game . . . a complex character. . . .

April 28th, 1789.

. . . My friend the major's malady approaches its term—the last few days find him fearfully enfeebled. He knows that the end draws nigh; indeed he speaks of it often, with remarkable calmness. I had thought it might turn his mind toward religion, but while he has accepted the ministrations of his Church, I fear it is without the sincere repentance of a Christian. When the priest had left him, yesterday, he summoned me, remarking, "Well, all that is over with," rather more in the tone of a man who has just reserved a place in a coach than one who will shortly stand before his Maker.

"It does no harm," he said, reflectively. "And, after all, it might be true. Why not?" and he chuckled in a way that repelled me. Then he asked me to read to him—not the Bible, as I had expected, but some verses of the poet Gray. He listened attentively, and when I came to the passage, "Hands, that the rod of empire might have swayed," and its successor, "Some mute inglorious Milton here may rest," he asked me to repeat them. When I had done so, he said, "Yes, yes. That is true, very true. I did not think so in boyhood—I thought genius must force its own way. But your poet is right about it."

I found this painful, for I had hoped that his illness had brought him to a juster, if less arrogant, estimate of his own abilities.

"Come, major," I said, soothingly, "we cannot all be great men, you know. And you have no need to repine. After all, as you say, you have risen in the world——"

"Risen?" he said, and his eyes flashed. "Risen? Oh, God, that I should die alone with my one companion an Englishman with a soul of suet! Fool, if I had had Alexander's chance, I would have bettered Alexander! And it will come, too, that is the worst of it. Already Europe is shaking with a new birth. If I had been born under the Sun-King, I would be a Marshal of France;

if I had been born twenty years ago, I would mold a new Europe with my fists in the next half-dozen years. Why did they put my soul in my body at this infernal time? Do you not understand, imbecile? Is there no one who understands?"

I called Madame at this, as he was obviously delirious, and, after some trouble, we got him quieted.

May 8th, 1789.

... My poor friend is gone, and peacefully enough at the last. His death, oddly enough, coincided with the date of the opening of the States-General at Versailles. The last moments of life are always painful for the observer, but his end was as relatively serene as might be hoped for, considering his character. I was watching at one side of the bed and a thunderstorm was raging at the time. No doubt, to his expiring consciousness, the cracks of the thunder sounded like artillery, for, while we were waiting the death-struggle, he suddenly raised himself in the bed and listened intently. His eyes glowed, a beatific expression passed over his features. "The army! Head of the army!" he whispered ecstatically, and, when we caught him, he was lifeless ... I must say that, while it may not be very Christian, I am glad that death brought him what life could not, and that, in the very article of it, he saw himself at the head of victorious troops. Ah, Fame —delusive spectre ... (A page of disquisition by General Estcourt on the vanities of human ambition is here omitted.) ... The face, after death, was composed, with a certain majesty, even ... one could see that he might have been handsome as a youth. ...

May 26th, 1789.

. . . I shall return to Paris by easy stages and reach
Stokely sometime in June. My health is quite restored
and all that has kept me here this long has been the
difficulty I have met with in attempting to settle my
poor friend, the major's affairs. For one thing, he appears to have been originally a native of Corsica, not of
Sardinia as I had thought, and while that explains
much in his character, it has also given occupation to
the lawyers. I have met his rapacious family, individu-
ally and in conclave, and, if there are further gray hairs
on my head, you may put it down to them. . . . However, I have finally assured the major's relict of her
legitimate rights in his estate, and that is something—
my one ray of comfort in the matter being the behavior
of her son by the former marriage, who seems an excellent and virtuous young man. . . .

. . . You will think me a very soft fellow, no doubt,
for wasting so much time upon a chance acquaintance
who was neither, in our English sense, a gentleman nor
a man whose Christian virtues counterbalanced his lack
of true breeding. Yet there was a tragedy about him
beyond his station, and that verse of Gray's rings in my
head. I wish I could forget the expression on his face
when he spoke of it. Suppose a genius born in circum-
stances that made the development of that genius impossible—well, all this is the merest moonshine. . . .

. . . To revert to more practical matters, I discover
that the major has left me his military memoirs, papers
and commentaries, including his maps. Heaven knows
what I shall do with them! I cannot, in courtesy, burn
them *sur-le-champ,* and yet they fill two huge packing

cases and the cost of transporting them to Stokely will be considerable. Perhaps I will take them to Paris and quietly dispose of them there to some waste-paper merchant. . . . In return for this unsought legacy, Madame has consulted me in regard to a stone and epitaph for her late husband, and, knowing that otherwise the family would squabble over the affair for weeks, I have drawn up a design which I hope meets with their approval. It appears that he particularly desired that the epitaph should be writ in English, saying that France had had enough of him, living—a freak of dying vanity for which one must pardon him. However, I have produced the following, which I hope will answer.

Here lies
NAPOLEONE BUONAPARTE
Major of the Royal Artillery
of France.
Born August 15th, 1737
at Ajaccio, Corsica.
Died May 5th, 1789
at St. Philippe-des-Bains

"Rest, perturbed spirit . . ."

. . . I had thought, for some hours, of excerpting the lines of Gray's—the ones that still ring in my head. But, on reflection, though they suit well enough, they yet seem too cruel to the dust.

THE SOBBIN' WOMEN

THEY came over the Pass one day in one big wagon —all ten of them—man and woman and hired girl and seven big boy children, from the nine-year-old who walked by the team to the baby in arms. Or so the story runs—it was in the early days of settlement and the town had never heard of the Sobbin' Women then. But it opened its eyes one day, and there were the Pontipees.

They were there but they didn't stay long—just time enough to buy meal and get a new shoe for the lead horse. You couldn't call them unsociable, exactly— they seemed to be sociable enough among themselves. But you could tell, somehow, from the look of them, that they weren't going to settle on ground other people had cleared. They were all high-colored and dark-haired—handsome with a wilderness handsomeness— and when you got them all together, they looked more like a tribe or a nation than an ordinary family. I don't know how they gave folks that feeling, but they did. Yes, even the baby, when the town women tried to handle him. He was a fine, healthy baby, but they said it was like trying to pet a young raccoon.

Well, that was all there was to it, at the start. They paid for what they bought in good money and drove on up into Sobbin' Women Valley—only it wasn't called Sobbin' Women Valley then. And pretty soon, there was smoke from a chimney there that hadn't been there before. But you know what town gossip is when it gets started. The Pontipees were willing enough to let other folks alone—in fact, that was what they wanted. But, because it was what they wanted, the town couldn't see why they wanted it. Towns get that way, sometimes.

So, it was mostly cross questions and crooked answers when the Pontipees came into town, to trade off their pelts and such and buy at the store. There wasn't much actual trouble—not after two loafers at the tavern made fun of Pa Pontipee's fur cap and Pa Pontipee stretched them both before you could say "Jack Robinson." But there wasn't a neighborly feeling—yes, you could say that. The women would tell their children about the terrible Pontipees and the men would wag their heads. And when they came in to church—which they did once a year—there'd be a sort of rustle in the congregation, though they always took a back pew and listened perfectly respectful. But the minister never seemed to be able to preach as good a sermon as usual that Sunday—and naturally, he blamed the Pontipees for that. Till, finally, they got to be a sort of legend in the community—the wild folks who lived up the valley like bears in the woods—and, indeed, some said they turned into bears in the winter time, which just shows you what people will say. And, though the boys were well set up, they might as well have been deaf-mutes for all the notice the town-girls took of them—except to squeak and run to the other side of the road when the Pontipees came marching along.

While, as for the Pontipees—nobody knew what they made of it all, for they weren't much on talking. If one of them said "It's a fine day" and another admitted it was, that was conversation that would last them a long while. Besides, they had work enough and to spare, in their own valley, to keep them busy; and, if Ma Pontipee would have liked more society, she never let on. She did her duty by the boys and tried to give them some manners, in spite of their backwoods raising; and that was enough for any woman to do.

But things never stand still in this world, and soon enough, the boys weren't boys any more, they were men. And when the fall of a tree took Pa Pontipee, his wife didn't linger long after him. There was a terrible fuss about the funerals too—for the Pontipee boys got the minister, but they wouldn't let the burials take place in town. They said Pa and Ma wouldn't feel comfortable, all crowded up among strangers in the churchyard, so they laid them to rest in the Valley where they'd lived, and the town found that queerer than ever. But there's worse places to lie than looking out over the fields you've cleared.

After that, though, the town thought some of the boys, at least, would move in from the Valley and get more sociable. They figured they'd have to—they figured with their Pa and Ma gone, the boys would fight amongst themselves—they figured a dozen things. But none of the things they figured happened at all. The Pontipee boys stayed out in the Valley, and when they came to the town, they walked through it as proud as Lucifer, and when they came to the church, they put just the same money in the collection-plate they had when Ma and Pa Pontipee were alive. Some thought it was because they were stupid to count, but I don't think it was that.

They went on just the same, as I say, but things didn't go quite the same for them. For one thing, the hired girl couldn't keep the place the way Ma Pontipee kept it. And besides, she was getting old herself. Well, pretty soon, she up and died. They gave her as good a funeral as they knew how—she'd always been part of the family. But, after that, though the farm went ahead as well as ever, things in the house began to go from bad to worse.

Menlike, they didn't notice what was wrong at first, except there was a lot of dust around and things didn't get put away. But, after each one of them had tried a week of cooking for the others and all the others had cursed out the one who was cooking something proper, they decided something had to be done about it. It took them a long time to decide that—they were slow thinkers as well as slow talkers, the Pontipees. But, when they decided about a thing, it got done.

"The flapjacks are greasy again," said Harry Ponti-pee, one evening—Harry was the oldest. "You know what we've got to get, brothers? We've got to get a woman to take care of this place. I can lay a tree within two inches of where I want it to fall. I can shoot the eye out of a grey squirrel in a treetop. I can do all a man should do. But I can't cook and make it taste human."

"You're right, brother," said Hob Pontipee—Hob was the youngest. "I can tan deerskin better than an Injun squaw. I can wrestle underholt and overholt and throw any man in this county. I can play on a boxwood fiddle—but I can't sweep dust so it stays swept. It takes a woman to do that, for there seems to be a trick about it. We've got to get a woman."

Then they all joined in saying what they could do—and it was plenty—but they couldn't cook and they couldn't dust and they couldn't make a house comfortable because that was woman's business, and there seemed to be a trick about it. So they had to get a woman to keep house for them. But where were they going to get her?

"We could get a hired girl, maybe," said Hosea Pontipee—the middle one—but, even as he spoke, there wasn't much hope in his voice.

"That hired girl we had was the last one left in the East," said Harry Pontipee. "Some may have growed up, since her time, but I don't want to go back across the Pass on the chance of an out-and-out miracle."

"Well then," said Hob Pontipee, practical, "there's just one thing to do. One of us has to get married. And I think it ought to be Harry—he's the eldest."

Well, that remark nearly caused a break-up in the family. Harry kicked like a cow in fly-time at the bare idea of getting married, and tried to put it on to Halbert, who was next in line. And Halbert passed it on to Harvey, but Harvey said women was snares and delusions, or so he'd heard, and he wouldn't have a strange woman around him for a brand-new plow.

So it went on down to Hob and he wouldn't hear of it—and it wasn't till a couple of chairs had been broken and Hob had a black eye that the ruckus quieted at all. But, gradually, they came to see that one of 'em would have to get married, as a matter of family duty, or they'd all be eating spoiled flapjacks for the rest of their lives. Only then the question came up as to who it was to be, and that started a bigger disturbance than ever.

Finally, they agreed that the only fair way was drawing straws. So Hob held the straws and they drew—and, sure enough, Harry got the long one. Sick enough he looked about it—but there it was. The others started congratulating him and making jokes—especially Hob.

"You'll have to slick up, tomorrow," said Hob, glad it wasn't him. "You'll have to cut your hair and brush your clothes and act pretty, if you're going to be a bridegroom!"

Next morning they got him down and cut his hair and put bear's grease on it and dressed him up in the best clothes they had and sent him into town to look for a wife.

It was all right when he started out from the Valley. He even took a look at himself in a spring and was kind of surprised at the young man who looked back at him. But the nearer he got to town, the queerer and tremblier he felt, and the less able to go about doing what he'd promised.

He tried to remember how it had been when his Pa and Ma had been courting. But, naturally, as he hadn't been born then, he didn't know. Then he tried to think of various girls in the village, but the more he thought of them, the more they mixed in his mind—till, finally, all he could think of was a high, wild bank of rhododendron flowers that mixed and shimmered and laughed at you the closer you came to it.

"Oh, Lordy! It's a heavy responsibility to lay on a man!" he said and mopped his forehead with his sleeve.

Finally, however, he made up his mind. "I'll ask the first woman I see, pretty or ugly!" he said to himself, with the perspiration fairly rolling down his face, though it was a cold March day. And he gave his horse a lick.

But, when he got into town, the first woman he saw was the storekeeper's wife. The second he saw was a little girl in a pinafore—and the third was the minister's daughter. He was all set up to speak to her— but she squeaked and ran to the other side of the street as soon as she saw him and left him standing there with his hat in his hand. That sort of took the courage out of him.

"By the whiskers of Moses!" he said to himself, "this marryin' job is a harder job than I bargained for. I guess I'll go over to the tavern and get me a drink— maybe that will put some ideas in my head."

It was there he saw her—feeding the chickens out in the poultry-yard. Her name was Milly and she was a bound girl, as they had in those days. Next door to a slave she was, for all she'd come of good stock and had some education. She was young and thin, with a sharp little thoughtful face and ragged clothes, but she walked as straight as an Indian as she went about the yard. Harry Pontipee couldn't have said if she were pretty or plain, but, as he watched her through the window, feeding the chickens, something seemed to tell him that he might have better luck with her than he'd had with the others.

Well, he drank his drink and went out.

"Hello, girl," he said, in one of those big voices men use when they're pretending not to be embarrassed.

She looked up at him straight. "Hello, backwoodsman!" she said, friendly enough. She didn't look a bit scared of him and that put him off.

"It's a nice morning," said Harry, louder, trying to lead up to his point.

"It is for some," said the girl, perfectly polite but going on feeding the chickens.

Harry swallowed hard at that. "It'd be a nice morning to get married, they tell me," he said, with the perspiration breaking out all over him again. He'd meant to say something else, but when it came to the point, he couldn't.

Well, she didn't say anything to that so he had to start all over again.

"My name's Harry Pontipee," he said. "I've got a good farm up the Valley."

"Have you?" said the girl.

"Yes," he said. "It's a right good farm. And some folks seem to think I'd make a good husband."

"Do they?" said the girl. I guess she was smiling by now but Harry couldn't see it—she had her head turned.

"Yes they do," said Harry, kind of desperate, his voice getting louder and louder. "What do you think about it?"

"I couldn't tell on such short acquaintance," said the girl.

"Will you marry me and find out?" said Harry, in a perfect bellow, shaking all over.

"Yes, I will, if you don't ask me quite so loud," she

said, very prim—and even Harry could see she was smiling now.

Well, they made a queer pair when they went up to the minister—the girl still in her chicken-feed clothes, for she didn't have any others, and Harry in his backwoods finery. He'd had to buy out her time from the innkeeper for twelve beaver pelts and a hunting knife.

But when the wedding service was over, "Well, we're married," said Harry, with great relief. "And now we'll be going home."

"Oh, no we won't," said she. "We're going to the store first and buy me some cloth for a decent dress— for landless I may be and dowryless I may be, but I'm a married woman now, and what's fit for a chicken-girl isn't fit for a married woman."

In a sort of daze, he saw her lay out the price of twelve more beaver pelts in cloth and woman's fixings, and beat down the storekeeper on the price, too.

He only asked her a question about one thing—a little pair of slippers she bought. They were fancy slippers, with embroidery on them. "I thought you had a pair of shoes," he said. She turned to him, with a cocky sort of look on her face. "Silly," she said. "How could anyone tell your wife had pretty feet in the shoes I had?"

Well, he thought that over, and, after a while, something in the way she said it and the cocky look on her face made him feel pleased, and he began to laugh. He wasn't used to laughing in front of a girl, but he could see it might have its points.

Then they rode back to the Valley, her riding pillion, with her bundles in the saddlebags. And all the way back, she was trying him and testing him and trying to find out, by one little remark or another, just what kind of a man he was. She was a spunky little girl, and she had more education than she let on. And long ago, she'd made up her mind to get out of being a bound girl the first way that offered. But, all the same, marrying Harry Pontipee was a leap in the dark.

But the more she tried and tested Harry, the better bargain she seemed to think she'd made. And that took courage to admit—for the way was a wild one and a lonesome, and, naturally, she'd heard stories of Pontipee Valley. She couldn't quite believe they lived with bears, up there, but she didn't know.

And finally, they came to the house, and there were dark things moving outside it. "Bears!" thought Milly, kind of hopeless, and her heart went into her throat, but she didn't let on.

"W-what's that, Harry dear?" she said, holding on tight.

"Oh, that's just my brothers," said Harry, kind of careless, and with that those six hungry six-footers moved into the light.

"Oh!" said Milly, "you didn't tell me you had six brothers." But her voice wasn't reproachful, just sort of soft and quiet.

"I guess it was the wedding kind of knocked it out of my mind," said Harry. "But, there—you'll see enough of 'em anyhow, because we all live together."

"Oh," said Milly again, kind of soft. "I see." And the brothers came up, one by one, and shook hands. They'd intended to cut quite a few jokes on Harry if he did come home with a wife, but, somehow, when they looked at Milly, they forgot about that.

Well, they brought her into the house. It was a handsome house, for the times, with genuine window-glass. But Milly rubbed her finger along a window sill and saw it come off black and then she wrote her name in the dust on the mantelpiece.

"What a lovely big house!" she said, coughing a little with the dust she'd raised.

"It's mebbe a little dusty now," said Harry. "But now you're here——"

"Yes," said Milly and passed on to the kitchen. Well, the kitchen was certainly a sight. But Milly didn't seem to notice.

Presently, "What a great big jar of flapjack batter!" she said. "And what a big tub of salt pork!"

"That's for tonight," said Harry. "Me and my brothers is hearty eaters. We haven't been eating so well since we had to cook for ourselves, but now you're here——"

"Yes," said Milly and passed on to the laundry. The laundry was half full of huckaback shirts and such that needed washing—piles and piles of them.

"What a lot of wash!" said Milly.

"That's so," said Harry, kind of pleased. "Me and my brothers is kind of hard on our clothes—all seven of us—so there's lots of washing and mending, but now you're here——"

"Yes," said Milly, swallowing a little. "And now all you men clear out of my kitchen while I get supper. Clear out!" she said, smiling at them, though she didn't feel much like smiling.

I don't know what she said to herself when they'd left her alone. I know what a man would have said and I guess she said that, too. I know she thought at least once of the money in her stocking and how far it was back to town. And then her eye happened to fall on that great big jar of flapjack batter—and, all of a sudden the whole thing struck her as funny, and she laughed till she cried.

But then she found a clean handkerchief and blew her nose and straightened her hair and set about her work.

Those boys hadn't had a supper like that in months and they treated it respectful. And Milly didn't say a word to them about manners then, though, later on, she said plenty. She just sat and watched them, with a curious light in her eyes.

When it was over finally, and they were stuffed, "Mrs. Harry," said Howard. "You're a wonder, Mrs. Harry!" and "You're sure a wonder, Mrs. Harry!" chorused all the rest of them, down to Hob. She could see they meant it, too.

"Thanks," she said, very polite and gracious. "Thank you, Howard, and you, Hosea, and all my brothers."

At the end of three months, there wasn't one of those boys that wouldn't have laid down his life for Milly, and, as for Harry, he just worshipped the ground she walked on. With all that work to do, naturally, she got thinner and thinner and peakeder and peakeder, but she didn't complain. She knew what she wanted and how she was going to get it—and she waited her chance.

Finally Harry noticed how thin she was getting and he spoke to her about it.

"Can't you ever sit down and rest, Milly?" he said one day, watching her fly around the kitchen, doing six things at once.

But she just laughed at him and said, "I'm cooking for you and your six brothers, and that makes work, you know."

Well, he thought that over, inside him, but he didn't say anything, then. But he came up to her in the laundry another time, and when she was dusting the house another time—she was looking peakeder each day—and asked her if she couldn't rest a spell. The last time, he brought his fist down on the table with a bang.

"This has got to stop!" he said. "Me and my six brothers is wearing you to skin and bone with our victuals and our shirts and the dust we track in the house, and I won't have it no more! It's got to stop!"

"Well, Harry," she said, sort of quiet, "if it's got to stop, it's got to—and pretty soon, Harry. Because, I'm expecting, and a woman that's expecting can't work like a woman in her usual health."

Well, after he got his sense back, after hearing that, he called the whole family into consultation that evening and put it to them plain. They'd do anything for Milly by then.

She led the conversation where she wanted it to go, though she didn't seem to, and finally they decided it was up to Halbert, the second oldest, to get married, so his wife could take some of the work off Milly's hands. So next day, Halbert spruced up and went to town to look for a wife. But when he came home, he was alone and all dejected.

"They won't have me," he said, very mournful. "They won't none of 'em have me—and I asked fourteen of 'em."

"Why, what's the matter?" said Milly.

"Well," said Halbert, "it seems they've heard about the seven of us and the lot of victuals we eat and the wash and all—and they say only a fool would marry into a family like that and they don't see how you stand it, Milly."

"Oh, that's what they say, is it?" said Milly, with her eyes as bright as candles. "Well, your turn next, Harvey."

So Harvey tried it and Hosea tried it and all of them tried it. But none of them had any luck. And then, finally, Milly let loose at them, good and proper.

"You great big lumps of men!" she said, with the cocky look on her face. "There's more ways of killing a cat than choking it with cream. If they won't marry you after you've asked 'em—why don't you marry 'em first and ask 'em afterwards?"

"But how can we do that?" said Harvey, who was the stupidest.

"Well," said Milly—and here's where her education came in that I've made such a point of—"I read in a history book once about a bunch of people called Romans who were just in your fix." And she went on to tell them about the Romans—how they were settled in a country that was unfriendly to them, just like the Pontipees, and how they all needed wives, just like the Pontipees, and how, when they couldn't get them in the ordinary way from the other people of the country who were called the Sobbin's or the Sabbin's or some such name, they raided the Sobbin' town one night and carried off a lot of the Sobbin' women and married them.

"And, if you can't do as well for yourselves as a lot of old dead Romans," she ended, "you're no brothers of mine and you can cook your own suppers the rest of your lives."

They all sat around dumbfounded for a while. Finally Hob spoke up.

"That sounds all right, in history," he said, "but this is different. Supposing these women just cry and pine away when we've carried them off—supposing that?"

"Listen to me," said Milly. "I know what I'm talking about. Every one of those girls is crazy to get married—and there's not half enough men in town to go round. They think a lot of you boys, too, for I've heard them talk about you; but they're scared of your being backwoodsmen, and scared of the work, and each one is scared of being the first to leave the others. I'll answer for them, once you've married them. Is there anybody around here who can marry people, except the regular minister?"

"There's a sort of hedge-parson just come to town," said Hob. "I reckon he can tie a knot as tight as any preacher in the county."

"All right," said Milly. "That settles it."

It was the evening of the big sociable that it happened. They held it once a year, around Thanksgiving time, and those who had rifles and weapons left them at the door. The Pontipee boys had never attended before—so there was a good deal of stir when they marched in, all seven of them, with Milly in the middle. The brothers were shaved and clean and dressed up spick and span and Milly never looked better, in a dress she'd made out of store cloth and her embroidered slippers.

There was quite a bit of giggling from the town girls, as the Pontipees entered, and a buzz around the hall, but then the fiddler struck up and people began to dance and play games and enjoy themselves, and pretty soon they forgot the Pontipees were there at all, except that the Pontipee boys acted very polite to everybody—Milly'd taught 'em that—and, I guess, before the evening was over, some of the town girls were wondering why they'd turned down boys like that just because they lived in the backwoods.

But they didn't get much chance to think about it, at that. Because, just as they were all going to sit down to supper—"Ready, boys?" called Milly, in a voice that cut through all the talk and commotion. Everybody turned to look at her. And then there was a gasp and a cry, for "Ready!" chorused the six bachelor Pontipees; and suddenly, each one had one hand on a rifle and the other holding a girl, while Harry and Milly trained a couple more rifles on the rest of the community to keep them quiet. It happened so sudden, half the folks didn't even know it was happening—till the Pontipee boys had their girls outside in the street, and the big doors locked and bolted behind them.

Then there was Cain to raise for fair in the meeting-hall, and people started to beat and kick at the doors—but they built solid, in those days. There wasn't any use in trying to shoot the locks off, because the Pontipee boys had tied up the guard over the weapons and dumped him and them outside in a shed.

It wasn't till pretty near dawn that the doors gave way—and when they did, the townspeople took one look outside and groaned. For it was snowing, lickety split, till you couldn't see your hand before your face— and when it snows, in our part of the country, it certainly snows. The blizzard didn't let up for four days, either, and by that time, the pass through the hills to Pontipee Valley was blocked solid, and nothing to do but wait for Spring and the thaw.

And, meanwhile, Milly had her work cut out for her. It wasn't an easy job, convoying three sleigh-loads full of hysterics all that long, cold ride. But she let them hysteric away, and, by the time they got to the Pontipee house, the stolen brides were so tuckered out that they'd quieted down a good deal.

Still, at first, they swore they wouldn't take bite or sup till they were restored to their grieving families. But Milly had some tea ready for them, in a jiffy—and a woman will usually take tea, no matter how mad she is. Well, Milly let them get warm and a little cozy, and then, when they were on their second cups, she made her little speech.

"Ladies," she said, "this affair makes me mighty sad—to see fine girls like you stole away by a lot of uncouth backwoodsmen. And I'd never have lent a hand to it if I'd known the truth of the matter. But, you and me, we'll turn the tables on them yet. You can't get back to your families till the blizzard lets up, but, while you've got to stay here, I'll see you're treated respectful. And just to prove that"—and she took a bunch of keys from her pocket—"I'll lock this house up tight, with us inside it; and, as for those backwoods Pontipees, they can sleep and eat in the stable with the livestock. That'll teach them they can't fool us!"

Well, that little speech—and the tea—cheered the girls up quite a bit. And by the time Milly showed them to their rooms—nice-looking rooms, too—and let them bolt themselves in, they were pretty well convinced that Milly was their friend.

So a week or so went by like that—the girls keeping house for themselves and never seeing hide nor hair of a Pontipee.

At first, it was a regular picnic for the girls. They allowed as how they'd always wanted to live without any men around, and, now they were, it was even better than they'd thought. And Milly agreed with them as hard as she could agree. She made them little speeches about the worthlessness of men in general and husbands in particular that would have raised the hair off any man's head. And, at first, the other girls listened to her and chimed in, and then they listened, but you could see they were being polite. And, by the end of the week, it was awful hard for her to get a real audience.

So, when she began to catch them looking out of windows when they should have been dusting, and peeking from behind curtains to try and get a sight of the terrible Pontipees, she knew it was time for the next step. For things got duller and duller in the house and little spats and quarrels began to break out among the girls. So, one afternoon, she suggested, tactfully, just to break the monotony, that they all go up and rummage in the garret.

They rummaged around and had quite a bit of fun, until finally the minister's daughter opened a long box and gave a little squeal of joy.

"What a lovely wedding-dress—whose was it?" she said, and pulled out the long white veil and the dress itself, while the rest stood round and admired.

"Oh, shucks, that's just an old wedding-dress those backwoodsmen made me make when they thought you were going to marry 'em," said Milly, in a very disgusted voice. "Put it back!" But the girls weren't paying attention.

"Will it fit me, I wonder?" said the minister's daughter.

"It's bad luck, trying on wedding-dresses, if you're not going to have a wedding!" said Milly. "Let's go downstairs and have tea." But the minister's daughter was stepping out of her regular clothes already. The other girls helped fix her up—and then they oh-ed and ah-ed, for, I must say, she made a handsome-looking bride.

"That Pontipee boy named Hob's got curly hair," said the minister's daughter, trailing out her veil. "I always did have a liking for curly hair."

"Hob's not nearly as good-looking as Halbert," said the lawyer's niece, quite violent, and another one said, "Handsome is as handsome does—the one they call Harvey isn't so handsome, maybe, but he certainly has nice eyes."

"There's something about a man around the house

hat brisks things up remarkable," said a fourth one. "Not that I want to get married, but Howard's a nice name, even if Pontipee is hitched to it and——"

"Girls, girls—are you crazy, girls?" said Milly, shocked and horrified. But the minute she started to reprove them, they all turned on her, most ungratefully, and there was a regular revolt. So, at last, she had to give in and admit that there were five more wedding-dresses in the garret—and that if anybody was thinking of getting married, there just happened to be a hedge-parson, spending the winter with the Pontipees. But one thing she was firm about.

"Get married if you like," she said. "I can't stop you. But I'm responsible for you to your families—and, after the ceremony's ended, your husbands go back to the stable and stay there, till I know your families approve of them." She looked very fierce about it, and she made them promise. The hedge-parson married them all—all six in their wedding dresses—and then the boys went back to the stable. And, at dinner that night, the minister's daughter burst out crying.

"I hate men just as much as ever!" she wailed. "But it's terrible to be lawful married to a man you can't even see, except now and then out of a window!"

So Milly saw she had to make some new rules and she did. Three afternoons a week, the boys were allowed to call on their new wives, and once in a while, for a great treat, they could stay to supper. But, always with Milly to chaperon.

Well, at first, the husbands and wives were mighty stiff and formal with each other, but, gradually, they got better and better acquainted. Till, pretty soon, the

minister's daughter was letting Hob hold her hand
when she thought Milly wasn't looking, and the lawyer'
niece was asking permission to sew a button on Hal
bert's coat—and there was a general atmosphere o
courting around the Pontipee place that'd make an ol
bachelor sick.

Milly took it all in but she never stopped chaperon
ing.

Well, finally, it was one day along in January. Mill
woke up in the morning—and she knew she was nea
her time. But, first thing in the morning, as always
she reached underneath her pillow for her keys—and
then she smiled. For somebody must have stolen then
while she was sleeping—and when she got up, and
went to the window in her wrapper, the door of th
house was wide open. And there was Hob and his wife
helping each other shovel snow from the doorstep
and Halbert and his wife were throwing snowballs a
Harvey and his, and Howard was kissing the doc
tor's eldest behind the kitchen door. "Praise be!" sai
Milly. "I can have my baby in peace"—and she wen
down to congratulate them all.

Only then, there were the families and the relative
still to fix. But Milly had a plan for that—she had plan
for everything. When they stole the girls away, the
left a letter she drew up, signed by all the boys and
expressing all the honorable intentions you could pu
a name to. But she was afraid that wouldn't cool dow
the townspeople much, even when they thought it ove
and it didn't.

One day when the first thaws had come and Milly'

baby was about six weeks old, Hob came running in from his lookout post.

"They're coming, Milly!" he said. "The whole dum town! They've got rifles and scythes and ropes and they look mighty wild and bloodthirsty! What'll we do?"

"Do?" said Milly, perfectly calm. "You get the boys together and keep out of sight—and tell the girls to come here. For it's women's work, now, that'll save us, if anything will."

When she got the girls together, she gave them their orders. I guess they were a bit white-faced, but they obeyed. Then she looked out of the window—and there was the town, marching up the road, slow and steady. She'd have liked it better if they'd shouted or cried, but they didn't shout nor cry. The minister was in the lead, with his lips shut, and a six foot rifle in his hand, and his face like an iron mask.

She saw them come up to the gate of the Pontipee place. The gate was wide open and nobody there to hinder. She could see them take that in—and the little waver in the crowd. Because that made them feel queer.

Then they caught themselves and came tramping along toward the house, the minister still in the lead. Milly caught her breath, for they still looked awful mad. She knew what they'd expect when they got near the house—every window barred and every door bolted and red-hot bullets spitting through the loop-holes in the walls.

But the windows were open—you could see white curtains in them; there were plants on some of the sills. The door of the house stood ajar and Milly's cat was asleep on the doorstone, there in the sun.

They stood outside that door for quite a little bit, just milling around and staring. It was very quiet; they could hear their own breath breathe and their own hearts knock. Finally the minister brushed his face, as if he were brushing a cobweb away from it, and he gripped his gun and went up on the porch and knocked at the open door. He'd intended to stomp up those steps like a charge of cavalry, but he walked soft, instead. He couldn't have told you why.

He knocked once and he knocked again—and then Milly was standing in the door, with her baby in her arms.

Somebody at the back of the crowd dropped the scythe he was carrying, and another one coughed in his hand.

"You're just in time to christen my child, your reverence," said Milly. "Have you brought that rifle to help you christen my child?"

The minister's eyes dropped, after a minute, and he lowered his rifle but he still held it in the crook of his arm.

"Your child?" he said, and his voice was as low as Milly's, but there was a fierceness in it. "What about my child?"

"Listen!" said Milly, raising her hand, and the whole crowd fell dead still. Then from somewhere in the house came the hum of a spinning-wheel, low and steady, and a woman's voice, humming with the wheel.

"That's your child you hear, your reverence," said Milly. "Does she sound hurt, your reverence, or does she sound content?"

The minister hesitated for a moment and the crowd

fell dead still again. Then they all heard the hum of the wheel and the hum of the woman's voice, humming back and forth to each other, as they did their work in the world.

"She sounds content—heaven help me!" said the minister, and a twist went over his face. But then there was a sudden outburst of cries and questions from the others. "My child, what about my child?" "Where's Mary?" "Is Susy safe?"

"Listen!" said Milly again, and they all fell silent once more. And, from somewhere, there came the splash of a churn and the voice of a woman talking to the butter to make it come; and the rattling of pans in a kitchen and a woman singing at her work; and the slap of clothes on a laundry board and the little clatter a woman makes setting table.

"There's your children," said Milly. "Hear 'em? Don't they sound all right? And—dinner will be ready in about half an hour—and you're all staying, I hope."

Then the daughters came out and their folks rushed to them; and, after all the crying and conniptions were over, Milly introduced the parents to their sons-in-law.

THE DEVIL AND DANIEL WEBSTER

IT'S a story they tell in the border country, where Massachusetts joins Vermont and New Hampshire.

Yes, Dan'l Webster's dead—or, at least, they buried him. But every time there's a thunderstorm around Marshfield, they say you can hear his rolling voice in the hollows of the sky. And they say that if you go to his grave and speak loud and clear, "Dan'l Webster—Dan'l Webster!" the ground'll begin to shiver and the trees begin to shake. And after a while you'll hear a deep voice saying, "Neighbor, how stands the Union?" Then you better answer the Union stands as she stood, rock-bottomed and copper-sheathed, one and indivisible, or he's liable to rear right out of the ground. At least, that's what I was told when I was a youngster.

You see, for a while, he was the biggest man in the country. He never got to be President, but he was the biggest man. There were thousands that trusted in him right next to God Almighty, and they told stories about him that were like the stories of patriarchs and such. They said, when he stood up to speak, stars and stripes came right out in the sky, and once he spoke against a river and made it sink into the ground. They said, when he walked the woods with his fishing rod, Killall, the trout would jump out of the streams right into his pockets, for they knew it was no use putting up a fight against him; and, when he argued a case, he could turn on the harps of the blessed and the shaking of the earth underground. That was the kind of man he was, and his big farm up at Marshfield was suitable to him. The chickens he raised were all white meat down through the drumsticks, the cows were tended like children, and the big ram he called Goliath had horns with a curl like a morning-glory vine and could butt through an iron door. But Dan'l wasn't one of your gentlemen farmers; he knew all the ways of the land, and he'd be up by candlelight to see that the chores got done. A man with a mouth like a mastiff, a brow like a mountain and eyes like burning anthracite—that was Dan'l Webster in his prime. And the biggest case he argued never got written down in the books, for he argued it against the devil, nip and tuck and no holds barred. And this is the way I used to hear it told.

There was a man named Jabez Stone, lived at Cross Corners, New Hampshire. He wasn't a bad man to start with, but he was an unlucky man. If he planted corn, he got borers; if he planted potatoes, he got blight. He had good-enough land, but it didn't prosper him; he had a decent wife and children, but the more children he had, the less there was to feed them. If stones cropped up in his neighbor's field, boulders boiled up in his; if he had a horse with the spavins, he'd trade it for one with the staggers and give something extra. There's some folks bound to be like that, apparently. But one day Jabez Stone got sick of the whole business.

He'd been plowing that morning and he'd just

broke the plowshare on a rock that he could have sworn hadn't been there yesterday. And, as he stood looking at the plowshare, the off horse began to cough —that ropy kind of cough that means sickness and horse doctors. There were two children down with the measles, his wife was ailing, and he had a whitlow on his thumb. It was about the last straw for Jabez Stone. "I vow," he said, and he looked around him kind of desperate—"I vow it's enough to make a man want to sell his soul to the devil! And I would, too, for two cents!"

Then he felt a kind of queerness come over him at having said what he'd said; though, naturally, being a New Hampshireman, he wouldn't take it back. But, all the same, when it got to be evening and, as far as he could see, no notice had been taken, he felt relieved in his mind, for he was a religious man. But notice is always taken, sooner or later, just like the Good Book says. And, sure enough, next day, about suppertime, a soft-spoken, dark-dressed stranger drove up in a handsome buggy and asked for Jabez Stone.

Well, Jabez told his family it was a lawyer, come to see him about a legacy. But he knew who it was. He didn't like the looks of the stranger, nor the way he smiled with his teeth. They were white teeth, and plentiful—some say they were filed to a point, but I wouldn't vouch for that. And he didn't like it when the dog took one look at the stranger and ran away howling, with his tail between his legs. But having passed his word, more or less, he stuck to it, and they went out behind the barn and made their bargain. Jabez Stone had to prick his finger to sign, and the stranger lent him a silver pin. The wound healed clean, but it left a little white scar.

After that, all of a sudden, things began to pick up and prosper for Jabez Stone. His cows got fat and his horses sleek, his crops were the envy of the neighborhood, and lightning might strike all over the valley, but it wouldn't strike his barn. Pretty soon, he was one of the prosperous people of the county; they asked him to stand for selectman, and he stood for it; there began to be talk of running him for state senate. All in all, you might say the Stone family was as happy and contented as cats in a dairy. And so they were, except for Jabez Stone.

He'd been contented enough, the first few years. It's a great thing when bad luck turns; it drives most other things out of your head. True, every now and then, especially in rainy weather, the little white scar on his finger would give him a twinge. And once a year, punctual as clockwork, the stranger with the handsome buggy would come driving by. But the sixth year, the stranger lighted, and, after that, his peace was over for Jabez Stone.

The stranger came up through the lower field, switching his boots with a cane—they were handsome black boots, but Jabez Stone never liked the look of them, particularly the toes. And, after he'd passed the time of day, he said, "Well, Mr. Stone, you're a hummer! It's a very pretty property you've got here, Mr. Stone."

"Well, some might favor it and others might not," said Jabez Stone, for he was a New Hampshireman.

"Oh, no need to decry your industry!" said the

stranger, very easy, showing his teeth in a smile. "After all, we know what's been done, and it's been according to contract and specifications. So when—ahem—the mortgage falls due next year, you shouldn't have any regrets."

"Speaking of that mortgage, mister," said Jabez Stone, and he looked around for help to the earth and the sky, "I'm beginning to have one or two doubts about it."

"Doubts?" said the stranger, not quite so pleasantly.

"Why, yes," said Jabez Stone. "This being the U.S.A. and me always having been a religious man." He cleared his throat and got bolder. "Yes, sir," he said, "I'm beginning to have considerable doubts as to that mortgage holding in court."

"There's courts and courts," said the stranger, clicking his teeth. "Still, we might as well have a look at the original document." And he hauled out a big black pocketbook, full of papers. "Sherwin, Slater, Stevens, Stone," he muttered. "I, Jabez Stone, for a term of seven years—— Oh, it's quite in order, I think."

But Jabez Stone wasn't listening, for he saw something else flutter out of the black pocketbook. It was something that looked like a moth, but it wasn't a moth. And as Jabez Stone stared at it, it seemed to speak to him in a small sort of piping voice, terrible small and thin, but terrible human. "Neighbor Stone!" it squeaked. "Neighbor Stone! Help me! For God's sake, help me!"

But before Jabez Stone could stir hand or foot, the stranger whipped out a big bandanna handkerchief, caught the creature in it, just like a butterfly, and started tying up the ends of the bandanna.

"Sorry for the interruption," he said. "As I was saying——"

But Jabez Stone was shaking all over like a scared horse.

"That's Miser Stevens' voice!" he said, in a croak. "And you've got him in your handkerchief!"

The stranger looked a little embarrassed.

"Yes, I really should have transferred him to the collecting box," he said with a simper, "but there were some rather unusual specimens there and I didn't want them crowded. Well, well, these little contretemps will occur."

"I don't know what you mean by contertan," said Jabez Stone, "but that was Miser Stevens' voice! And he ain't dead! You can't tell me he is! He was just as spry and mean as a woodchuck, Tuesday!"

"In the midst of life——" said the stranger, kind of pious. "Listen!" Then a bell began to toll in the valley and Jabez Stone listened, with the sweat running down his face. For he knew it was tolled for Miser Stevens and that he was dead.

"These long-standing accounts," said the stranger with a sigh; "one really hates to close them. But business is business."

He still had the bandanna in his hand, and Jabez Stone felt sick as he saw the cloth struggle and flutter.

"Are they all as small as that?" he asked hoarsely.

"Small?" said the stranger. "Oh, I see what you mean. Why, they vary." He measured Jabez Stone with his eyes, and his teeth showed. "Don't worry, Mr.

Stone," he said. "You'll go with a very good grade. I wouldn't trust you outside the collecting box. Now, a man like Dan'l Webster, of course—well, we'd have to build a special box for him, and even at that, I imagine the wing spread would astonish you. But, in your case, as I was saying——

"Put that handkerchief away!" said Jabez Stone, and he began to beg and to pray. But the best he could get at the end was a three years' extension, with conditions.

But till you make a bargain like that, you've got no idea of how fast four years can run. By the last months of those years, Jabez Stone's known all over the state and there's talk of running him for governor—and it's dust and ashes in his mouth. For every day, when he gets up, he thinks, "There's one more night gone," and every night when he lies down, he thinks of the black pocketbook and the soul of Miser Stevens, and it makes him sick at heart. Till, finally, he can't bear it any longer, and, in the last days of the last year, he hitches up his horse and drives off to seek Dan'l Webster. For Dan'l was born in New Hampshire, only a few miles from Cross Corners, and it's well known that he has a particular soft spot for old neighbors.

It was early in the morning when he got to Marshfield, but Dan'l was up already, talking Latin to the farm hands and wrestling with the ram, Goliath, and trying out a new trotter and working up speeches to make against John C. Calhoun. But when he heard a New Hampshireman had come to see him, he dropped everything else he was doing, for that was Dan'l's way. He gave Jabez Stone a breakfast that five men couldn't eat, went into the living history of every man and woman in Cross Corners, and finally asked him how he could serve him.

Jabez Stone allowed that it was a kind of mortgage case.

"Well, I haven't pleaded a mortgage case in a long time, and I don't generally plead now, except before the Supreme Court," said Dan'l, "but if I can, I'll help you."

"Then I've got hope for the first time in ten years," said Jabez Stone, and told him the details.

Dan'l walked up and down as he listened, hands behind his back, now and then asking a question, now and then plunging his eyes at the floor, as if they'd bore through it like gimlets. When Jabez Stone had finished, Dan'l puffed out his cheeks and blew. Then he turned to Jabez Stone and a smile broke over his face like the sunrise over Monadnock.

"You've certainly given yourself the devil's own row to hoe, Neighbor Stone," he said, "but I'll take your case."

"You'll take it?" said Jabez Stone, hardly daring to believe.

"Yes," said Dan'l Webster. "I've got about seventy-five other things to do and the Missouri Compromise to straighten out, but I'll take your case. For if two New Hampshiremen aren't a match for the devil, we might as well give the country back to the Indians."

Then he shook Jabez Stone by the hand and said, "Did you come down here in a hurry?"

"Well, I admit I made time," said Jabez Stone.

"You'll go back faster," said Dan'l Webster, and he told 'em to hitch up Constitution and Constellation to the carriage. They were matched grays with one white forefoot, and they stepped like greased lightning.

Well, I won't describe how excited and pleased the whole Stone family was to have the great Dan'l Webster for a guest, when they finally got there. Jabez Stone had lost his hat on the way, blown off when they overtook a wind, but he didn't take much account of that. But after supper he sent the family off to bed, for he had most particular business with Mr. Webster. Mrs. Stone wanted them to sit in the front parlor, but Dan'l Webster knew front parlors and said he preferred the kitchen. So it was there they sat, waiting for the stranger, with a jug on the table between them and a bright fire on the hearth—the stranger being scheduled to show up on the stroke of midnight, according to specifications.

Well, most men wouldn't have asked for better company than Dan'l Webster and a jug. But with every tick of the clock Jabez Stone got sadder and sadder. His eyes roved round, and though he sampled the jug you could see he couldn't taste it. Finally, on the stroke of 11:30 he reached over and grabbed Dan'l Webster by the arm.

"Mr. Webster, Mr. Webster!" he said, and his voice was shaking with fear and a desperate courage. "For God's sake, Mr. Webster, harness your horses and get away from this place while you can!"

"You've brought me a long way, neighbor, to tell me you don't like my company," said Dan'l Webster, quite peaceable, pulling at the jug.

"Miserable wretch that I am!" groaned Jabez Stone. "I've brought you a devilish way, and now I see my folly. Let him take me if he wills. I don't hanker after it, I must say, but I can stand it. But you're the Union's stay and New Hampshire's pride! He mustn't get you, Mr. Webster! He mustn't get you!"

Dan'l Webster looked at the distracted man, all gray and shaking in the firelight, and laid a hand on his shoulder.

"I'm obliged to you, Neighbor Stone," he said gently. "It's kindly thought of. But there's a jug on the table and a case in hand. And I never left a jug or a case half finished in my life."

And just at that moment there was a sharp rap on the door.

"Ah," said Dan'l Webster, very coolly, "I thought your clock was a trifle slow, Neighbor Stone." He stepped to the door and opened it. "Come in!" he said.

The stranger came in—very dark and tall he looked in the firelight. He was carrying a box under his arm— a black, japanned box with little air holes in the lid. At the sight of the box, Jabez Stone gave a low cry and shrank into a corner of the room.

"Mr. Webster, I presume," said the stranger, very polite, but with his eyes glowing like a fox's deep in the woods.

"Attorney of record for Jabez Stone," said Dan'l Webster, but his eyes were glowing too. "Might I ask your name?"

"I've gone by a good many," said the stranger carelessly. "Perhaps Scratch will do for the evening. I'm often called that in these regions."

Then he sat down at the table and poured himself a

drink from the jug. The liquor was cold in the jug, but it came steaming into the glass.

"And now," said the stranger, smiling and showing his teeth, "I shall call upon you, as a law-abiding citizen, to assist me in taking possession of my property."

Well, with that the argument began—and it went hot and heavy. At first, Jabez Stone had a flicker of hope, but when he saw Dan'l Webster being forced back at point after point, he just scrunched in his corner, with his eyes on that japanned box. For there wasn't any doubt as to the deed or the signature—that was the worst of it. Dan'l Webster twisted and turned and thumped his fist on the table, but he couldn't get away from that. He offered to compromise the case; the stranger wouldn't hear of it. He pointed out the property had increased in value, and state senators ought to be worth more; the stranger stuck to the letter of the law. He was a great lawyer, Dan'l Webster, but we know who's the King of Lawyers, as the Good Book tells us, and it seemed as if, for the first time, Dan'l Webster had met his match.

Finally, the stranger yawned a little. "Your spirited efforts on behalf of your client do you credit, Mr. Webster," he said, "but if you have no more arguments to adduce, I'm rather pressed for time"—and Jabez Stone shuddered.

Dan'l Webster's brow looked dark as a thundercloud.

"Pressed or not, you shall not have this man!" he thundered. "Mr. Stone is an American citizen, and no American citizen may be forced into the service of a foreign prince. We fought England for that in '12 and we'll fight all hell for it again!"

"Foreign?" said the stranger. "And who calls me a foreigner?"

"Well, I never yet heard of the dev—of your claiming American citizenship," said Dan'l Webster with surprise.

"And who with better right?" said the stranger, with one of his terrible smiles. "When the first wrong was done to the first Indian, I was there. When the first slaver put out for the Congo, I stood on her deck. Am I not in your books and stories and beliefs, from the first settlements on? Am I not spoken of, still, in every church in New England? 'Tis true the North claims me for a Southerner and the South for a Northerner, but I am neither. I am merely an honest American like yourself—and of the best descent—for, to tell the truth, Mr. Webster, though I don't like to boast of it, my name is older in this country than yours."

"Aha!" said Dan'l Webster, with the veins standing out in his forehead. "Then I stand on the Constitution! I demand a trial for my client!"

"The case is hardly one for an ordinary court," said the stranger, his eyes flickering. "And, indeed, the lateness of the hour——"

"Let it be any court you choose, so it is an American judge and an American jury!" said Dan'l Webster in his pride. "Let it be the quick or the dead; I'll abide the issue!"

"You have said it," said the stranger, and pointed his finger at the door. And with that, and all of a sudden, there was a rushing of wind outside and a noise of footsteps. They came, clear and distinct, through the night. And yet, they were not like the footsteps of living men.

"In God's name, who comes by so late?" cried Jabez Stone, in an ague of fear.

"The jury Mr. Webster demands," said the stranger, sipping at his boiling glass. "You must pardon the rough appearance of one or two; they will have come a long way."

And with that the fire burned blue and the door blew open and twelve men entered, one by one.

If Jabez Stone had been sick with terror before, he was blind with terror now. For there was Walter Butler, the loyalist, who spread fire and horror through the Mohawk Valley in the times of the Revolution; and there was Simon Girty, the renegade, who saw white men burned at the stake and whooped with the Indians to see them burn. His eyes were green, like a catamount's, and the stains on his hunting shirt did not come from the blood of the deer. King Philip was there, wild and proud as he had been in life, with the great gash in his head that gave him his death wound, and cruel Governor Dale, who broke men on the wheel. There was Morton of Merry Mount, who so vexed the Plymouth Colony, with his flushed, loose, handsome face and his hate of the godly. There was Teach, the bloody pirate, with his black beard curling on his breast. The Reverend John Smeet, with his strangler's hands and his Geneva gown, walked as daintily as he had to the gallows. The red print of the rope was still around his neck, but he carried a perfumed handkerchief in one hand. One and all, they came into the room with the fires of hell still upon them, and the stranger named their names and their deeds as they came, till the tale of twelve was told. Yet the stranger had told the truth—they had all played a part in America.

"Are you satisfied with the jury, Mr. Webster?" said the stranger mockingly, when they had taken their places.

The sweat stood upon Dan'l Webster's brow, but his voice was clear.

"Quite satisfied," he said. "Though I miss General Arnold from the company."

"Benedict Arnold is engaged upon other business," said the stranger, with a glower. "Ah, you asked for a justice, I believe."

He pointed his finger once more, and a tall man, soberly clad in Puritan garb, with the burning gaze of the fanatic, stalked into the room and took his judge's place.

"Justice Hathorne is a jurist of experience," said the stranger. "He presided at certain witch trials once held in Salem. There were others who repented of the business later, but not he."

"Repent of such notable wonders and undertakings?" said the stern old justice. "Nay, hang them —hang them all!" And he muttered to himself in a way that struck ice into the soul of Jabez Stone.

Then the trial began, and, as you might expect, it didn't look anyways good for the defense. And Jabez Stone didn't make much of a witness in his own behalf. He took one look at Simon Girty and screeched, and they had to put him back in his corner in a kind of swoon.

It didn't halt the trial, though; the trial went on, as trials do. Dan'l Webster had faced some hard juries and hanging judges in his time, but this was the hardest he'd ever faced, and he knew it. They sat there with a kind of glitter in their eyes, and the stranger's smooth voice went on and on. Every time he'd raise an objection, it'd be "Objection sustained," but whenever Dan'l objected, it'd be "Objection denied." Well, you couldn't expect fair play from a fellow like this Mr. Scratch.

It got to Dan'l in the end, and he began to heat, like iron in the forge. When he got up to speak he was going to flay that stranger with every trick known to the law, and the judge and jury too. He didn't care if it was contempt of court or what would happen to him for it. He didn't care any more what happened to Jabez Stone. He just got madder and madder, thinking of what he'd say. And yet, curiously enough, the more he thought about it, the less he was able to arrange his speech in his mind.

Till, finally, it was time for him to get up on his feet, and he did so, all ready to bust out with lightnings and denunciations. But before he started he looked over the judge and jury for a moment, such being his custom. And he noticed the glitter in their eyes was twice as strong as before, and they all leaned forward. Like hounds just before they get the fox, they looked, and the blue mist of evil in the room thickened as he watched them. Then he saw what he'd been about to do, and he wiped his forehead, as a man might who's just escaped falling into a pit in the dark.

For it was him they'd come for, not only Jabez Stone. He read it in the glitter of their eyes and in the way the stranger hid his mouth with one hand. And if he fought them with their own weapons, he'd fall into their power; he knew that, though he couldn't have told you how. It was his own anger and horror that burned in their eyes; and he'd have to wipe that out or the case was lost. He stood there for a moment, his black eyes burning like anthracite. And then he began to speak.

He started off in a low voice, though you could hear every word. They say he could call on the harps of the blessed when he chose. And this was just as simple and easy as a man could talk. But he didn't start out by condemning or reviling. He was talking about the things that make a country a country, and a man a man.

And he began with the simple things that everybody's known and felt—the freshness of a fine morning when you're young, and the taste of food when you're hungry, and the new day that's every day when you're a child. He took them up and he turned them in his hands. They were good things for any man. But without freedom, they sickened. And when he talked of those enslaved, and the sorrows of slavery, his voice got like a big bell. He talked of the early days of America and the men who had made those days. It wasn't a spread-eagle speech, but he made you see it. He admitted all the wrong that had ever been done. But he showed how, out of the wrong and the right, the suffering and the starvations, something new had come. And everybody had played a part in it, even the traitors.

Then he turned to Jabez Stone and showed him as he was—an ordinary man who'd had hard luck and

wanted to change it. And, because he'd wanted to
change it, now he was going to be punished for all
eternity. And yet there was good in Jabez Stone, and
he showed that good. He was hard and mean, in some
ways, but he was a man. There was sadness in being a
man, but it was a proud thing too. And he showed what
the pride of it was till you couldn't help feeling it.
Yes, even in hell, if a man was a man, you'd know it.
And he wasn't pleading for any one person any more,
though his voice rang like an organ. He was telling
the story and the failures and the endless journey of
mankind. They got tricked and trapped and bamboozled, but it was a great journey. And no demon that
was ever foaled could know the inwardness of it—it
took a man to do that.

The fire began to die on the hearth and the wind
before morning to blow. The light was getting gray in
the room when Dan'l Webster finished. And his words
came back at the end to New Hampshire ground, and
the one spot of land that each man loves and clings to.
He painted a picture of that, and to each one of that
jury he spoke of things long forgotten. For his voice
could search the heart, and that was his gift and his
strength. And to one, his voice was like the forest and
its secrecy, and to another like the sea and the storms
of the sea; and one heard the cry of his lost nation in
it, and another saw a little harmless scene he hadn't
remembered for years. But each saw something. And
when Dan'l Webster finished he didn't know whether or
not he'd saved Jabez Stone. But he knew he'd done a
miracle. For the glitter was gone from the eyes of judge

and jury, and, for the moment, they were men again, and knew they were men.

"The defense rests," said Dan'l Webster, and stood there like a mountain. His ears were still ringing with his speech, and he didn't hear anything else till he heard Judge Hathorne say, "The jury will retire to consider its verdict."

Walter Butler rose in his place and his face had a dark, gay pride on it.

"The jury has considered its verdict," he said, and looked the stranger full in the eye. "We find for the defendant, Jabez Stone."

With that, the smile left the stranger's face, but Walter Butler did not flinch.

"Perhaps 'tis not strictly in accordance with the evidence," he said, "but even the damned may salute the eloquence of Mr. Webster."

With that, the long crow of a rooster split the gray morning sky, and judge and jury were gone from the room like a puff of smoke and as if they had never been there. The stranger turned to Dan'l Webster, smiling wryly.

"Major Butler was always a bold man," he said. "I had not thought him quite so bold. Nevertheless, my congratulations, as between two gentlemen."

"I'll have that paper first, if you please," said Dan'l Webster, and he took it and tore it into four pieces. It was queerly warm to the touch. "And now," he said, "I'll have you!" and his hand came down like a bear trap on the stranger's arm. For he knew that once you bested anybody like Mr. Scratch in fair fight, his power on you was gone. And he could see that Mr. Scratch knew it too.

The stranger twisted and wriggled, but he couldn't get out of that grip. "Come, come, Mr. Webster," he said, smiling palely. "This sort of thing is ridic—ouch! —is ridiculous. If you're worried about the costs of the case, naturally, I'd be glad to pay——"

"And so you shall!" said Dan'l Webster, shaking him till his teeth rattled. "For you'll sit right down at that table and draw up a document, promising never to bother Jabez Stone nor his heirs or assigns nor any other New Hampshireman till doomsday! For any hades we want to raise in this state, we can raise ourselves, without assistance from strangers."

"Ouch!" said the stranger. "Ouch! Well, they never did run very big to the barrel, but—ouch!—I agree!"

So he sat down and drew up the document. But Dan'l Webster kept his hand on his coat collar all the time.

"And, now, may I go?" said the stranger, quite humble, when Dan'l'd seen the document was in proper and legal form.

"Go?" said Dan'l, giving him another shake. "I'm still trying to figure out what I'll do with you. For you've settled the costs of the case, but you haven't settled with me. I think I'll take you back to Marshfield," he said, kind of reflective. "I've got a ram there named Goliath that can butt through an iron door. I'd kind of like to turn you loose in his field and see what he'd do."

Well, with that the stranger began to beg and to plead. And he begged and he pled so humble that finally Dan'l, who was naturally kindhearted, agreed to let him go. The stranger seemed terrible grateful for that and said, just to show they were friends, he'd tell Dan'l's fortune before leaving. So Dan'l agreed to that, though he didn't take much stock in fortune-tellers ordinarily. But, naturally, the stranger was a little different.

Well, he pried and he peered at the lines in Dan'l's hands. And he told him one thing and another that was quite remarkable. But they were all in the past.

"Yes, all that's true, and it happened," said Dan'l Webster. "But what's to come in the future?"

The stranger grinned, kind of happily, and shook his head.

"The future's not as you think it," he said. "It's dark. You have a great ambition, Mr. Webster."

"I have," said Dan'l firmly, for everybody knew he wanted to be President.

"It seems almost within your grasp," said the stranger, "but you will not attain it. Lesser men will be made President and you will be passed over."

"And, if I am, I'll still be Daniel Webster," said Dan'l. "Say on."

"You have two strong sons," said the stranger, shaking his head. "You look to found a line. But each will die in war and neither reach greatness."

"Live or die, they are still my sons," said Dan'l Webster. "Say on."

"You have made great speeches," said the stranger. "You will make more."

"Ah," said Dan'l Webster.

"But the last great speech you make will turn many of your own against you," said the stranger. "They will call you Ichabod; they will call you by other names. Even in New England, some will say you have turned your coat and sold your country, and their voices will be loud against you till you die."

"So it is an honest speech, it does not matter what men say," said Dan'l Webster. Then he looked at the stranger and their glances locked.

"One question," he said. "I have fought for the Union all my life. Will I see that fight won against those who would tear it apart?"

"Not while you live," said the stranger, grimly, "but it will be won. And after you are dead, there are thousands who will fight for your cause, because of words that you spoke."

"Why, then, you long-barreled, slab-sided, lantern-jawed, fortune-telling note shaver!" said Dan'l Webster, with a great roar of laughter, "be off with you to your own place before I put my mark on you! For, by the thirteen original colonies, I'd go to the Pit itself to save the Union!"

And with that he drew back his foot for a kick that would have stunned a horse. It was only the tip of his shoe that caught the stranger, but he went flying out of the door with his collecting box under his arm.

"And now," said Dan'l Webster, seeing Jabez Stone beginning to rouse from his swoon, "let's see what's left in the jug, for it's dry work talking all night. I hope there's pie for breakfast, Neighbor Stone."

But they say that whenever the devil comes near

Marshfield, even now, he gives it a wide berth. And he hasn't been seen in the state of New Hampshire from that day to this. I'm not talking about Massachusetts or Vermont.

DANIEL WEBSTER AND THE
SEA SERPENT

IT happened, one summer's day, that Dan'l Webster and some of his friends were out fishing. That was in the high days of his power and his fame, when the question wasn't if he was going to be President but when he was going to be President, and everybody at Kingston depot stood up when Dan'l Webster arrived to take the cars. But in spite of being Secretary of State and the biggest man in New England, he was just the same Dan'l Webster. He bought his Jamaica personal and in the jug at Colonel Sever's store in Kingston, right under a sign saying ENGLISH AND WEST INDIA GOODS, and he never was too busy to do a hand's turn for a friend. And, as for his big farm at Marshfield, that was just the apple of his eye. He buried his favorite horses with their shoes on, standing up, in a private graveyard, and wrote Latin epitaphs for them, and he often was heard to say that his big Hungarian bull, Saint Stephen, had more sense in his rear off hoof than most politicians. But, if there was one thing he loved better than Marshfield itself, it was the sea and the waters around it, for he was a fisherman born.

This time, he was salt-water fishing in the Comet well out of sight of land. It was a good day for fishing, not too hazy, but not too clear, and Dan'l Webster en joyed it, as he enjoyed everything in life, except maybe listening to the speeches of Henry Clay. He'd stolen a half-dozen days to come up to Marshfield, and well he needed the rest, for we'd nearly gone to war with England the year before, and now he was trying to fix up a real copper-riveted treaty that would iron out all the old differences that still kept the two countries unfriendly. And that was a job, even for Dan'l Webster. But as soon as he stepped aboard the Comet, he was carefree and heartwhole. He had his real friends around him and he wouldn't allow a word of politics talked on the boat—though that rule got broken this time, and for a good reason, as you'll see. And when he struck his first cod, and felt the fish take the hook, a kind of big slow smile went over his features, and he said, "Gentlemen, this is solid comfort." That was the kind of man he was.

I don't know how many there were of them aboard —half a dozen or so—just enough for good company. We'll say there were George Blake and Rufus Choate and young Peter Harvey and a boy named Jim Billings. And, of course, there was Seth Peterson, Dan'l's boat captain, in his red flannel shirt, New England as cod and beach plums, and Dan'l Webster's fast friend. Dan'l happened to be Secretary of State, and Seth Peterson happened to be a boat captain, but that didn't make any difference between them. And, once the Comet left dock, Seth Peterson ran the show, as it's right that a captain should.

Well, they'd fished all morning and knocked off for a bite of lunch, and some had had segars and snoozes afterward, and some hadn't, but in any case, it was around midafternoon, and everybody was kind of comfortable and contented. They still fished, and they fished well, but they knew in an hour or so they'd be heading back for home with a fine catch on board. So maybe there was more conversation than Seth Peterson would have approved of earlier, and maybe some jokes were passed and some stories told. I don't know, but you know how it is when men get together at the end of a good day. All the same, they were still paying attention to their business—and I guess it was George Blake that noticed it first.

"Dan'l," he said, breathing hard, "I've got something on my line that pulls like a Morgan horse."

"Well, yank him in!" sang out Dan'l, and then his face changed as his own line began to stiffen and twang. "George," he said, "I beat you! I got something on my line that pulls like a pair of steers!"

"Give 'em more line, Mr. Webster!" yells Seth Peterson, and Dan'l did. But at that, the line ran out so fast it smoked when it hit the water, and any hands but Dan'l Webster's would have been cut to the bone. Nor you couldn't see where it went to, except Something deep in the waters must be pulling it out as a cat pulls yarn from a ball. The veins in Dan'l Webster's arm stood out like cords. He played the fish and played the fish; he fought it with every trick he knew. And still the little waves danced and the other men gaped at the fight—and still he couldn't bring the Something to time.

"By the big elm at Marshfield!" he said at last, with his dark face glowing and a fisherman's pride in his eyes. "Have I hooked on to a frigate with all sails set?

I've payed out a mile of my own particular line, and she still pulls like ten wild horses. Gentlemen, what's this?"

And even as he said it, the tough line broke in two with a crack like a musket-shot, and out of the deep of ocean, a mile away, the creature rose, majestic. Neighbors, that was a sight! Shaking the hook from its jaw, it rose, the sea serpent of the Scriptures, exact and to specifications as laid down in the Good Book, with its hairy face and its furlong on furlong of body, wallowing and thrashing in the troubled sea. As it rose, it gave a long low melancholy hoot, like a kind of forsaken steamboat; and when it gave out that hoot, young Jim Billings, the boy, fainted dead away on the deck. But nobody even noticed him—they were all staring at the sea serpent with bulging eyes.

Even Dan'l Webster was shaken. He passed his hand for a moment across his brow and gave a sort of inquiring look at the jug of Jamaica by the hatch.

"Gentlemen," he said in a low voice, "the evidence—the ocular evidence would seem to be conclusive. And yet, speaking as a lawyer——"

"Thar she blows! I never thought to see her again!" yells Seth Peterson, half driven out of his mind by the sight, as the sea serpent roiled the waters. "Thar she blows, by the Book of Genesis! Oh, why ain't I got a harpoon?"

"Quiet, Seth," said Dan'l Webster. "Let us rather give thanks for being permitted to witness this glorious and unbelievable sight." And then you could see the real majesty of the man, for no sooner were the words out of his mouth than the sea serpent started swimming straight toward the Comet. She came like a railway train and her wake boiled out behind her for an acre. And yet, there was something kind of skittish about her, too—you might say that she came kind of shaking her skirts and bridling. I don't know what there was about her that made you sure she was a female, but they were all sure.

She came, direct as a bullet, till you could count the white teeth shining in her jaws. I don't know what the rest of them did—though doubtless some prayers were put up in a hasty way—but Dan'l Webster stood there and faced her, with his brow dark and his eyes like a sleepy lion's, giving her glance for glance. Yes, there was a minute, there, when she lifted her head high out of water and they looked at each other eye to eye. They say hers were reddish but handsome. And then, just as it seemed she'd crash plumb through the Comet, she made a wide wheel and turned. Three times she circled the boat, hooting lonesomely, while the Comet danced up and down like a cork on the waves. But Dan'l Webster kept his footing, one hand gripping the mast, and whenever he got a chance, he fixed her with his eye. Till finally, on the third circuit, she gave one last long hoot—like twenty foghorns at once, it was, and nearly deafened them all—and plunged back whence she'd come, to the bottomless depths of the sea.

But even after the waters were calm again, they didn't say anything for quite a while. Till, finally, Seth Peterson spoke.

"Well, Mr. Webster," he said, "that one got away" —and he grinned a dry grin.

"Leviathan of the Scriptures! Give me paper and

)en," said Dan'l Webster. "We must write this down
ind attest it." And then they all began to talk.

Well, he wrote an account of just what they'd seen,
ery plain and honest. And everybody there signed his
iame to it. Then he read it over to them again aloud.
And then there was another silence, while they looked
it one another.

Finally, Seth Peterson shook his head, slow and
houghtful.

"It won't do, Dan'l," he said, in a deep voice.

"Won't do?" said Dan'l Webster, with his eyes blaz-
ing. "What do you mean, Seth?"

"I mean it just won't do, Dan'l," said Seth Peterson,
)erfectly respectful, but perfectly firm. "I put it up to
ou, gentlemen," he said, turning to the others. "I can
;o home and say I've seen the sea serpent. And every-
)ody'll say, 'Oh, that's just that old liar, Seth Peterson.'
3ut if it's Dan'l Webster says so—can't you see the
difference?"

He paused for a minute, but nobody said a word.

"Well, I can," he said. He drawled out the words
ery slow. "Dan'l Webster—Secretary of State—sees and
alks to a sea serpent—off Plymouth Bay. Why, it would
)lumb ruin him! And I don't mind being ruint, but
t's different with Dan'l Webster. Would you vote for
 man for President who claimed he'd saw the sea
erpent? Well, would you? Would anybody?"

There was another little silence, and then George
3lake spoke.

"He's right, Dan'l," he said, while the others
odded. "Give me that paper." He took it from Dan'l
Vebster's hand and threw it in the sea.

"And now," he said in a firm voice, "I saw cod
Nothing but cod. Except maybe a couple of halibut
Did any gentleman here see anything else?"

Well, at that, it turned out, of course, that nobod
aboard had seen anything but cod all day. And with
that, they put back for shore. All the same, they al
looked over their shoulders a good deal till they go
back to harbor.

And yet Dan'l Webster wasn't too contented tha
evening, in spite of his fine catch. For, after all, he ha
seen the sea serpent, and not only seen her but playe
her on the line for twenty-seven minutes by his gol
repeater, and, being a fisherman, he'd like to have sai
so. And yet, if he did—Seth was right—folks woul
think him crazy or worse. It took his mind off Lor
Ashburton and the treaty with England—till, finall
he pushed aside the papers on his desk.

"Oh, a plague on the beast!" he said, kind of crossl
"I'll leave it alone and hope it leaves me alone." So h
took his candle and went up to bed. But just as he wa
dropping off to sleep, he thought he heard a long lo
hoot from the mouth of Green Harbor River, two mile
away.

The next night the hooting continued, and the thir
day there was a piece in the Kingston paper about th
new Government foghorn at Rocky Ledge. Well, th
thing began to get on Dan'l Webster's nerves, and whe
his temper was roused he wasn't a patient man. Mor
over, the noises seemed to disturb the stock—at leas
his overseer said so—and the third night his favorit
gray kicked half the door out of her stall. "That se
serpent's getting to be an infernal nuisance," though

Dan'l Webster. "I've got to protect my property." So, the fourth night he put on his old duck-shooting clothes and took his favorite shotgun, Learned Selden, and went down to a blind at the mouth of Green Harbor River, to see what he could see. He didn't tell anybody else about his intentions, because he still felt kind of sensitive about the whole affair.

Well, there was a fine moon that night, and sure enough, about eleven o'clock, the sea serpent showed up, steaming in from ocean, all one continuous wave length, like a giant garden hose. She was quite a handsome sight, all speckled with the moonlight, but Dan'l Webster couldn't rightly appreciate it. And just as she came to the blind, she lifted her head and looked sorrowfully in the direction of Marshfield and let out a long low soulful hoot like a homesick train.

Dan'l Webster hated to do it. But he couldn't have a sea serpent living in Green Harbor River and scaring the stock—not to speak of the universal consternation and panic there'd be in the countryside when such a thing was known. So he lifted Learned Selden and gave her both barrels for a starter, just a trifle over her head. And as soon as the gun exploded, the sea serpent let out a screech you could hear a mile and headed back for open sea. If she'd traveled fast before, she traveled like lightning now, and it wasn't any time before she was just a black streak on the waters.

Dan'l Webster stepped out of the blind and wiped his brow. He felt sorry, but he felt relieved. He didn't think she'd be back, after that sort of scare, and he wanted to leave everything shipshape before he went down to Washington, next morning. But next day,

when he told Seth Peterson what he'd done, he didn't
feel so chipper. For, "You shouldn't have done that,
Mr. Webster," said Seth Peterson, shaking his head, and
that was all he would say except a kind of mutter that
sounded like "Samanthy was always particular set in
her likes." But Dan'l didn't pay any attention to that,
though he remembered it later, and he was quite short
with Seth for the first time in their long relationship.
So Seth shut up like a quahog, and Dan'l took the cars
for Washington.

When he got there he was busy enough, for the
British treaty was on the boil, and within twenty-four
hours he'd forgot all about the sea serpent. Or thought
he had. But three days later, as he was walking home
to his house on Lafayette Square, with a senator friend
of his, in the cool of the evening, they heard a curious
noise. It seemed to come from the direction of the
Potomac River.

"Must have got a new whistle for the Baltimore
night boat," said the senator. "Noisy too."

"Oh, that's just the bullfrogs on the banks," said
Dan'l Webster steadily. But he knew what it was, just
the same, and his heart sank within him. But nobody
ever called Dan'l Webster a coward. So, as soon as he'd
got rid of the senator, he went down to the banks of the
Potomac. Well, it was the sea serpent, all right.

She looked a little tired, as well she might, having
swum from Plymouth Bay. But as soon as she saw Dan'l
Webster, she stretched out her neck and gave a long
low loving hoot. Then Dan'l knew what the trouble
was and, for once in his life, he didn't know what to do.
But he'd brought along a couple of roe herring, in a

paper, just in case; so he fed them to her and she hooted, affectionate and grateful. Then he walked back to his house with his head bowed. And that very night he sent a special express letter to Seth Peterson at Marshfield, for, it seemed to him, Seth must know more about the business than he let on.

Well, Seth got to Washington as fast as the cars would bring him, and the very evening he arrived Dan'l sent him over to interview the serpent. But when Seth came back, Dan'l could see by his face that he hadn't made much progress.

"Could you talk to her, Seth?" he said, and his voice was eager. "Can she understand United States?"

"Oh, she can understand it all right," said Seth. "She's even picking up a few words. They was always a smart family, those Rock Ledge serpents, and she's the old maid of the lot, and the best educated. The only trouble with 'em is, they're so terrible sot in their ways."

"You might have warned me, Seth," said Dan'l Webster, kind of reproachful, and Seth looked uncomfortable.

"Well, to tell you the truth," he said, "I thought all of 'em was dead. Nor I never thought she'd act up like this—her father was as respectable a serpent as you'd see in a long summer's day. Her father———"

"Bother her father!" said Dan'l Webster and set his jaw. "Tell me what she says."

"Well, Mr. Webster," said Seth, and stared at his boots, "she says you're quite a handsome man. She says she never did see anybody quite like you," he went on. "I hate to tell you this, Mr. Webster, and I feel kind of responsible, but I think you ought to know. And I told you that you oughtn't to have shot at her—she's pretty proud of that. She says she knows just how you meant it. Well, I'm no great hand at being embarrassed, Mr. Webster, but, I tell you, she embarrassed me. You see, she's been an old maid for about a hundred and fifty years, I guess, and that's the worst of it. And being the last of her folks in those particular waters, there's just no way to restrain her—her father and mother was as sensible, hard-working serpents as ever gave a feller a tow through a fog, but you know how it is with those old families. Well, she says wherever you go, she'll follow you, and she claims she wants to hear you speak before the Supreme Court——"

"Did you tell her I'm a married man?" said Dan'l. "Did you tell her that?"

"Yes, I told her," said Seth, and you could see the perspiration on his forehead. "But she says that doesn't signify—her being a serpent and different—and she's fixing to move right in. She says Washington's got a lovely climate and she's heard all about the balls and the diplomatic receptions. I don't know how she's heard about them, but she has." He swallowed. "I got her to promise she'd kind of lie low for two weeks and not come up the Potomac by daylight—she was fixing to do that because she wants to meet the President. Well, I got her to promise that much. But she says, even so, if you don't come to see her once an evening, she'll hoot till you do, and she told me to tell you that you haven't heard hooting yet. And as soon as the fish market's open, I better run down and buy a barrel of flaked cod, Mr. Webster—she's partial to flaked cod and she usually takes it in the barrel. Well, I don't want to worry you, Mr. Webster, but I'm afraid that we're in a fix."

"A fix!" said Dan'l Webster. "It's the biggest fix I ever was in in my life!"

"Well, it's kind of complimentary, in a way, I guess," said Seth Peterson, "but——"

"Does she say anything else?" said Dan'l Webster, drawing a long breath.

"Yes, Mr. Webster," said Seth Peterson, his eyes on his boots. "She says you're a little shy. But she says she likes that in a man."

Dan'l Webster went to bed that night, but he didn't sleep. He worked and worked those great brains of his till he nearly wore out the wheels, but he still couldn't think of a way to get rid of the sea serpent. And just about the time dawn broke, he heard one long low hoot, faithful and reminiscent, from the direction of the Potomac.

Well, the next two weeks were certainly bad ones for him. For, as the days wore on, the sea serpent got more and more restive. She wanted him to call her Samanthy, which he wouldn't, and she kept asking him when he was going to introduce her into society, till he had to feed her Italian sardines in olive oil to keep her quiet. And that ran up a bill at the fish market that he hated to think of—besides, her continually threatening to come up the Potomac by day. Moreover, and to put the cap on things, the great Webster-Ashburton treaty that was to make his name as Secretary of State had struck a snag and England didn't seem at all partial to admitting the American claims. Oh, it was a weary fortnight and a troublesome one!

The last afternoon of the fortnight, he sat in his office and he didn't know where to turn. For Lord Ashburton was coming to see him for a secret conference that night at nine, and he had to see the sea serpent at ten, and how to satisfy either of them he didn't know. His eyes stared wearily at the papers on his desk. He rang the bell for his secretary.

"The corvette Benjamin Franklin reports——" he said. "This should have gone to the Navy Department, Mr. Jones." Then he glanced at the naval report again and his eyes began to glow like furnaces. "By the bones of Leviathan! I've got it!" he said, with a shout. "Where's my hat, Mr. Jones. I must see the President at once!"

There was a different feeling about the house on Lafayette Square that evening, for Dan'l Webster was himself again. He cracked a joke with Seth Peterson and took a glass of Madeira and turned it to the light. And when Lord Ashburton was announced—a nice, white-haired old gentleman, though a little stiff in his joints—he received him with all the courtesy of a king.

"I am glad to see you so much restored, Mr. Webster," said Lord Ashburton, when the greetings had been exchanged. "And yet I fear I bring you bad news. Concerning clauses six and seven of the proposed treaty between Her Majesty's Government and the United States of America, it is my duty to state——"

"My lord, let us drop the clauses for a moment and take the wider view," said Dan'l Webster, smiling. "This is a matter concerning the future welfare and peace of two great nations. Your government claims the right to search our ships; that right we deny. And our attitude seems to you preposterous. Is that not so?"

"I would hesitate to use the word 'preposterous,' " said Lord Ashburton cautiously. "Yet——"

"And yet," said Dan'l Webster, leaning forward, "there are things which may seem preposterous, and yet are not. Let me put a case. Let us say that Great Britain has the strongest navy afloat."

"Britannia rules the waves," said Lord Ashburton, with a noble smile.

"There were a couple she didn't rule in 1812," said Dan'l Webster, "but let that pass. Let me ask you, Lord Ashburton, and let me ask you solemnly, what could even the power and might of Britain's navy avail against Leviathan?"

"Leviathan?" said Lord Ashburton, rather coldly. "Naturally, I understand the Biblical allusion. Yet——"

"The sea serpent," said Dan'l Webster, kind of impatient. "What could all Britain's navy do against the sea serpent out of the Scriptures?"

Lord Ashburton stared at him as if he had gone mad. "God bless my soul, Mr. Secretary!" he said. "But I fail to see the point of your question. The sea serpent doesn't exist!"

"Doesn't he—I mean she?" said Dan'l Webster, calmly. "And suppose I should prove to you that it does exist?"

"Well, 'pon my word! God bless my soul!" said Lord Ashburton, kind of taken aback. "Naturally—in that case—however—but even so——"

Dan'l Webster touched a bell on his desk. "Lord

Ashburton," he said, kind of solemn, "I am putting my life, and what is dearer to me, my honor and reputation, in your hands. Nevertheless, I feel it necessary, for a better understanding between our two countries."

Seth Peterson came into the room and Dan'l nodded at him.

"Seth," he said, "Lord Ashburton is coming with us to see Samanthy."

"It's all right if you say so, Mr. Webster," said Seth Peterson, "but he'll have to help carry the sardines."

"Well, 'pon my word! Bless my soul! A very strange proceeding!" said Lord Ashburton, but he followed along.

Well, they got to the banks of the Potomac, the three of them, and when they were there, Seth whistled. Samanthy was lying mostly under water, behind a little brushy island, but when she heard the whistle, she began to heave up and uncoil, all shining in the moonlight. It was what you might call a kind of impressive sight. Dan'l Webster looked at Lord Ashburton, but Lord Ashburton's words seemed sort of stuck in his throat.

Finally he got them out. "Bless my soul!" he said. "You Americans are very extraordinary! Is it alive?"

But then all he could do was goggle, for Samanthy had lifted her head, and giving a low friendly hoot, she commenced to swim around the island.

"Now, is that a sea serpent or isn't it?" said Dan'l Webster, with a kind of quiet pride.

"Indubitably," said Lord Ashburton, staring through his eyeglass. "Indubitably," and he kind of cleared his throat. "It is, indeed and in fact, a serpent of the sea. And I am asleep and in bed, in my room at the British Embassy." He pinched himself. "Ouch!" he said. "No, I am not."

"Would you call it sizable, for a sea serpent?" persisted Dan'l Webster.

Lord Ashburton stared again through his eyeglass. "Quite," he said. "Oh, yes, quite, quite!"

"And powerful?" asked Dan'l.

"I should judge so," said Lord Ashburton, faintly, as the sea serpent swam around and around the island and the waves of its wake broke crashing on the bank. "Yes, indeed, a very powerful engine of destruction. May I ask what it feeds upon?"

"Italian sardines, for preference," said Dan'l. "But that's beside the point." He drew a long breath. "Well, my lord," he said, "we're intending to commission that sea serpent as a regular and acknowledged war vessel in the United States Navy. And then, where's your wooden walls?"

Lord Ashburton, he was a diplomat, and his face didn't change expression as he stared first at the sea serpent and then at the face of Dan'l Webster. But after a while, he nodded. "You need not labor the point, Mr. Secretary," he said. "My government, I am sure, will be glad to reconsider its position on the last two clauses and on the right of search."

"Then I'm sure we can reach an agreement," said Dan'l Webster, and wiped the sweat from his brow. "And now, let's feed Samanthy."

He whistled to her himself, a long musical whistle, and she came bounding and looping in toward shore. It took all three of them to heave her the barrel of sardines, and she swallowed it down in one gulp. After that, she gave a hoot of thanks and gratitude, and Lord Ashburton sat down on the bank for a minute and took snuff. He said that he needed something to clear his mind.

"Naturally," he said, after a while, "Her Majesty's Government must have adequate assurances as to the good conduct of this—this lady." He'd meant to say "creature" at first, but Samanthy rolled her eye at him just then, and he changed the word.

"You shall have them," said Dan'l Webster, and whistled Samanthy even closer. She came in kind of skittish, flirting her coils, and Lord Ashburton closed his eyes for a minute. But when Dan'l Webster spoke, it was in the voice that hushed the Senate whenever he rose.

"Samanthy," he said, "I speak to you now as Secretary of State of the United States of America." It was the great voice that had rung in the Supreme Court and replied to Hayne, and even a sea serpent had to listen respectful. For the voice was mellow and deep, and he pictured Samanthy's early years as a carefree young serpent, playing with her fellows, and then her hard life of toil and struggle when she was left lone and lorn, till even Seth Peterson and Lord Ashburton realized the sorrow and tragedy of her lonely lot. And then, in the gentlest and kindest way you could ask, he showed her where her duty lay.

"For, if you keep on hooting in the Potomac, Samanthy," he said, "you'll become a public menace to navigation and get sat upon by the Senate Committee for Rivers and Harbors. They'll drag you up on land,

Samanthy, and put you in the Smithsonian Institution;
they'll stick you in a stagnant little pool and children
will come to throw you peanuts on Sundays, and their
nurses will poke you with umbrellas if you don't act
lively enough. The U. S. Navy will shoot at you for
target practice, Samanthy, and the scientists will exam-
ine you, and the ladies of the Pure Conduct League
will knit you a bathing suit, and you'll be bothered
every minute by congressmen and professors and visitors
and foreign celebrities till you won't be able to call
your scales your own. Oh, yes, it'll be fame, Samanthy,
but it won't be good enough. Believe me, I know something about fame and it's begging letters from strangers
and calls from people you don't know and don't want
to know, and the burden and wear and tear of being a
public character till it's enough to break your heart.
It isn't good enough, Samanthy; it won't give you back
your free waters and your sporting in the deep. Yes,
Samanthy, it'd be a remarkable thing to have you here
in Washington, but it isn't the life you were meant for
and I can't take advantage of your trust. And now,"
he said to Seth Peterson, "just what does she say?"

Seth Peterson listened, attentive, to the hootings.

"She says the Washington climate isn't what she
thought it was," he said. "And the Potomac River's too
warm; it's bad for her sciatica. And she's plumb tired of
sardines."

"Does she say anything about me?" asked Dan'l
Webster, anxiously.

"Well," said Seth Peterson, listening, "she says—if
you'll excuse me, Mr. Webster—that you may be a
great man, but you wouldn't make much of a sea

serpent. She says you haven't got enough coils. She says
—well, she says no hard feelings, but she guesses it was
a mistake on both sides."

He listened again. "But she says one thing," he said.
"She says she's got to have recognition and a husband,
if she has to take this Lord Ashburton. She says he
doesn't look like much, but he might get her introduced at Court."

A great light broke over Dan'l's face and his voice
rang out like thunder. "She shall have them both," he
said. "Come here, Samanthy. By virtue of the authority
vested in me as Secretary of State, and by special order
of the President of the United States and the Secretary
of the Navy, as witness the attached commission in
blank which I now fill in with your name, I hereby at-
tach you to the United States Navy, to rank as a forty-
four-gun frigate on special duty, rating a rear admiral's
flag and a salute of the appropriate number of guns,
wherever encountered in American waters. And, by
virtue of the following special order, I hereby order
you to the South Seas, there to cruise until further
orders for the purpose of seeking a suitable and proper
husband, with all the rights, privileges, duties and ap-
purtenances pertaining to said search and said American citizenship, as aforesaid and Hail Columbia. Signed
John Tyler, President. With which is subjoined a pass-
port signed by Daniel Webster, Secretary of State, bid-
ding all foreign nations let pass without hindrance the
American citizen, Samanthy Doe, on her lawful jour-
neys and errands." He dropped his voice for a moment
and added reflectively, "The American corvette, Benjamin Franklin, reports sighting a handsome young male

sea serpent on February third of the present year, just off the coast of the Sandwich Islands. Said serpent had forty-two coils by actual count, and when last sighted was swimming SSW at full speed."

But hardly had he spoken when Samanthy, for the last time, lifted her head and gave out a last long hoot. She looked upon Dan'l Webster as she did so, and there was regret in her eye. But the regret was tinctured with eagerness and hope.

Then she beat the water to a froth, and, before they really saw her go, she was gone, leaving only her wake on the moonlit Potomac.

"Well," said Dan'l Webster, yawning a little, "there we are. And now, Lord Ashburton, if you'll come home with me, we can draw up that treaty."

"Gladly," said Lord Ashburton, brushing his coat with his handkerchief. "Is it really gone? 'Pon my soul! You know, for a moment, I imagined that I actually saw a sea serpent. You have a very vivid way of putting things, Mr. Webster. But I think I understand the American attitude now, from the—er—analogy you were pleased to draw between such a—er—fabulous animal and the young strength of your growing country."

"I was confident that you would appreciate it, once it was brought to your attention," said Dan'l Webster. But he winked one eye at Seth Peterson, and Seth Peterson winked back.

And I'll say this for Dan'l Webster, too—he kept his promises. All through the time he was Secretary of State, he saw to it that the forty-four-gun frigate, Samanthy Doe, was carried on a special account on the books of the Navy. In fact, there's some people say that she's still so carried, and that it was her give Ericsson the idea for building the Monitor in the Civil War—if she wasn't the Monitor herself. And when the White Fleet went around the world in Teddy Roosevelt's time —well, there was a lookout in the crow's-nest of the flagship, one still calm night, as they passed by the palmy isles of the South Seas. And all of a sudden, the water boiled, tremendous and phosphorescent, and there was a pair of sea serpents and seven young ones, circling, calm and majestic, three times around the fleet. He rubbed his eyes and he stared, but there they were. Well, he was the only one that saw it, and they put him in the brig for it next morning. But he swore, till the day he died, they were flying the Stars and Stripes.

IV

GLAMOUR

I USED to read quite a lot of books when I was younger, but now they just make me sore. Marian keeps on bringing them back from the lending library and, occasionally, I'll pick one up and read a few chapters, but sooner or later you're bound to strike something that makes you sick. I don't mean dirt or anything —just foolishness, and people acting the way they never act. Of course, the books she reads are mostly love stories. I suppose they're the worst kind.

But what I understand least is the money angle. It takes money to get drunk and it takes money to go around with a girl—at least that's been my experience. But the people in those books seem to have invented a special kind of money—it only gets spent on a party or a trip. The rest of the time they might as well be paying their bills with wampum, as far as you can figure it out.

Of course, often enough, the people in books are poor. But then they're so darn poor, it's crazy. And, often enough, just when everything's at its worst, some handy little legacy comes along and the new life opens out before them right away, like a great big tulip. Well, I only had one legacy in my life and I know what I did with that. It darn near ruined me.

Uncle Bannard died up in Vermont in 1924, and

when his estate was settled, it came to $1237.62 apiece for Lou and me. Lou's husband put her share in Greater Los Angeles real estate—they live out on the Coast—and I guess they've done pretty well. But I took mine and quit the firm I was with, Rosenberg and Jenkins, mechanical toys and novelties, and went to Brooklyn to write a novel.

It sounds crazy, looking back on it. But I was a bug about reading and writing in those days, and I'd done some advertising copy for the firm that pulled. And that was the time when everybody was getting steamed up about "the new American writers," and it looked like a game without much overhead. I'd just missed the war—I was seventeen when it finished—and I'd missed college because of father's death. In fact, I hadn't done much of anything I really wanted since I had to quit high school—though the novelty business was all right as businesses go. So when I got a chance to cut loose, I cut.

I figured I could easily live a year on the twelve hundred, and, at first, I thought of France. But there'd be the nuisance of learning frog-talk and the passage there and back. Besides, I wanted to be near a big library. My novel was going to be about the American Revolution, if you can picture it. I'd read "Henry Esmond" over and over and I wanted to write a book like that.

I guess it must have been a bunch of my New England ancestors that picked Brooklyn for me. They were pioneers, all right—but, gosh, how they hated to take any chance but a big one! And I'm like that myself. I like to feel tidy in my mind when I'm taking a chance.

I figured I could be as solitary in Brooklyn as I could in Pisa, and a lot more comfortable. I knew how many words it took to make a novel—I'd counted some of them—so I bought enough paper and a second-hand typewriter and pencils and erasers. That about cleaned out my ready cash. I swore I wouldn't touch the legacy till I was really at work. But I felt like a million dollars —I swear I felt as if I were looking for treasure—when I got into the subway that shiny autumn day, and started across the river to look for a room.

It may have been my ancestors that sent me to Brooklyn, but I don't know what landed me at Mrs. Forge's. Old Wrestling Southgate, the one who was bothered with witches, would probably have called it a flowered snare of the fiend. And I'm not so sure, looking back, that he'd have been wrong.

Mrs. Forge opened the door herself—Serena was out. They'd talked about putting an ad in the paper but they'd just never got around to it; and, naturally, they wouldn't have put up a card. If it hadn't looked like the sort of house I'd wanted, I'd never have rung the bell. As it was, when she came to the door, I thought that I had made a mistake. So the first thing I did was beg her pardon.

She had on her black silk dress—the one with the white ruffles—just as if she were going out calling in the barouche. The minute she started to speak, I knew she was Southern. They all had that voice. I won't try to describe it. There's nothing worse than a whiny one —it beats the New England twang. But theirs didn't whine. They made you think of the sun and long after-noons and slow rivers—and time, time, time, just sliding along like a current, not going anywhere particular, but gay.

I think she liked my begging her pardon, for she took me in and gave me a slice of fruit cake and some lemonade. And I listened to her talk and felt, somehow, as if I'd been frozen for a long time and was just beginning to get warm. There was always a pitcher of lemonade in the ice-box, though the girls drank "coke," mostly. I've seen them come in from the snow, in the dead of winter, and drink it. They didn't think much of the cold, anyway, so they more or less pretended it didn't exist. They were that way.

The room was exactly what I wanted—big and sunny, with an outlook over a little backyard where there was the wreck of a forsythia bush and some spindly grass. I've forgotten to say the house was in one of those old-fashioned side-streets, not far from Prospect Park. But it doesn't matter where it was. It must be gone, now.

You know, it took all my nerve to ask Mrs. Forge the price. She was very polite, but she made me feel like a guest. I don't know if you can understand that. And then she couldn't tell me.

"Well, now, Mr. Southgate," she said, in that soft, gentle, helpless voice that ran on as inexorably as water, "I wish my daughter Eva had been here to receive you. My daughter Eva has accepted a business position since we came here for my daughter Melissa's art training. And I said, only this morning, 'Eva, honey, suppose Serena's away and some young person comes here, askin' for tnat room. I'll be bound to say somethin' to them, sugar, and I'll feel right embarrassed.' But just then some little boys started shoutin' down the street and I never did rightly hear what she answered. So if you're in a hurry, Mr. Southgate, I don't just know what we can do."

"I could leave a deposit," I said. I'd noticed, by this time, that the black silk had a tear in it and that she was wearing a pair of run-down ball-slippers—incredibly small they were. But, all the same, she looked like a duchess.

"Why, I suppose you could, Mr. Southgate," she said, with an obvious lack of interest. "I suppose that would be businesslike. You gentlemen in the North are always so interested in business. I recollect Mr. Forge sayin' before he died, 'Call them d——— Yankees if you like, Milly, but we've all got to live in the same country and I've met some without horns.' Mr. Forge was always so humorous. So, you see, we're quite accustomed to Northerners. You don't happen to be kin to the Mobile Southgates, do you, Mr. Southgate? You'll excuse an old lady's askin'—but you seem to favor them a little, now your face is in the light."

I'm not trying to put down just the way she talked —she didn't say "ah" and "nah"—it was something lighter and suaver. But her talk went on like that. They all did it. It wasn't nervousness or trying to impress you. They found it as easy and restful to talk as most of us do to keep still; and, if the talk never got anywhere, they'd never expected it would. It was like a drug—it made life into a dream. And, of course, it isn't that.

Finally, I simply went for my stuff and moved in. I didn't know how much I was paying or what meals

would be included in it, but I somehow felt that these
things would be shown unto me when the time was
ripe. That's what an hour and a half with Mrs. Forge
did to me. But I did resolve to have a clear understanding with "my daughter, Eva," who seemed to be the
business head of the family.

Serena let me in when I came back. I gave her
fifty cents to get in her good graces and she took an
instant dislike to me which never wavered. She was
small and black and withered, with bright little sparks
of eyes. I don't know how long she'd been with them,
but I thought of her growing on the family, like mistle-
toe, from immemorial time.

Whenever I heard her singing in the kitchen, I felt
as if she were putting a private curse on me. "Honey-
bird—" she'd croon—"honey-bird, no one gwine tuh
fly away wid mah honey-bird. Ole buzzard, he try his
wings—he flap and he flap—man wid a gun he see him
—hi, hi, hi—shoot ole buzzard wid a buckshot and
never tetch mah honey-bird."

I knew who the old buzzard was, all right. And it
may sound funny—but it wasn't. It was spooky. Eva
wouldn't see it; they'd all treat Serena like a combina-
tion of unavoidable nuisance and troublesome child.
I don't understand how they can treat servants that way.
I mean friendly and grand at the same time. It isn't
natural.

It sounds as if I were trying to keep from telling
about Eva. I don't know why I'm doing that.

I got unpacked and pretty well settled. My room
was on the third floor, back, but I could hear the girls
coming home. There'd be the door and steps and a

voice saying, "Honey, I'm so tired—I'm just plumb dragged out," and Mrs. Forge saying, "Now, honey, you rest yourself." There were three of those. I kind of wondered why they were all so tired. Later on, I found that was just something they said.

But then Mrs. Forge would begin to talk and they wouldn't be tired any more. They'd be quite excited and there'd be a good deal of laughter. I began to feel very uncomfortable. And then I got stubborn. After all, I'd rented the room.

So, when Eva finally knocked at the door, I just grunted, "Come in!" the way you would to a chambermaid. She opened the door and stood in the doorway, hesitant. I imagine Melissa had bet her she wouldn't have the nerve.

"Mr. Southgate, I believe?" she said, quite vaguely, as if I might be anything from a cloud to a chest of drawers.

"Dr. Livingstone, I presume?" I said. There was an old picture on the wall—the two Englishmen meeting formally in the middle of a paper jungle. But I'll hand her something—she saw I wasn't trying to be fresh.

"I reckon we have been making a lot of racket," she said. "But that's mostly Melissa. She never was rightly raised. Won't you give us the favor of your company downstairs, Mr. Southgate? We-all don't act crazy. We just sound like it."

She was dark, you know, and yet she had that white skin. There's a kind of flower called freesia—when the petals are very white, they have the color of her skin. And there's a strong sweetness to it—strong and ghostly at the same time. It smells like spring with the ghosts in it, between afternoon and dusk. And there's a word they call glamour. It was there.

She had small white teeth and red lips. There was one little freckle in the hollow of her throat—I don't know how she happened to have only one. Louisa was the beauty and Melissa the artist. They'd settled it that way. I couldn't have fallen in love with Louisa or Melissa. And yet, I liked to see them all together—the three sisters—I'd liked to have lived in a big, cool house by a river and spent my life seeing them all together. What fool thoughts you get, when you're young. I'd be the Northern cousin who managed the place. I used to send myself to sleep with it, every night, for months.

Mrs. Forge wasn't in it, or Serena. It was a big place—it went on for miles and miles. Most of the land wasn't good for much and the Negroes were bone-lazy, but I made them work. I'd get up in the first mist of morning and be in the saddle all day, overseeing and planning. But, always, I'd be coming back, on a tired horse, up that flowery avenue and they'd be waiting for me on the porch, the three white dresses bunched like a bouquet.

They'd be nice to me, because I was weary, and I'd go upstairs to the room looking over the river and change out of my hot clothes and wash. Then Eva would send me up a long drink with mint in it and I'd take it slowly. After supper, when I wasn't doing accounts, they'd sing or we'd all play some foolish sort of round game with ivory counters. I guess I got most of it out of books, but it was very real to me. That's one trouble with books—you get things out of them.

Often we got old, but it never seemed to change

us much. Once in a while the other girls were married and, sometimes, I married Eva. But we never had any children and none of us ever moved away. I kept on working like a dog and they accepted it and I was content. We had quite a few neighbors, at first, but I got tired of that. So I made it a river island you could only reach by boat, and that was more satisfactory.

It wasn't a dream, you know, or anything sappy like that. I just made it up in my head. Toward the end of the year, I'd lie awake for hours, making it up, but it never seemed to tire me. I never really told Eva about it at all, not even when we were engaged. Maybe it would have made a difference, but I don't think so.

She wasn't the kind of person you'd tell any dreams to. She was in the dream. I don't mean she was noble or fatal or like a ghost. I've had her in my arms and she was warm and alive and you could have had children by her, because things are that way. But that wasn't the point—that wasn't the point at all.

She didn't even have much imagination. None of them had. They just lived, like trees. They didn't plan or foresee. I've spent hours trying to explain to Mrs. Forge that, if you had ten dollars, it wasn't just ten dollars, it was something you could put in a savings bank. She'd listen, very politely. But ten dollars, to her, was just something that went away. They thought it was fine if you had money, but they thought it was equally fine if you had a good-looking nose. Money was rather like rain to them—it fell or it didn't—and, they knew there wasn't any way to make it rain.

I'm sure they'd never have come North at all, if it hadn't been for some obscure family dispute. They often seemed to wonder about it themselves. And I heard the dispute talked about dozens of times but I never really got the gist of it, except that it was connected with two things, the new spur-track to the turpentine plant, and Cousin Belle. "Cousin Belle, she just acted so mean—she gave up her manners," Mrs. Forge would say, placidly. "She left us no reco'se, Bannard— no reco'se at all." And then the girls would chime in. I suppose they got the money to come North from selling land to the turpentine plant, but even of that I am not sure.

Anyhow, they had golden visions, as they would have. Louisa was going to be a great actress and Melissa a great artist—and Eva—I don't know exactly what Eva expected, even now. But it was something. And it was all going to happen without any real work, it was going to fall from a cloud. Oh, yes, Melissa and Louisa went to classes and Eva had a job, but those, you felt, were stop-gaps. They were passing the time till the cloud opened and the manna fell.

I'll say this for them—it didn't seem to hurt them to have their visions fail. The only person it really hurt was me.

Because I believed them, at first. How could I help it? The dream I had wasn't so wrong. They were living on an island—an island in the middle of Brooklyn— a piece of where they came from. People came to the house—art students and such—there were always plenty of young men. But, once inside the house, they submitted to the house. Serena would pass the cold ham, at supper, and you'd look out of the window and be surprised to find it snowing, for the window should have been open and the warm night coming through. I don't know what roomers they'd ever had before, but in my time there was only myself and Mr. Budd. He was a fat little clerk of fifty, very respectable, and he stayed because of the food, for Serena was a magnificent, wasteful cook.

Yes, I believed it, I believed in it all. It was like an enchantment. It was glamour. I believed in all they said and I saw them all going back to Chantry—the three famous sisters with their three distinguished husbands —like people in a fairy-tale.

We'd all have breakfast together, but the only person who talked much then was Mr. Budd. The Forges never were properly alive till later in the day. At breakfast, you saw them through a veil. Sometimes I'd feel my heart beat, staring at Eva, because she looked like one of those shut flowers in greenhouses—something shut and mysterious so you fairly held your breath, waiting for it to open. I suppose it was just because she took a long time to wake up.

Then Mr. Budd and the girls would go away, and, when my bed was made, I'd go up and work. I'm not saying much about the novel, but I worked hard on it. I'd made a little chart on cardboard with 365 squares and each day I'd ink one in.

I'd go out for lunch and take a walk afterwards. A man has to have regular exercise, and that's free. Then I'd work some more, until they started to come home. I couldn't work after that—not after the first months. But I'd make myself not listen for Eva's step.

The first time I kissed Eva was the New Year's party. One of Louisa's beaus had brought some red wine and we were singing and fooling around. Serena was off for the evening and Eva and I were out in the kitchen, looking for clean glasses. We were both feeling gay and it just seemed natural. I didn't even think of it again till the next afternoon, when we'd all gone to the movies. And then I suddenly began to shake all over, as if I had a chill, remembering, and she said, "What is it, honey?" and her hand slipped into my hand.

That was how it began. And that night I started inventing the river plantation. And I'm not a fool and I've been around. But I held hands with that girl through January, February, and most of March before I really kissed her again. I can't explain it at all. She wasn't being coy or mean or trying to fight me. It was as if we were floating downstream in a boat together, and it was so pleasant to look at her and be near her, you didn't need any more. The pain hadn't started, then.

And yet, all through that time, something in me was fighting, fighting, to get out of the boat, to get away from the river. It wasn't my river at all, you know. It never was. And part of me knew it. But, when you're in love, you haven't got common sense.

By the end of March, the novel was more than half finished. I'd allowed two months for revision and making contacts, which seemed sensible. And, one evening, it was cold, and Eva and I took a walk in the park. And when we came in, Mrs. Forge made us some hot cocoa —the other girls had gone to bed early, for once—and, while we were drinking it, Mrs. Forge fell asleep in her chair. And we put down our cups, as if it were a signal, and kissed—and the house was very quiet and we could hear her breathing, like sleep itself, through the long kiss.

Next morning, I woke up and the air felt warm and, when I looked out in the yard, there were leaves on the forsythia bush. Eva was just the same at breakfast, shut and mysterious, and I was just the same. But, when I went up to work, I shook my fist at old Wrestling Southgate, the fellow that was bothered with witches. Because I was going to marry Eva, and he could go to grass.

I tell you, they didn't plan or foresee. I told Mrs. Forge very straight just how I stood—finances and everything—and they treated it like a party. They were all as kind and excited as they could be, except Serena. She just refused to believe it and sang a lot more about buzzards. And, somehow or other, that made me feel queerer than ever. Because I knew Serena hated me but I knew she was a real person. I could understand her, she was close to the ground. And I loved the others but I didn't understand them, and sometimes I wouldn't be sure they were quite real. It was that way with Eva, even though we were in love.

I could kiss her but I couldn't be sure that she was always there when I kissed her. It wasn't coldness, it was merely another climate. I could talk for hours about what we were going to do when we were married and every time I stopped she'd say, "Go on, honey, it makes me feel so nice to hear you talk." But she'd have been as pleased if I'd sung it instead. God knows I didn't expect her to understand the novelty business, or even writing. But, sometimes, I'd honestly feel as

if we didn't speak the same language. Which was fool
ish, because she wasn't foreign.

I remember getting angry with her one evening be
cause I found out she was still writing to this boy
friend, down South, and hadn't even told him about us.
She opened her eyes very wide.

"Why, honey," she said, in the most reasonable of
voices, "I couldn't stop writing Furfew right off like
that. I've just always been sort of engaged to Furfew."

"Well, now you're engaged to me," I said.

"I know," she said. "That's why I can't stop writing
him, honey. It would hurt Furfew something dreadful
if he knew I had to stop writing him because I was
engaged to you."

"Look here," I said, wondering which of us was
crazy, "are we going to be married?"

"Of co'se, honey."

"Then what," I said, "has this Furfew got to with
it? Are you engaged to him or me?"

"Of co'se I'm engaged to you, honey, and we're
going to get married. But Furfew, he's kind of like kin,
and we been engaged a long time. It seems right mean
and uncivil to break off with him short like that."

"I don't believe it," I said, "I don't believe there
are any Furfews. It sounds like something you grow
under glass. What's he like?"

She thought for a long time.

"He's right cute," she said finally. "But he's got a
little doin's of a black moustache."

I managed to find out, however, that he owned the
turpentine plant and was considered quite the John D.
Rockefeller of Chantry. I was so used to no one in

Chantry ever having any money that was worth any-thing, that this came as an unpleasing surprise. After that, Furfew used to try to come to the river plantation in a very shiny motor-launch with a red-and-white awn-ing and I would warn him off with a shotgun.

But then the money business began. You like to give a girl presents when you're in love—you like to do things right. Well, Lord knows, Eva was no gold-digger—she was as likely to be pleased with a soda as a pair of imported gloves. On the other hand, she was as likely to be pleased with the gloves.

I kept on schedule with the work, but I couldn't with the money. Each week, I'd be just a little over the line. I tell you, the people in books don't know about money. The people who write them can tell what it's like to be broke. But they don't tell what it's like to go around with clothes enough to cover you and food enough to satisfy you, and still have your heart's desire depend on money you haven't got.

Sure, I could have gone back in the novelty business and Eva could have kept on working. That would have been right for nine people out of ten. But it wouldn't have been right for the way I felt about Eva. It can be like that.

I wanted to come to her—oh, like a rescuer, I sup-pose. Like a prince, like the Northern cousin that saved the plantation. I didn't want to make the best of things —I wanted it all. You can't compromise with glamour. Or that's the way I feel.

Besides, I'd put in eight months' work on that novel and it didn't seem sensible to throw it all away. It might be a ladder to climb out on. It might have been.

Eva never complained, but she never understood She'd just say we could all go back and live in Chantry Well, I'm not that kind of man. If it had only been the river plantation! But, by now, I knew Chantry as well as if I'd been born there, and there wasn't a thing for me to do. Except maybe a job in Furfew's turpentine plant. And wouldn't that have been pretty?

Then, gradually, I got to know that the Forges, too were almost at the end of their string. I had to get it casually—they never talked about those things directly But when you keep on spending what you've got, there comes a time when you don't have it any more. Only it always surprised them. I wish I was built that way

It was the middle of July by this time, and one Saturday afternoon Eva came home and said she'd been let off at her office. They were cutting down the staff I'd just been going over my accounts, and when she told me that, I started laughing as if I couldn't stop

She looked rather surprised at first, but then she laughed, too.

"Why, honey," she said, "you're the killin'est. You always take things so serious. And then, sometimes, you don't take them serious a bit."

"It's an old Northern custom," I said. "They call it 'Laugh, clown, laugh.' For God's sake, Eva, what are we going to do?"

"Why, honey," she said, "I suppose I could get me another position." She never told me it was up to me She never would have. "But I just sort of despise those mean old offices. Do you think I ought to get me another position, honey?"

"Oh, darling, it doesn't matter," I said, still laugh-ing. "Nothing matters but us."

"That's mighty sweet of you, honey," she said and she looked relieved. "That's just the way I feel. And, when we get married, we'll fix things up right nice for Melissa and Louisa, won't we? And mother, of co'se, because she just can't stand Cousin Belle."

"Sure," I said. "Sure. When we're married, we'll fix up everything." And we went out in the back yard to look at the forsythia bush. But that night, Furfew brought his launch inshore and landed on the lower end of the island. He pitched camp there, and I could see his fire at night, through a glass.

I can't describe the next two months very well. They were all mixed up, the reality and the dream. Melissa and Louisa had to give up their classes, so we were all home, and lots of people came to the house. Some of them were callers and some of them were bill-collectors but, whoever they were, they generally stayed to a meal. Serena never minded that, she liked company. I remem-ber paying a grocery bill, with almost the last of my legacy, toward the end. There were eight hams on the bill and ten cases of "coke." It hadn't been paid for a long time.

Often, we'd all pile into an old Ford that belonged to one of the art students and go down to a public beach for the day. Eva didn't care so much about swimming but she loved to lie in the sand. And I'd lie beside her, painfully happy, and we'd hardly say anything at all. My God, but she was beautiful against those beach colors—the clear greens of the water and the hot white and tan of the sand. But then, she was just as beautiful, sitting in the plush rocker in the front parlor, under that green lamp.

They say the time between the Ordinance of Secession and the firing on Sumter was one of the gayest seasons Charleston ever had. I can understand that. They'd come to the brink of something, and fate was out of their hands. I got to feel that way.

Everything mixed, I tell you, everything mixed. I'd be sitting on the beach with Eva and, at the same time, I'd be riding around the river plantation, getting reports from my foreman and planning years ahead. I got to love that place. Even toward the end, it was safe, it didn't change. Of course, we kept having more and more trouble with Furfew; he kept extending his lines from the lower end of the island, but it never came to actual warfare—just fights between our men.

Meanwhile, I finished the novel and started revising it. And sometimes Eva would say why didn't we get married, anyway, and I knew we couldn't. You can't get married without some future ahead of you. So we started having arguments, and that was bad.

Why didn't I just seduce her like the big, brave heroes in books? Well, there were times when I thought it might be the answer for both of us. But it never happened. It wasn't shame or good principles. It just isn't so awfully easy to seduce a dream.

I knew they were writing letters but I didn't want to know any more. I knew the legacy was gone and my savings account was going, but I didn't care. I just wanted things to go on.

Finally, I heard that Furfew was coming North. I was going around like a sleepwalker most of the time, then, so it didn't hit me, at first. And then it did hit me.

Eva and I were out in the back yard. We'd fixed up an old swing seat there and it was dusky. Serena was humming in the kitchen. "Ole buzzard he fly away now —buzzard he fly away." I can't sing, but I can remember the way she sang it. It's funny how things stick in your head.

Eva had her head on my shoulder and my arms were around her. But we were as far away as Brooklyn and New York with the bridges down. Somebody was making love, but it wasn't us.

"When's he coming?" I said, finally.

"He's drivin' up in his car," she said. "He started yesterday."

"Young Lochinvar complete with windshield," I said. "He ought to be careful of those roads. Has he got a good car?"

"Yes," she said. "He's got a right pretty car."

"Oh, Eva, Eva," I said. "Doesn't it break your heart?"

"Why, honey," she said. "Come here to me."

We held each other a long time. She was very gentle. I'll remember that.

I stayed up most of that night, finishing revision on the novel. And, before I went to sleep, Furfew came to the house on the river plantation and walked in. I was standing in the hall and I couldn't lift a hand to him. So then I knew how it was going to be.

He came in the flesh, next afternoon. Yes, it was a good car. But he didn't look like Benedict Arnold. He was tall and black-haired and soft-voiced and he had on the sort of clothes they wear. He wasn't so old, either, not much older than I was. But the minute I saw him beside Eva, I knew it was all up. You only had to look at them. They were the same kind.

Oh, sure, he was a good business man. I got that in a minute. But, underneath all the externals, they were the same kind. It hadn't anything to do with the faithfulness or meanness. They were just the same breed of cats. If you're a dog and you fall in love with a cat, that's just your hard luck.

He'd brought up some corn with him and he and I sat up late, drinking it. We were awfully polite and noble in our conversation but we got things settled just the same. The funny thing is, I liked him. He was Young Lochinvar, he was little Mr. Fix-it, he was death and destruction to me, but I couldn't help liking him. He could have come to the island when Eva and I were married. He'd have been a great help. I'd have built him a house by the cove. And that's queer.

Next day, they all went out in the car for a picnic, and I stayed home, reading my novel. I read it all through—and there was nothing there. I'd tried to make the heroine like Eva, but even that hadn't worked. Sometimes you get a novelty like that—it looks like a world-beater till you get it into production. And then, you know you've just got to cut your losses. Well, this was the same proposition.

So I took it down to the furnace and watched it burn. It takes quite a while to burn four hundred sheets of paper in a cold furnace. You'd be surprised.

On my way back, I passed through the kitchen where Serena was. We looked at each other and she put her hand on the bread-knife.

"I'll like to see you burning in hell, Serena," I said. I'd always wanted to say that. Then I went upstairs, feeling her eyes on my back like the point of the bread-knife.

When I lay down on the bed, I knew that something was finished. It wasn't only Eva or the novel. I guess it was what you call youth. Well, we've all got to lose it, but generally it just fades out.

I lay there a long time, not sleeping, not thinking. And I heard them coming back and, after a while, the door opened gently and I knew it was Eva. But my eyes were shut and I didn't make a move. So, after another while, she went away.

There isn't much else to tell. Furfew settled everything up—don't tell me Southerners can't move fast when they want to—and the packers came and four days later they all started back for Chantry in the car. I guess he wasn't taking any chances, but he needn't have worried. I knew it was up. Even hearing Cousin Belle had "come around" didn't excite me. I was past that.

Eva kissed me goodbye—they all did, for that matter—the mother and the three sisters. They were sort of gay and excited, thinking of the motor-trip and getting back. To look at them, you wouldn't have said they'd ever seen a bill-collector. Well, that was the way they were.

"Don't write," I said to Eva. "Don't write, Mrs. Lochinvar."

She puckered her brows as she did when she was really puzzled.

"Why, honey, of co'se I'll write," she said. "Why wouldn't I write you, honey?"

I am sure she did, too. I can see the shape of the letters. But I never got them because I never left an address.

The person who was utterly dumbfounded was Mr. Budd. We camped in the house for a week, getting our own meals and sleeping under overcoats—the lease wasn't up till the first and Furfew had made an arrangement with the owner. And Mr. Budd couldn't get over it.

"I always knew they were crazy," he said. "But I'll never get such cooking again." I could see him looking into a future of boarding-houses. "You're young," he said. "You can eat anything. But when a man gets my age——"

He was wrong, though. I wasn't young. If I had been, I wouldn't have spent that week figuring out three novelties. Two of them were duds, but the third was Jiggety Jane. You've seen her—the little dancing doll that went all over the country when people were doing the Charleston. I made the face like Serena's at first, but it looked too lifelike, so we changed the face. The other people made most of the money, but I didn't care. I never liked the darn thing anyway. And it gave me a chance to start on my own.

They couldn't stop me after that. You're harder to stop, once you get rid of your youth. No, I don't think it was ironic or any of those things. You don't, outside of a book. There wasn't any connection between the two matters.

That fall I met Marian and we got married a year

later. She's got a lot of sense, that girl, and it's worked out fine. Maybe we did have the children a little quick, but she'd always wanted children. When you've got children and a home, you've got something to keep you steady. And, if she gets a kick out of reading love stories, let her. So I don't have to.

In a book, I'd have run across Eva, or seen Furfew's name in a paper. But that's never happened and I suppose it never will. I imagine they're all still in Chantry, and Chantry's one of those places that never gets in the news. The only thing I can't imagine is any of them being dead.

I wouldn't mind seeing Furfew again, for that matter. As I say, I liked the man. The only thing I hold against him is his moving them back, that way, before the lease was up. It was all right and he had his reasons. But they had two weeks left—two weeks till the first. And that would just have finished the year.

And when I get to sleep nowadays, Marian's there in the next bed, so that's all right, too. I've only tried to go back to the river plantation once, after a convention in Chicago when I was pretty well lit. And then, I couldn't do it. I was standing on the other side of the river and I could see the house across the water. Just the way it always was, but it didn't look lived in. At least nobody came to the window—nobody came out.

EVERYBODY WAS VERY NICE

YES, I guess I have put on weight since you last saw me—not that you're any piker yourself, Spike. But I suppose you medicos have to keep in shape —probably do better than we downtown. I try to play golf in the week-ends, and I do a bit of sailing. But four innings of the baseball game at reunion was enough for me. I dropped out, after that, and let Art Corliss pitch.

You really should have been up there. After all, the Twentieth is quite a milestone—and the class is pretty proud of its famous man. What was it that magazine article said: "most brilliant young psychiatrist in the country"? I may not know psychiatry from marbles, but I showed it to Lisa, remarking that it was old Spike Garrett, and for once she was impressed. She thinks brokers are pretty dumb eggs. I wish you could stay for dinner—I'd like to show you the apartment and the twins. No, they're Lisa's and mine. Boys, if you'll believe it. Yes, the others are with Sally—young Barbara's pretty grown up, now.

Well, I can't complain. I may not be famous like you, Spike, but I manage to get along, in spite of the brain trusters, and having to keep up the place on Long Island. I wish you got East oftener—there's a pretty view from the guest house, right across the Sound—

and if you wanted to write a book or anything, we'd know enough to leave you alone. Well, they started calling me a partner two years ago, so I guess that's what I am. Still fooling them, you know. But, seriously, we've got a pretty fine organization. We run a conservative business, but we're not all stuffed shirts, in spite of what the radicals say. As a matter of fact, you ought to see what the boys ran about us in the last Bawl Street Journal. Remind me to show it to you.

But it's your work I want to hear about—remember those bull-sessions we used to have in Old Main? Old Spike Garrett, the Medical Marvel! Why, I've even read a couple of your books, you old horse thief, believe it or not! You got me pretty tangled up on all that business about the id and the ego, too. But what I say is, there must be something in it if a fellow like Spike Garrett believes it. And there is, isn't there? Oh, I know you couldn't give me an answer in five minutes. But as long as there's a system—and the medicos know what they're doing.

I'm not asking for myself, of course—remember how you used to call me the 99 per-cent normal man? Well, I guess I haven't changed. It's just that I've gotten to thinking recently, and Lisa says I go around like a bear with a sore head. Well, it isn't that. I'm just thinking. A man has to think once in a while. And then, going back to reunion brought it all up again.

What I mean is this—the thing seemed pretty clear when we were in college. Of course, that was back in '15, but I can remember the way most of us thought. You fell in love with a girl and married her and settled down and had children and that was that. I'm not being simple-minded about it—you knew people get divorced, just as you knew people died, but it didn't seem something that was likely to happen to you. Especially if you came from a small Western city, as I did. Great Scott, I can remember when I was just a kid and the Prentisses got divorced. They were pretty prominent people and it shook the whole town.

That's why I want to figure things out for my own satisfaction. Because I never expected to be any Lothario—I'm not the type. And yet Sally and I got divorced and we're both remarried, and even so, to tell you the truth, things aren't going too well. I'm not saying a word against Lisa. But that's the way things are. And it isn't as if I were the only one. You can look around anywhere and see it, and it starts you wondering.

I'm not going to bore you about myself and Sally. Good Lord, you ushered at the wedding, and she always liked you. Remember when you used to come out to the house? Well, she hasn't changed—she's still got that little smile—though, of course, we're all older. Her husband's a doctor, too—that's funny, isn't it?—and they live out in Montclair. They've got a nice place there and he's very well thought of. We used to live in Meadowfield, remember?

I remember the first time I saw her after she married McConaghey—oh, we're perfectly friendly, you know. She had on red nail polish and her hair was different, a different bob. And she had one of those handbags with her new initials on it. It's funny, the first time, seeing your wife in clothes you don't know. Though Lisa and I have been married eight years, for that matter, and Sally and I were divorced in '28.

Of course, we have the children for part of the summer. We'll have Barbara this summer—Bud'll be in camp. It's a little difficult sometimes, but we all cooperate. You have to. And there's plenty to do on Long Island in the summer, that's one thing. But they and Lisa get along very well—Sally's brought them up nicely that way. For that matter, Doctor McConaghey's very nice when I see him. He gave me a darn good prescription for a cold and I get it filled every winter. And Jim Blake—he's Lisa's first husband—is really pretty interesting, now we've got to seeing him again. In fact, we're all awfully nice—just as nice and polite as we can be. And sometimes I get to wondering if it mightn't be a good idea if somebody started throwing fits and shooting rockets, instead. Of course I don't really mean that.

You were out for a week end with us in Meadowfield—maybe you don't remember it—but Bud was about six months old then and Barbara was just running around. It wasn't a bad house, if you remember the house. Dutch Colonial, and the faucet in the pantry leaked. The landlord was always fixing it, but he never quite fixed it right. And you had to cut hard to the left to back into the garage. But Sally liked the Japanese cherry tree and it wasn't a bad house. We were going to build on Rose Hill Road eventually. We had the lot picked out, if we didn't have the money, and we made plans about it. Sally never could remember to put in the doors in the plan, and we laughed about that.

It wasn't anything extraordinary, just an evening. After supper, we sat around the lawn in deck chairs and drank Sally's beer—it was long before Repeal.

We'd repainted the deck chairs ourselves the Sunday before and we felt pretty proud of them. The light stayed late, but there was a breeze after dark, and once Bud started yipping and Sally went up to him. She had on a white dress, I think—she used to wear white a lot in the summers—it went with her blue eyes and her yellow hair. Well, it wasn't anything extraordinary—we didn't even stay up late. But we were all there. And if you'd told me that within three years we'd both be married to other people, I'd have thought you were raving.

Then you went West, remember, and we saw you off on the train. So you didn't see what happened, and, as a matter of fact, it's hard to remember when we first started meeting the Blakes. They'd moved to Meadowfield then, but we hadn't met them.

Jim Blake was one of those pleasant, ugly-faced people with steel glasses who get right ahead in the law and never look young or old. And Lisa was Lisa. She's dark, you know, and she takes a beautiful burn. She was the first girl there to wear real beach things or drink a special kind of tomato juice when everybody else was drinking cocktails. She was very pretty and very good fun to be with—she's got lots of ideas. They entertained a good deal because Lisa likes that—she had her own income, of course. And she and Jim used to bicker a good deal in public in an amusing way —it was sort of an act or seemed like it. They had one little girl, Sylvia, that Jim was crazy about. I mean it sounds normal, doesn't it, even to their having the kind of Airedale you had then? Well, it all seemed normal enough to us, and they soon got to be part of the crowd. You know, the young married crowd in every suburb.

Of course, that was '28 and the boom was booming and everybody was feeling pretty high. I suppose that was part of it—the money—and the feeling you had that everything was going faster and faster and wouldn't stop. Why, it was Sally herself who said that we owed ourselves a whirl and mustn't get stodgy and settled while we were still young. Well, we had stuck pretty close to the grindstone for the past few years, with the children and everything. And it was fun to feel young and sprightly again and buy a new car and take in the club gala without having to worry about how you'd pay your house account. But I don't see any harm in that.

And then, of course, we talked and kidded a lot about freedom and what have you. Oh, you know the kind of talk—everybody was talking it then. About not being Victorians and living your own life. And there was the older generation and the younger generation. I've forgotten a lot of it now, but I remember there was one piece about love not being just a form of words mumbled by a minister, but something pretty special. As a matter of fact, the minister who married us was old Doctor Snell and he had the kind of voice you could hear in the next county. But I used to talk about that mumbling minister myself. I mean, we were enlightened, for a suburb, if you get my point. Yes, and pretty proud of it, too. When they banned a book in Boston, the lending library ordered six extra copies. And I still remember the big discussion we had about perfect freedom in marriage when even the straight Republicans voted the radical ticket. All except Chick

Bewleigh, and he was a queer sort of bird, who didn't even believe that stocks had reached a permanently high plateau.

But, meanwhile, most of us were getting the 8:15 and our wives were going down to the chain store and asking if that was a really nice head of lettuce. At least that's the way we seemed. And, if the crowd started kidding me about Mary Sennett, or Mac Church kissed Sally on the ear at a club revel, why, we were young, we were modern, and we could handle that. I wasn't going to take a shotgun to Mac, and Sally wasn't going to put on the jealous act. Oh, we had it all down to a science. We certainly did.

Good Lord, we had the Blakes to dinner, and they had us. They'd drop over for drinks or we'd drop over there. It was all perfectly normal and part of the crowd. For that matter, Sally played with Jim Blake in the mixed handicap and they got to the semifinals. No, I didn't play with Lisa—she doesn't like golf. I mean that's the way it was.

And I can remember the minute it started, and it wasn't anything, just a party at the Bewleighs'. They've got a big, rambling house and people drift around. Lisa and I had wandered out to the kitchen to get some drinks for the people on the porch. She had on a black dress, that night, with a big sort of orange flower on it. It wouldn't have suited everybody, but it suited her.

We were talking along like anybody and suddenly we stopped talking and looked at each other. And I felt, for a minute, well, just the way I felt when I was first in love with Sally. Only this time, it wasn't Sally. It happened so suddenly that all I could think of was,

"Watch your step!" Just as if you'd gone into a room in the dark and hit your elbow. I guess that makes it genuine, doesn't it?

We picked it up right away and went back to the party. All she said was, "Did anybody ever tell you that you're really quite a menace, Dan?" and she said that in the way we all said those things. But, all the same, it had happened. I could hear her voice all the way back in the car. And yet, I was as fond of Sally as ever. I don't suppose you'll believe that, but it's true.

And next morning, I tried to kid myself that it didn't have any importance. Because Sally wasn't jealous, and we were all modern and advanced and knew about life. But the next time I saw Lisa, I knew it had.

I want to say this. If you think it was all romance and rosebuds, you're wrong. A lot of it was merry hell. And yet, everybody whooped us on. That's what I don't understand. They didn't really want the Painters and the Blakes to get divorced, and yet they were pretty interested. Now, why do people do that? Some of them would carefully put Lisa and me next to each other at table and some of them would just as carefully not. But it all added up to the same thing in the end—a circus was going on and we were part of the circus. It's interesting to watch the people on the high wires at the circus and you hope they don't fall. But, if they did, that would be interesting too. Of course, there were a couple of people who tried, as they say, to warn us. But they were older people and just made us mad.

Everybody was so nice and considerate and understanding. Everybody was so nice and intelligent and fine. Don't misunderstand me. It was wonderful, being with Lisa. It was new and exciting. And it seemed to be wonderful for her, and she'd been unhappy with Jim. So, anyway, that made me feel less of a heel, though I felt enough of a heel, from time to time. And then, when we were together, it would seem so fine.

A couple of times we really tried to break it, too—at least twice. But we all belonged to the same crowd, and what could you do but run away? And, somehow, that meant more than running away—it meant giving in to the Victorians and that mumbling preacher and all the things we'd said we didn't believe in. Or I suppose Sally might have done like old Mrs. Pierce, back home. She horsewhipped the dressmaker on the station platform and then threw herself crying into Major Pierce's arms and he took her to Atlantic City instead. It's one of the town's great stories and I always wondered what they talked about on the train. Of course, they moved to Des Moines after that—I remember reading about their golden wedding anniversary when I was in college. Only nobody could do that nowadays, and, besides, Lisa wasn't a dressmaker.

So, finally, one day, I came home, and there was Sally, perfectly cold, and, we talked pretty nearly all night. We'd been awfully polite to each other for quite a while before—the way you are. And we kept polite, we kept a good grip on ourselves. After all, we'd said to each other before we were married that if either of us ever—and there it was. And it was Sally who brought that up, not me. I think we'd have felt better if we'd fought. But we didn't fight.

Of course, she was bound to say some things about Lisa, and I was bound to answer. But that didn't last long and we got our grip right back again. It was funny, being strangers and talking so politely, but we did it. I think it gave us a queer kind of pride to do it. I think it gave us a queer kind of pride for her to ask me politely for a drink at the end, as if she were in somebody else's house, and for me to mix it for her, as if she were a guest.

Everything was talked out by then and the house felt very dry and empty, as if nobody lived in it at all. We'd never been up quite so late in the house, except after a New Year's party or when Buddy was sick, that time. I mixed her drink very carefully, the way she liked it, with plain water, and she took it and said "Thanks." Then she sat for a while without saying anything. It was so quiet you could hear the little drip of the leaky faucet in the pantry, in spite of the door being closed. She heard it and said, "It's dripping again. You better call up Mr. Vye in the morning—I forgot. And I think Barbara's getting a cold—I meant to tell you." Then her face twisted and I thought she was going to cry, but she didn't.

She put the glass down—she'd only drunk half her drink—and said, quite quietly, "Oh, damn you, and damn Lisa Blake, and damn everything in the world!" Then she ran upstairs before I could stop her and she still wasn't crying.

I could have run upstairs after her, but I didn't. I stood looking at the glass on the table and I couldn't think. Then, after a while, I heard a key turn in a lock. So I picked up my hat and went out for a walk—I hadn't been out walking that early in a long time. Finally, I found an all-night diner and got some coffee.

Then I came back and read a book till the maid got down—it wasn't a very interesting book. When she came down, I pretended I'd gotten up early and had to go into town by the first train, but I guess she knew.

I'm not going to talk about the details. If you've been through them, you've been through them; and if you haven't, you don't know. My family was fond of Sally, and Sally's had always liked me. Well, that made it tough. And the children. They don't say the things you expect them to. I'm not going to talk about that.

Oh, we put on a good act, we put on a great show! There weren't any fists flying or accusations. Everybody said how well we did it, everybody in town. And Lisa and Sally saw each other, and Jim Blake and I talked to each other perfectly calmly. We said all the usual things. He talked just as if it were a case. I admired him for it. Lisa did her best to make it emotional, but we wouldn't let her. And I finally made her see that, court or no court, he'd simply have to have Sylvia. He was crazy about her, and while Lisa's a very good mother, there wasn't any question as to which of them the kid liked best. It happens that way, sometimes.

For that matter, I saw Sally off on the train to Reno. She wanted it that way. Lisa was going to get a Mexican divorce—they'd just come in, you know. And nobody could have told, from the way we talked in the station. It's funny, you get a queer bond, through a time like that. After I'd seen her off—and she looked small in the train—the first person I wanted to see wasn't Lisa, but Jim Blake. You see, other people are fine, but unless you've been through things yourself, you don't quite understand them. But Jim Blake was still in Meadowfield, so I went back to the club.

I hadn't ever really lived in the club before, except for three days one summer. They treat you very well, but, of course, being a college club, it's more for the youngsters and the few old boys who hang around the bar. I got awfully tired of the summer chintz in the dining room and the Greek waiter I had who breathed on my neck. And you can't work all the time, though I used to stay late at the office. I guess it was then I first thought of getting out of Spencer Wilde and making a new connection. You think about a lot of things at a time like that.

Of course, there were lots of people I could have seen, but I didn't much want to—somehow, you don't. Though I did strike up quite a friendship with one of the old boys. He was about fifty-five and he'd been divorced four times and was living permanently at the club. We used to sit up in his little room—he'd had his own furniture moved in and the walls were covered with pictures—drinking Tom Collinses and talking about life. He had lots of ideas about life, and about matrimony, too, and I got quite interested, listening to him. But then he'd go into the dinners he used to give at Delmonico's, and while that was interesting, too, it wasn't much help, except to take your mind off the summer chintz.

He had some sort of small job, downtown, but I guess he had an income from his family too. He must have. But when I'd ask him what he did, he'd always say, "I'm retired, my boy, very much retired, and how about a touch more beverage to keep out the sun?"

He always called it beverage, but they knew what he meant at the bar. He turned up at the wedding, when Lisa and I were married, all dressed up in a cutaway, and insisted on making us a little speech—very nice it was too. Then we had him to dinner a couple of times, after we'd got back, and somehow or other, I haven't seen him since. I suppose he's still at the club— I've got out of the habit of going there, since I joined the other ones, though I still keep my membership.

Of course, all that time, I was crazy about Lisa and writing her letters and waiting till we could be married. Of course I was. But, now and then, even that would get shoved into the background. Because there was so much to do and arrangements to make and people like lawyers to see. I don't like lawyers very much, even yet, though the people we had were very good. But there was all the telephoning and the conferences. Somehow, it was like a machine—a big machine—and you had to learn a sort of new etiquette for everything you did. Till, finally, it got so that about all you wanted was to have the fuss over and not talk about it any more.

I remember running into Chick Bewleigh in the club, three days before Sally got her decree. You'd like Chick—he's the intellectual type, but a darn good fellow too. And Nan, his wife, is a peach—one of those big, rangy girls with a crazy sense of humor. It was nice to talk to him because he was natural and didn't make any cracks about grass-bachelors or get that look in his eye. You know the look they get. We talked about Meadowfield—just the usual news—the Bakers were splitting up and Don Sikes had a new job and the Wilsons were having a baby. But it seemed good to hear it.

"For that matter," he said, drawing on his pipe, "we're adding to the population again ourselves. In the fall. How we'll ever manage four of them! I keep telling Nan she's cockeyed, but she says they're more fun than a swimming pool and cost less to keep up, so what can you do!"

He shook his head and I remembered that Sally always used to say she wanted six. Only now it would be Lisa, so I mustn't think about that.

"So that's your recipe for a happy marriage," I said. "Well, I always wondered."

I was kidding, of course, but he looked quite serious.

"Kinder, Küchen und Kirche?" he said. "Nope, that doesn't work any more, what with pre-schools, automats and the movies. Four children or no four children, Nan could still raise hell if she felt like raising hell. And so could I, for that matter. Add blessings of civilization," and his eyes twinkled.

"Well then," I said, "what is it?" I really wanted to know.

"Oh, just bull luck, I suppose. And happening to like what you've got," he answered, in a sort of embarrassed way.

"You can do that," I said. "And yet——"

He looked away from me.

"Oh, it was a lot simpler in the old days," he said. "Everything was for marriage—church, laws, society. And when people got married, they expected to stay that way. And it made a lot of people as unhappy as hell. Now the expectation's rather the other way, at least in this great and beautiful nation and among peo-

ple like us. If you get a divorce, it's rather like going
to the dentist—unpleasant sometimes, but lots of people have been there before. Well, that's a handsome
system, too, but it's got its own casualty list. So there
you are. You takes your money and you makes your
choice. And some of us like freedom better than the
institution and some of us like the institution better,
but what most of us would like is to be Don Juan on
Thursdays and Benedick, the married man, on Fridays,
Saturdays and the rest of the week. Only that's a bit
hard to work out, somehow," and he grinned.

"All the same," I said, "you and Nan——"

"Well," he said. "I suppose we're exceptions. You
see, my parents weren't married till I was seven. So I'm
a conservative. It might have worked out the other
way."

"Oh," I said.

"Yes," he said. "My mother was English, and you
may have heard of English divorce laws. She ran away
with my father and she was perfectly right—her husband was a very extensive brute. All the same, I was
brought up on the other side of the fence, and I know
something about what it's like. And Nan was a minister's daughter who thought she ought to be free. Well,
we argued about things a good deal. And, finally, I told
her that I'd be very highly complimented to live with
her on any terms at all, but if she wanted to get married, she'd have to expect a marriage, not a trip to
Coney Island. And I made my point rather clear by
blacking her eye, in a taxi, when she told me she was
thinking seriously of spending a week end with my
deadly rival, just to see which one of us she really

loved. You can't spend a romantic week end with some-body when you've got a black eye. But you can get married with one and we did. She had raw beefsteak on it till two hours before the wedding, and it was the prettiest sight I ever saw. Well, that's our simple story."

"Not all of it," I said.

"No," he said, "not all of it. But at least we didn't start in with any of this bunk about if you meet a handsomer fellow it's all off. We knew we were getting into something. Bewleigh's Easy Guide to Marriage in three installments—you are now listening to the Voice of Experience, and who cares? Of course, if we hadn't—ahem—liked each other, I could have blacked her eye till doomsday and got nothing out of it but a suit for assault and battery. But nothing's much good unless it's worth fighting for. And she doesn't look exactly like a downtrodden wife."

"Nope," I said, "but all the same——"

He stared at me very hard—almost the way he used to when people were explaining that stocks had reached a permanently high plateau.

"Exactly," he said. "And there comes a time, no matter what the intention, when a new face heaves into view and a spark lights. I'm no Adonis, God knows, but it's happened to me once or twice. And I know what I do then. I run. I run like a rabbit. It isn't courageous or adventurous or fine. It isn't even particularly moral, as I think about morals. But I run. Because, when all's said and done, it takes two people to make a love affair and you can't have it when one of them's not there. And, dammit, Nan knows it, that's the trouble. She'd ask Helen of Troy to dinner just to see me run. Well, goodbye, old man, and our best to Lisa, of course——"

After he was gone, I went and had dinner in the grill. I did a lot of thinking at dinner, but it didn't get me anywhere. When I was back in the room, I took the receiver off the telephone. I was going to call long distance. But your voice sounds different on the phone, and, anyway, the decree would be granted in three days. So when the girl answered, I told her it was a mistake.

Next week Lisa came back and she and I were married. We went to Bermuda on our wedding trip. It's a very pretty place. Do you know, they won't allow an automobile on the island?

The queer thing was that at first I didn't feel married to Lisa at all. I mean, on the boat, and even at the hotel. She said, "But how exciting, darling!" and I suppose it was.

Now, of course, we've been married eight years, and that's always different. The twins will be seven in May —two years older than Sally's Jerry. I had an idea for a while that Sally might marry Jim Blake—he always admired her. But I'm glad she didn't—it would have made things a little too complicated. And I like McConaghey—I like him fine. We gave them an old Chinese jar for a wedding present. Lisa picked it out. She has very good taste and Sally wrote us a fine letter.

I'd like to have you meet Lisa sometime—she's interested in intelligent people. They're always coming to the apartment—artists and writers and people like that.

Of course, they don't always turn out the way she expects. But she's quite a hostess and she knows how to handle things. There was one youngster that used to rather get in my hair. He'd call me the Man of Wall

Street and ask me what I thought about Picabia or one of those birds, in a way that sort of said, "Now watch this guy stumble!" But as soon as Lisa noticed it, she got rid of him. That shows she's considerate.

Of course, it's different, being married to a person. And I'm pretty busy these days and so is she. Sometimes, if I get home and there's going to be a party, I'll just say good night to the twins and fade out after dinner. But Lisa understands about that, and I've got my own quarters. She had one of her decorator friends do the private study and it really looks very nice.

I had Jim Blake in there one night. Well, I had to take him somewhere. He was getting pretty noisy and Lisa gave me the high sign. He's doing very well, but he looks pretty hard these days and I'm afraid he's drinking a good deal, though he doesn't often show it. I don't think he ever quite got over Sylvia's dying. Four years ago. They had scarlet fever at the school. It was a great shock to Lisa, too, of course, but she had the twins and Jim never married again. But he comes to see us, every once in a while. Once, when he was tight, he said it was to convince himself about remaining a bachelor, but I don't think he meant that.

Now, when I brought him into the study, he looked around and said, "Shades of Buck Rogers! What one of Lisa's little dears produced this imitation Wellsian nightmare?"

"Oh, I don't remember," I said. "I think his name was Slivovitz."

"It looks as if it had been designed by a man named Slivovitz," he said. "All dental steel and black glass.

I recognize the Lisa touch. You're lucky she didn't put murals of cogwheels on the walls."

"Well, there was a question of that," I said.

"I bet there was," he said. "Well, here's how, old man! Here's to two great big wonderful institutions, marriage and divorce!"

I didn't like that very much and told him so. But he just wagged his head at me.

"I like you, Painter," he said. "I always did. Sometimes I think you're goofy, but I like you. You can't insult me—I won't let you. And it isn't your fault."

"What isn't my fault?" I said.

"The setup," he said. "Because, in your simple little heart, you're an honest monogamous man, Painter—monogamous as most. And if you'd stayed married to Sally, you'd have led an honest monogamous life. But they loaded the dice against you, out at Meadowfield, and now Lord knows where you'll end up. After all, I was married to Lisa myself for six years or so. Tell me, isn't it hell?"

"You're drunk," I said.

"*In vino veritas*," said he. "No, it isn't hell—I take that back. Lisa's got her damn-fool side, but she's an attractive and interesting woman—or could be, if she'd work at it. But she was brought up on the idea of Romance with a big R, and she's too bone-lazy and bone-selfish to work at it very long. There's always something else, just over the horizon. Well, I got tired of fighting that, after a while. And so will you. She doesn't want husbands—she wants clients and followers. Or maybe you're tired already."

"I think you'd better go home, Jim," I said. "I don't want to have to ask you."

"Sorry," he said. *"In vino veritas.* But it's a funny setup, isn't it? What Lisa wanted was a romantic escapade—and she got twins. And what you wanted was marriage—and you got Lisa. As for me," and for a minute his face didn't look drunk any more, "what I principally wanted was Sylvia and I've lost that. I could have married again, but I didn't think that'd be good for her. Now, I'll probably marry some client I've helped with her decree—we don't touch divorce, as a rule, just a very, very special line of business for a few important patrons. I know those—I've had them in the office. And won't that be fun for us all! What a setup it is!" and he slumped down in his chair and went to sleep. I let him sleep for a while and then had Briggs take him down in the other elevator. He called up next day and apologized—said he knew he must have been noisy, though he couldn't remember anything he said.

The other time I had somebody in the study was when Sally came back there once, two years ago. We'd met to talk about college for Barbara and I'd forgotten some papers I wanted to show her. We generally meet downtown. But she didn't mind coming back—Lisa was out, as it happened. It made me feel queer, taking her up in the elevator and letting her in at the door. She wasn't like Jim—she thought the study was nice.

Well, we talked over our business and I kept looking at her. You can see she's older, but her eyes are still that very bright blue, and she bites her thumb when she's interested. It's a queer feeling. Of course, I was used to seeing her, but we usually met downtown. You know, I wouldn't have been a bit surprised if she'd pushed the bell and said, "Tea, Briggs. I'm home." She didn't, naturally.

I asked her, once, if she wouldn't take off her hat and she looked at me in a queer way and said, "So you can show me your etchings? Dan, Dan, you're a dangerous man!" and for a moment we both laughed like fools.

"Oh, dear," she said, drying her eyes, "that's very funny. And now I must be going home."

"Look here, Sally," I said, "I've always told you— but, honestly, if you need anything—if there's anything——"

"Of course, Dan," she said. "And we're awfully good friends, aren't we?" But she was still smiling.

I didn't care. "Friends!" I said. "You know how I think about you. I always have. And I don't want you to think——"

She patted my shoulder—I'd forgotten the way she used to do that.

"There," she said. "Mother knows all about it. And we really are friends, Dan. So——"

"I was a fool."

She looked at me very steadily out of those eyes.

"We were all fools," she said. "Even Lisa. I used to hate her for a while. I used to hope things would happen to her. Oh, not very bad things. Just her finding out that you never see a crooked picture without straightening it, and hearing you say: 'A bird can't fly on one wing,' for the dozenth time. The little things everybody has to find out and put up with. But I don't even do that any more."

"If you'd ever learned to put a cork back in a bottle," I said. "I mean the right cork in the right bottle. But——"

"I do so! No, I suppose I never will." And she laughed. She took my hands. "Funny, funny, funny," she said. "And funny to have it all gone and be friends."

"Is it all gone?" I said.

"Why, no, of course not," she said. "I don't suppose it ever is, quite. Like the boys who took you to dances. And there's the children, and you can't help remembering. But it's gone. We had it and lost it. I should have fought for it more, I suppose, but I didn't. And then I was terribly hurt and terribly mad. But I got over that. And now I'm married to Jerry. And I wouldn't give him up, or Jerry Junior, for anything in the world. The only thing that worries me is sometimes when I think it isn't quite a fair deal for him. After all, he could have married—well, somebody else. And yet he knows I love him."

"He ought to," I said rather stiffly. "He's a darn lucky guy, if you ask me."

"No, Dan. I'm the lucky girl. I'm hoping this minute that Mrs. Potter's X-rays turn out all right. He did a beautiful job on her. But he always worries."

I dropped her hands.

"Well, give him my best," I said.

"I will, Dan. He likes you, you know. Really he does. By the way, have you had any more of that bursitis? There's a new treatment—he wanted me to ask you——"

"Thanks," I said, "but that all cleared up."

"I'm glad. And now I must fly. There's always shopping when you come in from the suburbs. Give my best to Lisa and tell her I was sorry not to see her. She's out I suppose."

"Yes," I said. "She'll be sorry to miss you—you wouldn't stay for a cocktail? She's usually in around then."

"It sounds very dashing, but I mustn't. Jerry Junior lost one of his turtles and I've got to get him another. Do you know a good pet shop? Well, Bloomingdale's, I suppose—after all, I've got other things to get."

"There's a good one two blocks down on Lexington," I said. "But if you're going to Bloomingdale's——Well, goodbye, Sally, and good luck."

"Goodbye, Dan. And good luck to you. And no regrets."

"No regrets," I said, and we shook hands.

There wasn't any point in going down to the street with her, and besides I had to phone the office. But before I did, I looked out, and she was just getting into a cab. A person looks different, somehow, when they don't know you're seeing them. I could see the way she looked to other people—not young any more, not the Sally I'd married, not even the Sally I'd talked with, all night in that cold house. She was a nice married woman who lived in Montclair and whose husband was a doctor; a nice woman, in shopping for the day, with a new spring hat and a fifty-trip ticket in her handbag. She'd had trouble in her life, but she'd worked it out. And, before she got on the train, she'd have a black-and-white soda, sitting on a stool at the station, or maybe she didn't do that any more. There'd be lots of things in er handbag, but I wouldn't know about any of them or what locks the keys fitted. And, if she were dying, ey'd send for me, because that would be etiquette. nd the same if I were dying. But we'd had something nd lost it—the way she said—and that was all that was ft.

Now she was that nice Mrs. McConaghey. But she'd ever be quite that to me. And yet, there was no way to back. You couldn't even go back to the house in leadowfield—they'd torn it down and put up an apart- ent instead.

So that's why I wanted to talk to you. I'm not com- aining and I'm not the kind of fellow that gets nerves. ut I just want to know—I just want to figure it out. nd sometimes it keeps going round and round in your ead. You'd like to be able to tell your children some- ing, especially when they're growing up. Well, I know hat we'll tell them. But I wonder if it's enough.

Not that we don't get along well when Bud and arbara come to see us. Especially Barbara—she's very ctful and she's crazy about the twins. And now they're owing up, it's easier. Only, once in a while, some- ing happens that makes you think. I took Barbara out iling last summer. She's sixteen and a very sweet kid, I say it myself. A lot of kids that age seem pretty hard, ut she isn't.

Well, we were just talking along, and, naturally, you ke to know what your children's plans are. Bud thinks wants to be a doctor like McConaghey and I've no jection. I asked Barbara if she wanted a career, but e said she didn't think so.

"Oh, I'd like to go to college," she said, "and maybe

work for a while, afterwards, the way mother did, you
know. But I haven't any particular talents, dad. I could
kid myself, but I haven't. I guess it's just woman's func-
tion and home and babies for me."

"Well, that sounds all right to me," I said, feeling
very paternal.

"Yes," she said, "I like babies. In fact, I think I'll
get married pretty young, just for the experience. The
first time probably won't work, but it ought to teach
you some things. And then, eventually, you might find
somebody to tie to."

"So that's the way it is with the modern young
woman?" I said.

"Why, of course," she said. "That's what practically
all the girls say—we've talked it all over at school. Of
course, sometimes it takes you quite a while. Like
Helen Hastings' mother. She just got married for the
fourth time last year, but he really is a sweet! He took
us all to the matinee when I was visiting Helen and we
nearly died. He's a count, of course, and he's got the
darlingest accent. I don't know whether I'd like a count,
though it must be fun to have little crowns on your
handkerchiefs like Helen's mother. What's the matter,
daddy? Are you shocked?"

"Don't flatter yourself, young lady—I've been
shocked by experts," I said. "No, I was just thinking.
Suppose we—well, suppose your mother and I had
stayed together? How would you have felt about it
then?"

"But you didn't, did you?" she said, and her voice
wasn't hurt or anything, just natural. "I mean, almost
nobody does any more. Don't worry, daddy. Bud and

understand all about it—good gracious, we're grown up! Of course, if you and mother had," she said, rather dutifully, "I suppose it would have been very nice. But then we'd have missed Mac, and he really is a sweet, and you'd have missed Lisa and the twins. Anyhow, it's all worked out now. Oh, of course, I'd rather hope it would turn out all right the first time, if it wasn't too stodgy or sinister. But you've got to face facts, you know."

"Face facts!" I said. "Dammit, Barbara!"

Then I stopped, because what did I have to say?

Well, that's the works, and if you've got any dope on it, I wish you'd tell me. There are so few people you can talk to—that's the trouble. I mean everybody's very nice, but that's not the same thing. And, if you start thinking too much, the highballs catch up on you. And you can't afford that—I've never been much of a drinking man.

The only thing is, where does it stop, if it does? That's the thing I'm really afraid of.

It may sound silly to you. But I've seen other people—well, take this Mrs. Hastings, Barbara talked about. Or my old friend at the club. I wonder if he started in, wanting to get married four times. I know I didn't—I'm not the type and you know it.

And yet, suppose, well, you do meet somebody who treats you like a human being. I mean somebody who doesn't think you're a little goofy because you know more about American Can than who painted what. Supposing, even, they're quite a lot younger. That shouldn't make all the difference. After all, I'm no Lothario. And Lisa and I aren't thinking of divorce or anything like that. But, naturally, we lead our own lives, and you ought to be able to talk to somebody. Of course, if it could have been Sally. That was my fault. But it isn't as if Maureen were just in the floor show. She's got her own specialty number. And, really, when you get to know her, she's a darned intelligent kid.

A DEATH IN THE COUNTRY

FTER the years, Tom Carroll was going back to Waynesville—to stand by a kinswoman's grave, in the country of his youth. The names of the small, familiar stations were knots on a thread that led back into the darkness of childhood. He was glad Claire had not come. She hated death and memories. She hated cramped, local trains that smelled of green plush and cinders. Most of all she would hate Waynesville, even in mid-September and the grave light of afternoon.

Well, he wasn't looking forward to a pleasant time. He felt fagged and on edge already. There was work for the active partner of Norman, Buckstone, and Carroll in his brief-case, but he could not get down to the work. Instead he remembered, from childhood, the smell of dyed cloth and poignant, oppressive flowers, the black wisp tied on the knocker, the people coming to the door. The house was full of a menace—full of a secret—there were incomprehensible phrases, said in a murmur, and a man in black gloves who came, and a strangeness behind a shut door. Run out and play, run out and play; but there was no right way to play any more—even out in the yard you could smell the sweet, overpowering flowers—even out in the street you could see the people coming and coming, making that little pause as they saw the black wisp. Beautiful, they said, she looks beautiful; but the glimpse of the face was not mother, only somebody coldly asleep. Our sister has gone to dear Jesus . . we shall meet on that beautiful shore . . . but the man spoke words, and the harsh box sank into the hole, and from it nothing arose, not even a white thing, not even silver vapor; the clay at the sides of the hole was too yellow and thick and cold. He's too young to realize, said a great many voices— but for months nothing was right. The world had stopped being solid, and people's smiles were different, and mother was Jesus's sister, and they gave her clothes away. Then, after a long time, the place was green again and looked just like the other graves, and the knife in your pocket was a comfort, going out there Sundays in the street car.

Barbarous. And to-morrow would be barbarous, as well. The family met only at funerals and weddings, now; and there had been more funerals than weddings for the past ten years. The big Christmas tree was gone from the house on Hessian Street—the majestic tree whose five-pointed, sparkling star had scratched against the ceiling of heaven in the back parlor, spreading wide its green boughs to shelter all generations and tribes of the Pyes and Merritts and Chipmans, their wives and their children, their menservants and their maidservants, their Noah's arks and cigar-cases and bottles of *eau-de-cologne.* The huge tablecloth of Thanksgiving lay folded away at the bottom of a chest—the tables now were too small. There would never be another turkey, with a breast like a mountainside, to fall into endless slices under the shining magic of Uncle Melrose's knife. Aunt Louise and Aunt Emmy had been the last of Hessian Street and, after to-morrow, there would only be Aunt Emmy and the ghosts.

The faces around the table had been masterful and full of life. They had been grown-up and permanent—one could not imagine them young or growing old. Together, they made a nation; they were the earth. If one took the trains of the morning, even as far as Bradensburg, lo, Uncle Melrose was there, at his desk with the little brass postage-scale on top of it, as it had been from the first. If one walked out to Mount Pleasant through the buckeye fall, at the end there was the white gate of Cousin Edna and the iron nigger boy with the rainstreaked face, holding out his black hand stiffly for the buckboards that drove no more. There were princes and dominations and thrones and powers; but what were these beside Aunt Emmy and Cousin Millie, beside the everlasting forms of Mrs. Bache and Mr. Beaver, of the ladies at the Women's Exchange and the man who lighted the gas street-lamps with a long brass spike? Then, suddenly, the earth had begun to crumble. A wind blew, a bell sounded, and they were dispersed. There were shrunken old people, timorous and pettish, and a small, heart-stifling town. These and the grown-up children, more strange than strangers. But Hessian Street was over—the great tree was down.

"And Uncle Melrose was a pompous old windbag," thought Tom Carroll. "And yet, if he were alive, I'd be calling him 'Sir.' Oh, Claire's right—the jungle's the jungle—she's saner than I am, always."

It was one of the many maxims Claire found in books. The family was the jungle that you grew up in and, if you did not, somehow, break through to light and air of your own when you were young, you died, quickly or slowly but surely, stifled out, choked down by the overpowering closeness of your own kin. Tom Carroll knew this much—that New York, after Waynesville, had been like passing from the large, squabbling, overheated room of Christmas afternoon into the anonymous peace of a bare and windy street. He had been lonely, often—he had missed Hessian Street and them all. But, oh the endless, intricate, unimportant diplomacy—the feuds and the makings-up—the inflexible machine of the Family, crushing all independence. Not again, not ever again! And yet, here he was, on the train.

Well, nobody could say that he shirked it. He would have to take charge when he got there, like it or not. It wouldn't be easy, straightening everything out—he'd rather handle the Corliss case any day—but he'd done it in other emergencies and he supposed he could do it again. After all, who else was there? Jerry Pye? His mouth narrowed, thinking of Jerry.

The conductor bawled the names of familiar stations, the long, autumnal twilight began beyond the window. If only things could go smoothly just this once! But something always cropped up—something always had to be smoothed over and explained. *Morton Center, Morton Center!* If Aunt Louise had left no will— and she very probably hadn't—there'd be the dickens of a time, securing the estate to Aunt Emmy. But it must be done—he'd ride roughshod over Jerry Pye if necessary. *Brandy Hill! Brandy Hill!* . . If only nobody would tell him to be sure and notice Mrs. Bache! He could easily fix a pension for Aunt Emmy, but how to do it best? She'd have to leave Hessian Street, of course. Even cutting the old house into apartments hadn't really solved the problem. She could get a small, comfortable, modern flat over in the new section. The silver candlesticks were the only things Claire would have liked, but they would go to Jerry because Jerry had always failed.

Waynesville, next stop! The flowers had been wired from New York. *Waynesville!* We're coming in. There's an A. & P. on Main Street, and Ellerman's Bazaar is gone. *Waynesville!* . . . And God bless Uncle Melrose and Aunt Louise and Aunt Emmy and all my dear relations and friends and Spot and make me a good boy and not afraid of the dark. *Waynesville!*

Right down the middle of Main Street the train clanged till it stopped in front of the bald, new station. Tom Carroll sighed. It was as he had prophesied. Jerry Pye was there to meet him.

He got off the train, and the cousins shook hands. "Have a good trip, Tom?"

"Not bad. Real fall weather, isn't it?"

"Yes, it's a real fall. You took the limited as far as Bradensburg, I suppose?"

"Yes, that seemed the quickest thing for me to do."

"They say she's quite a train," said Jerry Pye. "I was on her once—three years ago, you know. Well, I thought, here's where the old man blows himself for once. Minnie would hardly believe me when I told her. 'Jerry Pye!' she said, 'I don't know what's come over you. You never take me on any limiteds!' 'Well,' I said, 'maybe it is extra-fare, but I just decided the old man could blow himself for once!' Well, you should have seen her expression! Though I guess it wouldn't mean much to you, at that. I guess extra-fare trains don't mean much in people's lives when they come from New York."

"I could have taken a slower train," said Tom Carroll, carefully, "but it wouldn't have saved any time."

This remark seemed to amuse Jerry Pye intensely. His thin, sallow face—the face of a dyspeptic fox— gloated with mirth for an instant. Then he sobered himself, abruptly and pointedly.

"You always were a case, Tom," he said, "always. But this is a sad occasion."

"I didn't mean to be funny," said Tom Carroll. "Had I better get a taxi or is that your car?"

"Oh, we've got the family mistake—a dollar down and a dollar whenever they catch you!" Jerry Pye grinned and sobered himself again with the automatism of a mechanical figure. "I drove up in her night before last," he said, pointedly, as they got in. "Evans is a good man and all that, but he's apt to figure a little close on the cars; and as long as ours is dark blue, it'll look perfectly dignified."

"I telegraphed Aunt Emmy," said Tom Carroll and stopped. There was no possible use in trying to explain oneself to Jerry Pye.

"Yes, indeed," said Jerry, instantly. "Aunt Emmy appreciated it very much. Very much indeed. 'Tom's always very busy,' I told her. 'But don't you worry, Aunt Emmy. Tom may be a big man now, but his heart's in the right place. He'll be here.'"

"I told her," said Tom Carroll, distinctly and in

spite of himself, "that in case anything of the sort came up, she had only to—"

"Oh," said Jerry, brightly, "we all knew that. We all knew you couldn't be expected to send one of your big cars all the way from New York to Waynesville. How's Claire?"

"Claire was very sorry indeed not to be able to come," said Tom, his hands gripping his knees. "We have one car," he said.

"That's just what I said," said Jerry Pye triumphantly. "I told Aunt Emmy—'you couldn't expect Tom to take the car away from Claire—she'll need it when he's away, shopping and seeing her friends—and naturally she hardly knew Aunt Louise. You wait and see. She'll send handsome flowers,' I said."

"Oh, God, make me a good boy!" prayed Tom Carroll, internally. "It can't last more than ten minutes. Ten minutes isn't really long." He braced himself. "How is Aunt Emmy?" he said.

Their speed instantly dropped to a respectful twenty miles an hour.

"She's wonderful," said Jerry Pye. "Simply wonderful. Of course, Minnie's been a great help to her and then, the end was very peaceful. Just seemed to breathe away." His voice had an obvious relish. "One minute she was there—as bright as a button, considering everything—and the next minute—" He shook his head.

"I'm glad," said Tom Carroll. "I mean——"

"Oh, we wouldn't have wanted her to suffer," said Jerry Pye in a shocked voice, as if he were denying some uncouth suggestion of Tom's. "No, sir, we wouldn't have wanted that. Now when Minnie's mother passed over—I don't know whether I ever told you the whole story, Tom—but from the Friday before—"

He continued, but had only come to the personal idiosyncrasies of the first night nurse when they turned into Hessian Street.

They got out of the car. Jerry Pye was mopping his forehead, though the day was chill. Yes, there was the black wisp on the knocker. But there was a row of bell-pushes where the old name-plate had been. The bricks in the sidewalk were rose-red and old and worn—the long block of quiet houses kept its faded dignity, in spite of a sign, "Pappas' Smoke Shop," a sign, "The Hessian Sergeant—Tea and Antiques." The linden trees had not perished, though their shade was thin.

"If this were a city," thought Tom Carroll, "people would have found out by now that it was quaint and painted the doors green and had studio-parties. Well, anyhow, that hasn't happened."

"Everyone's been very respectful," said Jerry Pye, nodding at the black wisp. "I mean, some people might be touchy when everybody has to use the same front-door. But Mr. Rodman came to me himself—they're the second-floor back. Just leave your bag in the car, Tom. It won't be in the way. I think Minnie's seen us —we figured out if you came to-day this ought to be the train."

Tom Carroll did not repeat that he had telegraphed or that there was only one afternoon train to Waynes-ville. He kissed his cousin-in-law's flustered cheek and was kissed by her in return. Minnie was always flus-tered; she had been a plump, flustered robin of a girl at her wedding; she was unaltered now save for the dust of gray in her abundant, unbecoming hair; they had never exchanged three words, except on family matters; and yet, they always kissed. He wondered if Minnie, too, ever found this circumstance strange. He should not wonder, of course, especially now.

"How's Aunt Emmy?" said Jerry Pye, in the anxious tones of one just returned from a long absence. "There isn't any change?"

"No, dear," said Minnie, solemnly, "she's just the same. She's wonderful. Mrs. Robinson and Mrs. Bache are with her, now. Remember—we must all be very nice to Mrs. Bache, Cousin Tom."

"I did put a tick-tack on her window, once," said Tom Carroll, reflectively. "But I haven't done that for a long time. Not for thirty years."

Minnie, the robin, was shocked for a moment, but brightened.

"That's right," she said. "We must all keep up for Aunt Emmy. Now, if you'll just go in—" She stood aside.

The spare, small, hawk-nosed figure rose from the stiff-backed chair as Tom Carroll entered. "Good evening, Thomas. I am glad you are here," said the unfaltering voice. "I think you know my good neighbors, Mrs. Bache and Mrs. Robinson."

Tom Carroll took the thin, dry, forceful hands. By God, she is wonderful, he thought, in spite of their saying it—it's taken me years to unlearn what she taught me, but she's remarkable. Why don't they let her alone? *Aunt Emmy, Aunt Emmy, you have grown so small! You rapped on my chapped knuckles with a steel thimble when I was cold; you ran me through and*

*through like the emery-bag in your workbox with your
sharp and piercing eyes; you let me see that you thought
my father a rascal; you made me lie and cheat because
of the terror of your name—and now you have grown
small and fragile and an old woman, and there is not
even injustice left in Hessian Street.*

The moment passed. Tom Carroll found himself
mechanically answering Mrs. Bache's questions while
his eyes roved about the room. The conch-shell was still
on the mantelpiece, but one of the blue vases was gone.
This was the front-parlor—the room of reward and
punishment, of visitors and chill, the grandest room in
the world—this room with the shabby carpet and the
huge forbidding pieces of black walnut that never could
have come in through a mortal door. What could you
do with it all, what could you do? What could be done
with a conch-shell and an iron oak-leaf and a set of
yellowed pictures for a broken stereopticon? It was incredible that civilized people should ever have cher-
ished such things. It was incredible that he had ever
put the conch-shell to his ear and held his breath with
wonder, hearing the sea.

"It was just like another home to the Major and
myself. Always," said Mrs. Bache. "I can hear your dear
grandmother now, before the Major was taken, when
he had his trouble. 'Alice, my child, you're young,' she
said. 'But, young or old, we all have to bear our cross.
The Major is a good man—he'll always be welcome in
Hessian Street.' The Major never forgot it. He was very
badly treated but he never forgot a kindness. And now,
Emmy and I are the last—Emmy and I are the last."

She fumbled for her handkerchief in her vast lap.

"There, there, Mrs. Bache," said Tom Carroll, inadequately, "Grandmother must have been a wonderful woman."

"You never even saw her," said Mrs. Bache, viciously, "Tom Carroll saw to that. Oh, why couldn't it have been me, instead of Louise?" she said. "I've been ready to go so long!"

Tom Carroll's face felt stiff, but he found the handkerchief. After a moment Mrs. Bache arose, enormously yet with a curious dignity.

"Come, Sarah," she said to the dim figure in black that was Mrs. Robinson, "It's time for us to go. I've been making a fool of myself. Good-by, Emma. Frank will take us to the church to-morrow. Try to get some rest."

Minnie was whispering to him that Mrs. Bache was very much broken and that Cousin Tom must not mind. Tom Carroll whispered back at appropriate intervals. He did not mind Mrs. Bache. But there was always so much whispering, and it hurt one's head.

Now they were all standing in the narrow hall, and the others were looking at him.

"We can just slip in for a minute before anyone else comes," whispered Minnie, "I know Cousin Tom would rather—"

"Of course," said Tom Carroll. "Thank you, Cousin Minnie." He must have been working too hard, he thought—perhaps he and Claire could go off for a trip together when he got back. Because, after all, it was Aunt Louise who was dead. He knew that perfectly well. And yet, until Minnie had spoken, he hadn't been thinking about her at all.

The statue lay on the walnut bed in the partitioned room that had once been part of the back parlor. Over the head of the bed was a cross of dry, brittle palm-leaves tied with a purple ribbon, and a church-calendar. Against the opposite wall was the highboy that he remembered, with the small china slipper upon it, and above it the ageless engraving of the great Newfound-land dog, head lifted, lying upon the stone blocks of an English quay. "A Member of the Royal Humane Society." There were brown spots on the margin of the engraving now, Tom Carroll noticed. The window was a little open, but everywhere were the massed, triumphant flowers.

A white, transparent veil lay on the face of the statue. The features showed dimly through it, as if Aunt Louise lay in a block of ice. Tom Carroll felt cold. Now Aunt Emmy, putting Minnie aside, went slowly to lift the veil.

Tom Carroll, waking at three o'clock in the morn-ing in his room at the Penniquit House, knew in-stantly what was in store for him. He might lie on the hillocks of his bed as long as he liked but he would not be allowed to sleep any more.

"You're acting like somebody on the edge of a first-class nervous breakdown," he told himself sternly. "And yet, you haven't been working so hard."

The last year hadn't been easy, but no year was. When times were good, you worked hard to take ad-vantage of them. And when they were bad, you nat-urally had to work. That was how you got to be somebody, in a city. It was something Waynesville could never understand.

He thought of their life in the city—his and Claire's —for solace. It was cool and glittering and civilized as a cube of bright steel and glass. He thought of the light, pleasant furniture in the apartment, the clean, bright colors, the crisp sunlight on stone and metal, the bright, clean, modern, expensive school where a doctor looked down the boys' throats every morning and they had special blocks of wood to hammer nails in, since apartments were hardly the places to hammer nails. He thought of his office and the things on his desk and the crowded elevators of morning and night. He thought of the crammed red moving vans of October and the spring that bloomed before April in the flowershops and the clever men, putting in the new telephones. He thought of night beside Claire, hearing the dim roar of the city till at last the uneasy lights of the sky were quieted in the breathing-space before dawn.

It was she who had really held their life to its pattern. She had not let them be trapped; she had kept them free as air from the first day. There had been times when he had weakened—he admitted it—but she had kept her level head and never given in.

It had been that way about the old farmhouse in Connecticut and the cooperative apartment in town. He had wanted to buy them both, at different times. It was the Waynesville coming out in him, he supposed. But she had demurred.

"Oh, Tom, let's not tie ourselves up yet!" she had said. "Yes, I know it does seem silly just going on paying rent and having nothing to show for it but a leak in the washstand. But the minute you buy places to live in, they start to own you. You aren't free. You aren't young. You're always worrying. Don't talk to me about just playing with a few acres, not really farming. That was the way Grandfather started. Oh, Tom, don't you see—we're so *right* the way we are! Now, let's go over it sensibly, figures and all."

And she had been right. The old farmhouse, with its lilac hedge, now stood twenty feet away from a four-lane road; the cooperative apartment had failed and crippled its owner-tenants. She had been precisely right. She almost always was.

She had been entirely and unsentimentally right about her mother's coming to live with them for six months out of the year, when that had seemed unescapable.

"It's darling of you, Tom, but, dear old man, it never would work in the world. We've got to be modern and intelligent about the important things. Mother had me, and I'm devoted to her; but, when we're together for more than a week we get on each other's nerves like the very devil. It'll actually be a help to Hattie to have her for the winters—Hattie's always having a fearful time with the children. And we can have her for a long visit in the summer, and in between she can take the trips she's always wanted to take with that terrible Mrs. Tweed. Of course, I don't mean we ought to leave the whole financial end to Hattie and Joe. I'll insist on our doing our share. But I do think people ought to have *some* independence even when they are old and not just be shipped around from one relative to another like parcels, the way they did with

Aunt Vi! It's more than sweet of you, Tom, darling. But you see how it is."

Tom Carroll had seen, with some relief, that they were not likely to have Mrs. Fanshawe as a permanent addition to their household, and he had acquiesced. Not that he disliked Mrs. Fanshawe. He got on very well with the rather nervous little lady—which was strange, considering how unlike she was to Claire. It struck him at times that Mrs. Fanshawe, from what he knew of her, had never been a remarkably independent person, and that to begin one's complete independence at the age of sixty-seven might be something of a task. But Claire must know her mother better than he did.

She did get on Claire's nerves and she did spoil the children—he could see that plainly enough. But, then, her visits were seldom very long. Claire would hardly have time to decline three or four invitations because mother was with them for a quiet little time before something would happen to call Mrs. Fanshawe away. And yet she seemed to like his calling her Mother May and pretending he was jealous of Hattie and Joe for stealing away his best girl. She'd laugh her brisk, nervous laugh and say he'd better look out or sometime she'd take him at his word and stay forever. And Claire would be saying, patiently, "Now, mother, are you sure that you have your ticket? And Tom will get you some magazines to read on the train." Afterwards Claire would say, "Oh, Tom, how can you? But she adores it!" and he would mumble something and feel rather pleased. Then Claire would kiss him and go to the telephone.

Only one of the visits had been in the least unfortunate. Claire had been tired that evening, and it was a pity that the conversation had happened to run on the future of the children. "But, of course, you and Tom are planning to make a real home for them sometime?" Mrs. Fanshawe had said. Well, naturally, she could hardly be expected to understand the way he and Claire happened to feel about "homes" in the Waynesville sense. And it had all come right the following morning —had not Mrs. Fanshawe nervously stayed an extra two days in proof? But the evening had carried him back to the hurt feelings of Hessian Street. Tom Carroll was glad there had been another visit before Mrs. Fanshawe died.

She had died in the waiting room of the Auburndale Station, on her way back to Hattie's, after a pleasant month with her old friend, Mrs. Tweed. Even so, she had been considerate; for the station agent knew her and got hold of the Morrises at once—there had been some mix-up about her telegram. Later, they had found out that she had known about her heart trouble for some time.

He had expected to take Claire on to the funeral, but Claire had been adamant. "I will not have you do it, Tom. It'll be bad enough by myself. But I will not have you mixed up in it—it isn't fair. We can have bad memories separately, but I won't have us have them together." She had grown almost hysterical about it— Claire! And so she had gone alone.

He had been very much worried till she returned, with a white changed face that refused to give any details of those three days. "Don't ask me, Tom. I've told you everything I can—oh, yes, everybody was kind and they had her hymns . . . but, oh Tom, it's so terrible. Terrible. The most barbarous, the most humiliating custom I know! I'll tell you this right now, I'm not going to wear mourning. I don't believe in it and I won't submit to it. All the black dresses—mother didn't really like black. Oh, Tom, Tom, when I die don't dare wear mourning for me!"

He had got her to bed and quieted at last. But she had not been herself—the true Claire—for months afterward, though, as soon as she could, she had taken up the strands of their life again and woven the pattern even more deftly and swiftly, as if each new thread were precious and each second not to be recalled.

Naturally, then, it was only right for him to come to this death in his own country alone. Any other course would have been a monstrous selfishness. And yet he wished that he could go to sleep.

Perhaps, if he thought once more of that shining cube of steel and glass that was their planned security, sleep would come. Even death in New York was different and impersonal. Except for the very mighty, it was an anonymous affair. The man in 10B died and, the next fall, they redecorated the apartment for other tenants. In a month or so even the doorman had forgotten; the newsdealer wrote another name on the morning papers. A name dropped out of the 'phone book . . . you had moved again, with October . . . moved to another city—the city at the sprawling edge of town where lie the streets and avenues of the numberless, quickly buried dead. There, too, you would be part of the crowd, and your neighbors would be strangers, as it had been in life. Your dwelling would be well kept-up, for that was written in the contract. No ghosts could ever arise from that suburban earth. For this, John Merritt and Samuel Pye had built a house in the wilderness to be a shelter and a refuge for them and their seed to the generations of generations. It was just.

Something cracked in the shining cube of glass and steel. The girders crunched on one another, wrenching apart; the glass tumbled into nothingness, falling a long way. There was nothing left but the perplexed, forgotten spirit, roused out of long sleep at last to strive, unprepared, against its immortal adversary.

Claire was all right, but she was afraid of death. He was all right, but he was afraid of death. The clever people they knew were entirely right, but most of them were deadly afraid of death.

If the life they led was rich—if it was the good life —why were they so afraid? It was not because they so joyed in all things under the sun that it was bitter to leave them. That was mortal and understandable, that had always been. But this was a blinder fear.

It had not been in sorrow or remorse that Claire had grieved for her mother. She had grieved the most because she had been afraid. And that made Claire a monster, which she was not. But there was something in it, all the same. He could admit it in her because he could admit it in himself. He lay sleepless, dreading the morrow. And yet he was not a coward so far as he knew.

They had won, but where was the victory? They had escaped from Waynesville and Hessian Street, from Fanshawe and Pye and Merritt, but where was the escape? If they were afraid in these years, how were they to deal with the years to come? Tom Carroll heard the clock in the courthouse strike five strokes. And then, when it seemed to him he could never sleep again, he fell asleep.

They drove at the slow pace down Hessian Street into Main, through the bright, morning sunlight. Tom Carroll felt ashamed of the dreams and waking of the night. He had never felt more solid and confident and assured than he did now, sitting beside Aunt Emmy, his tact and his shoulder ready for her the moment the inevitable breakdown came. Thank God! Jerry Pye was driving his own car. Jerry muddled things so. As for what was to come, that would merely be pathetic—the few old people painfully come together to mourn not only one of their own but a glory that had departed, the Waynesville of their youth. He hoped Aunt Emmy would not notice how few they were. But she, too, was old; and the old lived in the past. She could people the empty pews with the faces that once had been there. It was better so. The lords of Hessian and Bounty Streets had ruled the town with a high hand, even as they sank into poverty, but that was ended. You had only to look along Main to see the new names on the shop-fronts. They knew not Hessian Street, these Caprellos and Szukalskis, but they thrived and inherited the land. Even Waynesville was growing up—there was little charm left in it, but it was alive. And here was the old brick church of the memories.

He helped Aunt Emmy expertly from the car, but she would not take his arm. Well, he respected her courage. He stood tactfully to shield her from the sight of the coffin, just being lifted down from that other, windowless car. But before he knew it Jerry Pye was beside them.

"Aunt Emmy," said Jerry Pye incredibly, "did Aunt Louise really want old Zenas to be one of the coffin-bearers? Because he's there now, and it'll be too late unless somebody tells him . . ."

He actually made a gesture with his hand. Tom Carroll would have been glad to strangle his cousin. But miraculously Aunt Emmy did not break.

She even walked past Tom Carroll to look deliberately at the six black-suited negroes who now had their burden ready to carry into the church. Tom Carroll looked as well. They were none of them under forty, and their faces were grave and sober, but there was something ceremonial in their attitude that struck Tom Carroll strangely. They were sad but they were not constrained—they were doing something they felt to be right and they did it naturally and with ceremony. They would remember the ceremony always when the sadness had passed.

"Zenas, Joram, Joseph, William, Henry, Devout," said Aunt Emmy, in a half-whisper. "Yes, that's right. That's right. Zenas should be there. Louise would have missed Zenas. No, Tommy, we will let them pass, please."

When the coffin had passed, to the sway of the easy shoulders, they followed it in. It was the beginning of Tom Carroll's astonishment. The astonishment did not lessen when he found the church half full, and not only with the old.

He had always thought of Aunt Louise as Aunt Emmy's shadow—in his boyhood as someone always hurried but vaguely sweet whose peppermint-drops took away the taste of Aunt Emmy's wrath; in his manhood as a responsibility at the back of his mind. But the minister was a young man, and neither Pye nor Merritt, and he spoke of the Louise Pye, whose singlehanded effort had turned the ramshackle old School For The Instruction Of Freed Negroes into an institution model for its time, in terms that assumed his hearers knew and appreciated the difficulties of that task.

Phrases came to Tom Carroll's ears. They were the conventional phrases of oratory, yet the speaker meant them. "Unsparing of time or labor." "The rare gift of personality." "The quiet achievement of many years." "We can say to-day, in all truth, a light has gone from among us. . . ." But this was Aunt Louise!

And after the service, and on the way to the grave, and after the service there, the astonishment continued. He was by Aunt Emmy's side, and the people spoke to him. Nearly everyone who spoke to him knew his name. They did not find it odd or kind or a favor that he should be there—he was Julia Merritt's son, who was working in New York. You didn't hear as much about him as you did about Jerry Pye, but it was natural that he should return. Not only Mrs. Bache was under the impression that he had come principally to hear the reading of Aunt Louise's will. They did not think ill of him for it, merely prudent. He could explain nothing, even if he had wished to. There was nothing to explain.

He could not count the number of times he was

told that the cross of yellow roses was beautiful—did they know by telepathy that it was from him and Claire? He had thought it garish and out of place beside the other flowers, the late asters and first chrysanthemums, the zinnias and snapdragons, the bronzes and reds and golds of the country fall. But that he could not say.

The negroes who had borne the coffin knew him. They spoke to him gravely in their rich voices when all was done. Aunt Emmy had a curious phrase for each of them. "Thank you, Devout. Thank you, Joram. Miss Louise will be pleased." It would seem macabre, telling it to Claire. It was not; it was only simple. But that she would not believe.

He remembered, as if in a dream, his plans for succor and comfort when Aunt Emmy should collapse. But it was he who felt physically exhausted when they got back to the house.

This, too, was the moment that he had dreaded the most. Last night he had been able to have dinner at the hotel, but this time there was no escaping the cold meal laid in the basement dining room, the haunted and undue fragrance of flowers that had filled the house for a while. But, when the food was in front of him he was hungry and ate. They all ate, even Aunt Emmy. Minnie did what waiting was necessary and did it, for once, without fluster. Jerry Pye seemed tired and subdued. Once Tom Carroll caught himself feeling sorry for him, once he tried to help him out in a story that was meant to be cheerful and fell flat.

"You know," said Minnie, in a flat voice, pouring coffee, "it seems as if Aunt Louise hadn't gone away so far as before it happened."

Tom Carroll knew what she meant. He felt it too —that presence of the dead, but not grimly nor as a ghost. The presence was as real as the October sky, and as removed from flesh. It did not have to mean that all tired souls were immortal—it had its own peace.

After the meal was over, Tom Carroll walked in the back yard and smoked with Jerry Pye. Now and then he remembered from childhood the fear that had walked there with him, with the scent of the overpowering flowers. But, search as he would, he could not find that fear. The few flowers left in the beds were bronze and scentless; there was no fear where they bloomed.

It was time to go in for the reading of Aunt Louise's will. Tom Carroll listened obediently. He did not even mention the names of Norman, Buckstone, and Carroll. Once, when Mr. Dabney, the lawyer, looked at him and said, "You are a member of the New York Bar, I believe, Mr. Carroll?" he felt surprised at being able to say "yes."

It was a long and personal will made up of many small bequests. He could see Aunt Louise going through her innumerable boxes, trying hard to be fair.

"To my nephew, Thomas Carroll, and his wife, Claire Fanshawe Carroll, the pair of silver candlesticks belonging to my dear Father."

Tom Carroll felt the slow red creeping into his face.

They shook hands with Mr. Dabney. They spoke of what was to be done. Tom Carroll did not proffer assistance. There was no need.

Jerry Pye was offering him a lift as far as Bradensburg—Minnie would be staying with Aunt Emmy for the next week or so, but he must get back to work.

But Tom Carroll thought he had better wait till the morning.

"Well, I guess you'll be more comfortable here at that," said Jerry Pye. "I'll have to hit her up if I want to get home before 3 G.M. So long, Tom. You see Minnie doesn't step out with a handsomer fellow now the old man's away. And take care of the Pye candlesticks—at that, I guess they'll look better in your place than they would in ours. Our kids might use 'em for baseball bats. Say, give my best to Claire."

He was gone. "Now, Tommy," said Aunt Emmy in her tired, indomitable voice, "you go back to the hotel and get a rest—you look tuckered out. Nelly Jervis is coming in here to get the supper. Half-past six."

They were sitting in the front parlor again that evening, he and she. It wasn't late, but Minnie had been sent to bed, unwilling. She wouldn't close an eye, she said; but they knew she was already asleep.

"It's queer what a good nurse Minnie is," said Aunt Emmy reflectively. "Seems as if it was the only thing that ever got her shut of her fussiness—taking care of sick people. You'd think she'd drop crumbs in the bed, but she never does. I don't know what we'd have done without her. Well, she's a right to be tired."

"How about you, Aunt Emmy?"

"Oh," said Aunt Emmy, "they used to say there'd be some people the Fool Killer would still be looking for on Judgment Day. I guess I'm one of them. Of course I'm tired, Tommy. When I'm tired enough, I'll tell you and go to bed."

"Look here, Aunt Emmy," said Tom Carroll, "if there's anything I can do——"

"And what could you do, Tommy?"

"Well, wouldn't you like a car?" he said, awkwardly, "or somebody to stay with you—or another place. They say those apartments over by the——"

"I was born here," said Aunt Emmy, with a snap of her lips, "and now Louise has gone, I've got just enough money to die here. It isn't the same, but I'm suited. And, of all the horrors of age, deliver me from a paid companion. If I need anything like that I'll get Susan Bache to move in here. She's a fool and she's a tattler," said Aunt Emmy, clearly, "but I'm used to her. And Minnie'll come up, every now and then. Don't worry about me, Tom Carroll. We've all of us been on your back long enough."

"On my back?" said Tom Carroll, astounded.

"Well, I'd like to know where else it was," said Aunt Emmy. "You got Louise's money back from that rascal that bamboozled her, and I know twice you pulled Jerry Pye out of the mudhole, and then there was Cousin Edna all those years. Not to speak of what you did for Melrose. Melrose was my own brother, but he ought to have been ashamed of himself, the way he hindered you. Oh, don't you worry about Waynesville, Tommy—you've no call. You did right to get out when you did and as you did, and Waynesville knows it, too. Not that Waynesville would ever admit George Washington was any great shakes, once he'd moved away. But you wait till you die, Tom Carroll"—and she actually chuckled—"and you see what the *Waynesville Blade* says about her distinguished son. They told Louise for twenty years she was crazy, teaching negroes to read and write. But they've got two columns about her this evening and an editorial. I've cut it out and I'm going to paste it under her picture. Louise was always the loving one, and I never grudged her that. But I did grudge her forgiving where I didn't see cause to forgive. But that's all done." She rustled the paper in her lap.

"How are your boys, Tommy?" she said. "They look smart enough in their pictures."

"We think they are," said Tom Carroll. "I hope you're right."

"They ought to be," said Aunt Emmy. "The Fanshawes never lacked smartness, whatever else they lacked, and your father was a bright man. Well, I've seen Jeremiah's and Minnie's. Boy and girl. Don't laugh at me, because it doesn't seem possible, but Jeremiah makes a good father. I never could get on with children —you ought to know that if anyone does—but I think they'll amount to something. Well, it's time the family was getting some sense again."

"Aunt Emmy!" said Tom Carroll, protestingly.

"Was this a happy house?" said Aunt Emmy, fiercely. "For me it was—yes—because I grew up in it. And I always had Louise and I don't regret anything. But was it happy for your mother and you? You know it wasn't, and a good thing your father took her out of it, adventurer or no adventurer, and a bad thing she had to come back. Well, we did our duty according to our lights. But that wasn't enough. There's no real reason, you know, why families have to get that way, except they seem to. But they will get to thinking they're God Almighty, and, after a while, that gets taken notice of. I'll say this—it wasn't the money with us. We held up our heads with it or without it. But maybe we held them too stiff."

She sank into a brooding silence. Behind her in the corner the vague shadows of innumerable Pyes and Merritts seemed to gather and mingle and wait. After a while she roused herself.

"Where are you going to live, Tommy?" she said.

"I've been thinking about a place in the country sometime," said Tom Carroll. "If Waynesville were a little different——"

Aunt Emmy shook her head.

"You couldn't come back here, Tommy," she said. "It's finished here. And that's just as well. But, if you're going to build your own house, you'd better do it soon. You won't be happy without it—you've got too much Merritt in you. The Merritts made their own places. It was the Pyes that sat on the eggs till finally they tried to hatch chickens out of a doorknob, because it was easier than looking for a new roost. But you haven't much Pye. All the same, you won't be contented till you've got some roots put down. The Fanshawes, they could live in a wagon and like it, but the Bouverins were like the Merritts—when they'd rambled enough, they cleared ground. And Claire looks a lot more Bouverin than Fanshawe to me, whether she likes it or not."

"I didn't know you knew Claire's family," said Tom Carroll.

"She probably wouldn't tell you," said Aunt Emmy. "Well, that's natural enough. Good Goshen! I remember Claire Fanshawe, a peaked little slip of a child, at Anna Bouverin's funeral, just before they left Bradensburg. The coffin was still open, and some ignoramus

or other thought it would be fitting for all the grandchildren to come and kiss their grandma good-by. Mind
you, after they'd said good-by to her once already,
before she died. I could have told them better, little
as I know children. Well, it didn't make much difference to Hattie; she always had the nerves of an ox.
But Claire was just over typhoid and after they made
her do it she had what *I'd* call a shaking chill, in a
grown person. And *yet*, they made her get up and recite
the Twenty-Third Psalm in front of everybody—just
because she was smart for her age, and a little child
shall lead them. Her mother didn't stop them—too
proud of her knowing it, I guess. But that was the Fanshawe of it—they had to play-act whatever happened."

Tom Carroll had his head in his hands.

"She never told me," he said. "She never told me
at all."

"No?" said Aunt Emmy, looking at him sharply.
"Well, she was young and maybe she forgot it. I imagine Hattie did."

"Claire never has," said Tom Carroll.

"Well," said Aunt Emmy, "I'll tell you something,
Tommy. When you get to my age you've seen life and
death. And there's just one thing about death, once
you start running away from the thought of it, it runs
after you. Till finally you're scared even to talk about
it and, even if your best friend dies, you'll forget him
as quick as you can because the thought's always waiting. But once you can make yourself turn around and
look at it—it's different. Oh, you can't help the grief.
But you can get a child so it isn't afraid of the dark
—though if you scared it first it'll take a longer while."

"Tell me," said Tom Carroll in a low voice, "were there—very sweet flowers—when my mother died?"

"It was just before Easter," said Aunt Emmy softly. "You could smell the flowers all through the house. But we didn't have any play-acting," she added, quickly. "Not with you. Melrose had that bee in his bonnet, but Louise put her foot down. But it's hard to explain to a child."

"It's hard to explain anyway," said Tom Carroll.

"That's true," said Aunt Emmy. "It's a queer thing," she said. "I never smell lilac without thinking of Lucy Marshall. She was a friend of mine, and then we fell out, and when we were young we used to play by a lilac bush in her yard. It used to trouble me for a long time before I put the two things together. But the pain went out of it then."

"Yes. The pain goes out when you know," said Tom Carroll. "It's not knowing that makes you afraid."

"If Hattie was closer to her, she could do it," said Aunt Emmy. "But the way things are——"

"It'll have to be me," said Tom Carroll. "And I don't know how."

"Well, you're fond of her," said Aunt Emmy. "They say that helps." She rose. "I'll give you the candlesticks in the morning, Tom."

"Can't I leave them with you, Aunt Emmy?"

"What's the use?" said Aunt Emmy practically. "To tell you the truth, Tommy, I'd got right tired of shining them. Besides, they'll look well in your house, when you get your house."

BLOSSOM AND FRUIT

WHEN the spring was in its mid-term and the apple trees entirely white they would walk down by the river, talking as they went, their voice hardly distinguishable from the voices of birds or waters. Their love had begun with the winter; they were both in their first youth. Those who watched them made various prophecies—none of which was fulfilled—laughed, criticized, or were sentimental according to the turn of their minds. But these two were ignorant of the watching and, if they had heard the prophecies they would hardly have understood them.

Between them and the world was a wall of glass—between them and time was a wall of glass—they were not conscious of being either young or old. The weather passed over them as over a field or a stream—it was there but they took no account of it. There was love and being alive, there was the beating of the heart apart or together. This had been, this would be, this was—it was impossible to conceive of a world created otherwise. He knew the shape of her face, in dreams and out of them; she could shut her eyes, alone, and feel his hands on her shoulders. So it went, so they spoke and answered, so they walked by the river. Later on, once or twice, they tried to remember what they had said—a great deal of nonsense?—but the words

286

were already gone. They could hear the river running; he could remember a skein of hair; she, a blue shirt open at the throat and an eager face. Then, after a while, these two were not often remembered.

All this had been a number of years ago. But now that the old man had returned at last to the place where he had been born, he would often go down to the river-field. Sometimes a servant or a grandchild would carry the light camp chair and the old brown traveling-rug; more often he would go alone. He was still strong— he liked to do for himself; there was no use telling him he'd catch his death walking through the wet grass, it only set him in his ways.

When at last he had reached his goal—a certain ancient apple tree whose limbs were entirely crooked with bearing—he would set the chair under it, sit down, wrap his legs in the rug, and remain there till he was summoned to come in. He was alone but not lonely; if anyone passed by he would talk; if no one passed he was content to be silent. There was almost always a book in his lap, but he very seldom read it; his own life, after all, was the book that suited him best, it did not grow dull with rereading. There is little to add, he thought, little to add; but he was not sorry. The text remained; it was a long text, and many things that had seemed insignificant and obscure in the living took on sudden clarities and significances, now he re-membered.

Yes, he thought, that is how most people live their actual lives—skimming it through, in a hurry to get to the end and find out who got married and who got rich. Well, that's something that can't be helped. But when you know the end you can turn back and try to find out the story. Only most people don't want to, he thought, and smiled. Looks too queer to suit them —reading your own book backwards. But it's a great pleasure to me. He relaxed, let his hands lie idle in his lap, let the pictures drift before his eyes.

The picture of the boy and girl by the river. He could stand off from it now and regard it, without sorrow or longing; no ghost cried in his flesh because of it, though it was a part of that flesh and with that flesh would die. And yet, for a moment, he had almost been in the old mood again, recovered the old ecstasy. Whatever love was, he had been in love at that time. But what was love?

They met by stealth because of reasons no longer important; it lasted through all of one long dry summer in the small town that later became a city. Outside, the street baked, the white dust blew up and down, but it was fresh and pleasant in the house.

She was a dark-haired woman, a widow, some years older than he—he was a young man in a tall collar, his face not yet lined or marked but his body set in the pattern which it would keep. Her name was Stella. She had a cool voice, sang sometimes; they talked a great deal. They made a number of plans which were not accomplished—they were hotly in love.

He remembered being with her one evening toward the end of summer, in the trivial room. On the table was a bowl of winesaps—he had been teasing her about them—she said she liked the unripened color best.

They talked a little more, then she grew silent; her face, turned toward his, was white in the dusk.

That autumn an accident took him away from the town. When he came back, a year later, she had moved to another state. Later he heard that she had married again, and the name of the man. A great while later he read of her death.

The old man's rug had slipped from his knees; he gathered it up again and tucked it around him. He could not quite get back into the man who had loved and been loved by Stella, but he could not escape him, either. He saw that youth and the boy who had walked by the river. Each had a woman by his side, each stared at the other hostilely, each, pointing to his own companion, said, "This is love." He smiled a trifle dubiously at their frowning faces—both were so certain—and yet he included them both. Which was right, which wrong? He puzzled over the question but could come to no decision. And if neither were right—or both—why then, what was love?

You certainly strike some queer things when you read the book backwards, he thought. I guess I'd better call it a day and quit. But, even as he thought so, another picture arose.

They had been married for a little more than two years, their first child was eight months old. He was a man in his thirties, doing well, already a leader in the affairs of the growing town. She was five years younger, tall for a woman; she had high color in those days. They had known comparatively little of each other before their marriage—indeed, had not been very deeply in love; but living together had changed them.

He came back to the house on Pine Street, told the news of his day, heard about the neighbors, the errands, the child. After dinner they sat in the living room, he smoked and read the newspaper, she had sewing in her lap. They talked to each other in snatches; when their eyes met, something went, something came. At ten o'clock she went upstairs to feed the child; he followed some time later. The child was back in its crib again; they both looked at her a moment—sleep already lay upon her like a visible weight —how deeply, how swiftly she sank towards sleep! They went out, shut the door very softly, stood for a moment in the hallway, and embraced. Then the woman released herself.

"I'm going to bed now, Will," she said. "Be sure and turn out the lights when you come up."

"I won't be long," he said. "It's been a long day."

He stretched his arms, looking at her. She smiled deeply, turned away. The door of their room shut behind her.

When he had extinguished the lights and locked the doors he went up to the long garret that stretched the whole length of the house. They had had the house only two years, but the garret had already accumulated its collection of odds and ends; there were various discarded or crippled objects that would never be used again, that would stay here till the family moved, till someone died. But what he had come to see was a line of apples mellowing on a long shelf, in the dusty darkness. They had been sent in from the farm—you could smell their faint, unmistakable fragrance from the doorway. He took one up, turned it over in his hand, felt its weight and texture, firm and smooth and cool. You couldn't get a better eating apple than that, and this was the right place for them to mellow.

Mary's face came before him, looking at him in the hallway; the thought of it was like the deep stroke of a knife that left, as it struck, no pain. Yes, he thought, I'm alive—we're pretty fond of each other. Some impulse made him put down the apple and push up the little skylight of the garret to let the air blow in on his face. It was a clean cold—it was autumn; it made the blood run in him to feel it. He stood there for several minutes, drinking in cold autumn, thinking about his wife. Then at last he shut the skylight and went downstairs to their room.

A third couple had joined the others under the tree, a third image asserted itself, by every settled line in its body, the possessor not only of a woman but of a particular and unmistakable knowledge. The old man observed one and all, without envy but curiously. If they could only get to talking with one another, he thought, why then, maybe, we'd know something. But they could not do it—it was not in the cards. All each could do was to make an affirmation, "This is love."

The figures vanished, he was awake again. When you were old you slept lightly but more often, and these dreams came. Mary had been dead ten years; their children were men and women. He had always expected Mary to outlive him, but things had not happened so. She would have been a great comfort. Yet when he thought of her dead, though his grief was real, it came to him from a distance. He and she were nearer together than he and grief. And yet if he met her again it would be strange.

The flower came out on the branch, the fruit budded and grew. At last it fell or was picked, and the thing started over again. You could figure out every process of growth and decline, but that did not get you any nearer the secret. Only, he'd like to know.

He turned his eyes toward the house—somebody coming for him. His eyes were still better for far-away things than near, and he made out the figure quite plainly. It was the girl who had married his grand-nephew, Robert. She called him "Father Hancock" or "Gramp" like the rest of them, but still, she was different from the rest.

For a moment her name escaped him. Then he had it. Jenny. A dark-haired girl, pleasant spoken, with a good free walk to her—girls stepped out freer, on the whole, than they had in his day. As for cutting their hair and the rest of it—well, why shouldn't they? It was only the kind of people who wrote to newspapers who made a fuss about such things. And they always had to make a fuss about something. He chuckled deeply, wondering what a newspaper would make of it if a highly respected old citizen wrote and asked them what was love. "Crazy old fool—ought to be in an asylum." Well, maybe at that, they'd be right.

He watched the girl coming on as he would have watched a rabbit run through the grass or a cloud march along the sky. There was something in her walk that matched both rabbit and cloud—something light and free and unbroken. But there was something else in her walk as well.

"Lunch, Father Hancock!" she called while she was still some yards away. "Snapper beans and black-cherry pie!"

"Well, I'm hungry," said the old man. "You know me, Jenny—never lost appetite yet. But you can have my slice of the pie; you've got younger teeth than mine."

"Stop playing you're a centenarian, Father Hancock," said the girl. "I've seen you with Aunt Maria's pies before."

"I might take a smidgin', at that," said the old man reflectively, "just to taste. But you can have all I don't eat, Jenny—and that's a fair offer."

"It's too fair," said the girl. "I'd eat you out of house and home to-day." She stretched her arms toward the sky. "Gee, I feel hungry!" she said.

"It's right you should," said the old man, placidly. "And don't be ashamed of your dinner either. Eat solid and keep your strength up."

"Do I look as if I needed to keep my strength up?" she said with a laugh.

"No. But it's early to tell," said the old man, gradually disentangling himself from his coverings. He stood up, declining her offered hand. "Thank you, my dear," he said. "I never expected to see my own great-grandnephew. But don't be thinking of that. It'll be your baby, boy or girl, and that's what's important."

The girl's hand went slowly to her throat while color rose in her face. Then she laughed.

"Father Hancock!" she said. "You—you darned old

wizard! Why Robert doesn't know about it yet
and——"

"He wouldn't," said the old man briefly. "Kind of
inexperienced at that age. But you can't fool me, my
dear. I've seen too much and too many."

She looked at him with trouble in her eyes.

"Well, as long as you know . . ." she said. "But
you won't let on to the rest of them . . . of course I'll
tell Robert soon, but——"

"I know," said the old man. "They carry on. Never
could see so much sense in all that carrying on, but
relations do. And being the first great-grandchild. No,
I won't tell 'em. And I'll be as surprised as Punch when
they finally tell me."

"You're a good egg," said the girl gratefully.
"Thanks ever so much. I don't mind your knowing."

They stood for a moment in silence, his hand on
her shoulder. The girl shivered suddenly.

"Tell me, Father Hancock," she said suddenly, in
a muffled voice, not looking at him, "is it going to be
pretty bad?"

"No, child, it won't be so bad." She said nothing,
but he could feel the tenseness in her body relax.

"It'll be for around November, I expect?" he said,
and went on without waiting for her reply. "Well, that's
a good time, Jenny. You take our old cat, Marcella—
she generally has her second lot of kittens around in
October or November. And those kittens, they do right
well."

"Father Hancock! You're a positive disgrace!" So
she said, but he knew from the tone of her voice that
she was not angry with him and once more, as they went

together towards the house, he felt the stroke of youth upon him, watching her walk so well.

About the middle of summer, when the green of the fields had turned to yellow and brown, Will Hancock's old friend John Sturgis drove over one day to visit him.

A son and a granddaughter accompanied John Sturgis, as well as two other vaguer female relatives whom the young people called indiscriminately "Cousin" and "Aunt"; and for a while the big porch of the Hancock house knew the bustle of tribal ceremony. Everyone was a little anxious, everyone was a little voluble; this was neither a funeral nor a wedding but, as an occasion, it ranked with those occasions, and in the heart of every Hancock and Sturgis present was a small individual grain of gratitude and pride at being there to witness the actual meeting of two such perishable old men.

The relatives possessed the old men and displayed them. The old men sat quietly, their tanned hands resting on their knees. They knew they were being possessed, but they too felt pride and pleasure. It was, after all, remarkable that they should be here. The young people didn't know how remarkable it was.

Finally, however, Will Hancock rose.

"Come along down-cellar, John," he said gruffly. "Got something to show you."

It was the familiar opening of an immemorial gambit. And it brought the expected reply.

"Now, father," said Will Hancock's eldest daughter,

"if you'll only wait a minute, Maria will be out with the lemonade, and I had her bake some brownies."

"Lemonade!" said Will Hancock and sniffed. "Hold your tongue, Mary," he said gently. "I'm going to give John Sturgis something good for what ails him."

As he led the way down-cellar he smiled to himself. They would be still protesting, back on the porch. They would be saying that cellars were damp and old men delicate, that cider turned into acid, and that at their age you'd think they'd have more sense. But there would be no real heart in the protestations. And if the ceremonial visit to the cellar had been omitted there would have been disappointment. Because then their old men would not have been quite so remarkable, after all.

They passed through the dairy-cellar, with its big tin milk-pans, and into the cider-cellar. It was cool there but with a sweet-smelling coolness; there was no scent of damp or mold. Three barrels stood in a row against the wall; on the floor was a yellow patch of light. Will Hancock took a tin cup from a shelf and silently tapped the farthest barrel. The liquid ran in the cup. It was old cider, yellow as wheat-straw, and when he raised it toward his nostrils the soul of the bruised apple came to him. .

"Take a seat, John," he said, passing over the full cup. His friend thanked him and sank into the one disreputable armchair. Will Hancock filled another cup and sat down upon the middle barrel.

"Well, here's to crime, John!" he said. It was the time-honored phrase.

"Mud in your eye!" said John Sturgis fiercely. He sipped the cider.

"Ah!" he said, "tastes better every year, Will."

"She ought to, John. She's goin' along with us."

They both sat silent for a time, sipping appreciatively, their worn eyes staring at each other, taking each other in. Each time they met again now was a mutual triumph for both; they looked forward to each time and back upon it, but they had known each other so long that speech had become only a minor necessity between them.

"Well," said John Sturgis at last, when the cups had been refilled, "I hear you got some more expectations in your family, Will. That's fine."

"That's what they tell me," said Will Hancock. "She's a nice girl, Jenny."

"Yes, she's a nice girl," said John Sturgis indifferently. "It'll be some news for Molly when I get home. She'll be right interested. She was hopin' we might beat you to it, with young Jack and his wife. But no signs yet."

He shook his head and a shadow passed over his face.

"Well, I don't know that you set so much store by it," said Will Hancock consolingly, "though it's interesting."

"Oh, they'll have a piece in the paper," said John Sturgis with a trace of bitterness. "Four generations. Even if it isn't a great-grandchild, so to speak. I know 'em." He took a larger sip of cider.

"That won't do me a speck of good when I get home," he confided. "And Molly, she'll think I was crazy. But what's the use of livin' if you've got to live so tetchy all the time?"

"I never saw you looking better, John," said Will Hancock, heartily. "Never did."

"I'm spry enough most days," admitted John Sturgis. "And as for you, you look like a four-year-old. But it's the winter——"

He left the sentence uncompleted, and both fell silent for a moment, thinking of the coming winter. Winter, the foe of old men.

At last John Sturgis leaned forward. His cheeks had a ghost of color in them now, his eyes an unexpected brightness.

"Tell me, Will," he said, eagerly, "you and me—we've seen a good deal in our time. Well, tell me this —just how do you figure it all out?"

Will Hancock could not pretend to misunderstand the question. Nor could he deny his friend the courtesy of a reply.

"I haven't a notion," he said at last, slowly and gravely. "I've thought about it, Lord knows—but I haven't a notion, John."

The other sank back into his chair, disappointedly.

"Well now, that's too bad," he grumbled, "for I've been thinkin' about it. Seems to me as if I didn't do much else *but* think most of the time. But you're the educated one; and if you haven't a notion—well——"

His eyes stared into space, without fear or anger, but soberly. Will Hancock tried to think of some way to help his friend.

He saw again before him those three figures under the apple tree, each a part of himself, each with a woman beside it, each saying, "This is love." Now, as he fell into reverie, a fourth couple joined them—an old man, still erect, and a girl who still walked with a light step though her body was heavy now.

He stared at these last visitors, incredulously at first, and then with a little smile. Nearly every day of the summer Jenny had come to call him when he sat under his tree. He could see her looking across the gulf that separated them—and finding things not so bad as she had thought they might be. Why, I might have been an old tree myself, he thought. Or an old rock you went out to when you wanted to be alone.

There had been her relatives and his. There had been all the women. But it was to him that she had come. To the others he was and would be "Father Hancock" and their own remarkable old man. But Jenny was not really one of his own; and because of that she had from him a certain calming wisdom that he did not know he possessed.

He heard an insect cry in the deep grass and smelled the smell of the hay, the smell of summer days. Love? It was not love, of course, nor could be, by any stretch of language. To her it had been summer and an old tree; and to him, he knew what it had been. He was fond of her, naturally, but that was not the answer. It was not she who had moved him. But for an instant, on the cords of the defeated flesh, he had heard a note struck clearly, the vibration of a single and silver wire. As he thought of this, the wire vibrated anew, the imperishable accent rang. Then it was mute—it would not be struck again.

"I tried to figure it out the other day," he said to John Sturgis, "what love was, first. But——"

Then he stopped. It was useless. John Sturgis was his old friend, but there was no way to tell John Sturgis the thoughts in his mind.

"It's funny your sayin' that," said John Sturgis reflectively. "You know I came back to the house the other day, and there was Molly asleep in the chair. I was scared for a minute but then I saw she was sleeping. Only she didn't wake up right away—I guess I came in light. Well, I stood there looking at her. You came to our golden wedding, Will; but her cheeks were pink and she looked so pretty in her sleep. I just went over and kissed her, like an old fool. Now what makes a man act like that?"

He paused for a moment.

"It's so blame' hard to figure out," he said. "When you're young you've got the strength but you haven t got the time. And when you're old you've got time enough, but I'm always goin' to sleep."

He drained the last drop in his cup and rose.

"Well, Sam'll be lookin' for me," he said. "It was good cider."

As they passed through the dairy a black, whiskered face appeared at the small barred window and vanished guiltily at the sound of Will Hancock's voice.

"That old cat's always trying to get in to the milk," he said. "She ought to take shame on her, all the kittens she's had. But I guess this'll be her last litter, this fall. She's getting on."

The tribal ceremonies of departure were drawing toward a close. Will Hancock shook John Sturgis' hand.

"Come over again, John, and bring along Molly next time," he said. "There's always a drop in the barrel."

"And it's a prize drop," said John Sturgis. "Thank you, Will. But I don't figure on gettin' over again this summer. Next spring, maybe."

"Sure," said Will. But between them both, as they knew, lay the shadow of the cold months, the shadow to be lived through. Will Hancock watched his friend being helped into the car, watched the car drive away. "John's beginning to go," he thought with acceptance. "And that's probably just what John's telling Sam about me."

He turned back toward his family. He was tired, but he could not give in. The family clustered about him, talking and questioning. John's visit had made him, for the moment, an even more remarkable old man than ever; and he must play his role for the rest of them, worthily, now John had gone. So he played it, and they saw no difference. But he kept wondering what day the winter would set in.

The first gales of autumn had come and passed; when Will Hancock got up in the morning he saw white rime on the ground. It had melted away by eleven, but next morning it was back again. At last, when he walked down to his apple tree he walked under bare boughs.

That night he went early to his room, but before he got in bed he stood for a while at the window, looking at the sky. It was a winter sky, the stars were hard in it. Yet the day had been mild enough. Jenny wanted her child born in the Indian Summer. Perhaps she would still have her wish.

He slept more lightly than ever these nights—the first thing roused him. So when the noises began in the house he was awake at once. But he lay there for some time, dreamily, not even looking at his watch. The footsteps went up and down stairs, and he listened to them; a voice said something sharply and was hushed; somebody was trying to telephone. He knew them all, those sounds of whispering haste that wake up a house at night.

Yes, he thought, all the same it's hard on the women. Or the men too, for that matter. But sooner or later, the doctor would come and take from his small black bag the miraculous doll wrapped up in the single cabbage leaf. He himself had once been such a doll, though he couldn't remember it. Now they would not want him out there, but he would go all the same.

He rose, put on his dressing-gown, and tiptoed down the long corridor. He heard a shrill whisper in his ear, *"Father!* Are you *crazy?* Go back to *bed!"* But he shook his head at the whisper and went on. At the head of the stairs he met his grandnephew, Robert. There was sweat on the boy's face and he breathed as if he had been running. They looked at each other a moment, with sympathy but without understanding.

"How is she?" said Will Hancock.

"All right, thanks, Gramp," said the boy in a grateful voice as he kept fumbling in his dressing-gown pocket for a cigarette that was not there. "The doctor's coming over but we—we don't think it's the real thing yet."

Someone called to the boy, and he disappeared again. The corridor abruptly seemed very full of Will Hancock's family. They were clustering around him, buzzing reassuringly, but he paid little attention.

Suddenly, from behind a closed door, he heard Jenny's voice, clear and amused. "Why how perfectly sweet of Father Hancock, Bob! But I'm sorry they woke him—and all for a false alarm."

The reassuring buzzes around him recommenced. He shook them off impatiently and walked back toward his room. But when he was hidden from the others he gave a single guilty look behind him and made for the back stairs. They won't follow me, he thought; got too much to talk about.

He switched on the light in the cider-cellar, drawing his dressing-gown closer about him. It was cold in the cellar now and it would be colder still. But cider was always cider, and he felt thirsty.

He drank the yellow liquid reflectively, swinging his heels against the side of the barrel. Upstairs they would still be whispering and consulting. And maybe the doctor would come with his black bag after all, and to-morrow there would be a piece in the paper to make John Sturgis jealous. But there wasn't anything he could do about it.

No, even for Jenny, there was nothing more he could do. She had taken his wisdom, such as it was, and used it. And he was glad of that. But now he knew from the light tone of her voice that she was beyond such wisdom as he had. The wire had ceased its vibration, the leaves of the tree were shed, like dry wisdom on the ground. Well, she was a nice girl and Robert a decent boy. They would have other children doubtless, and those children children in their turn.

He heard a low sound from the other corner of the cellar and went over to see what had made it. Then he whistled. "Well, old lady," he said, "you certainly don't waste your time." It was the old black house-cat who had stared through the dairy window at himself and John Sturgis. Already she was licking the third of her new kittens while the two first-born nuzzled at her, squeaking from time to time.

He bent over and stroked her head. She looked at him troubledly. "It's all right," he said reassuringly. "They've forgotten about us both—and no wonder. But I'll stick around."

He refilled his cup and sat down upon the barrel, swinging his heels. There was nothing here that he could do, either—cats were wiser than humans in such matters. But, nevertheless, he would stay.

As the cider sank in the cup and he grew colder he fell into a waking dream. Now and then he went over to stroke the cat, but he did it automatically. He was here, in a bare old cellar, drinking cider which would doubtless disagree with him, and in all probability catching his death of cold. And upstairs, perhaps, were life and death and the doctor—new life fighting to come into the world and death waiting a chance to seize it as it came, as death always did. Moreover, these lives and deaths were his lives and deaths, after a fashion, for he was part of their chain. But, for the moment, he was disconnected from them. He was beyond life and death.

He saw again, in front of him, the three couples of

his first dream—and himself and Jenny—himself giving Jenny, unconsciously, the wisdom he did not know. "This is love—this is love—this is love—" and so it was, each phase of it, for each man there spoke the truth of his own heart. Then he looked at the apple tree and saw that it was in flower, but fruit hung on it as well, green fruit and ripe, and even as he looked a wind was blowing the last leaves from the bare bough.

He shivered a little, he was very cold. He put his cup back on the shelf and went over for a last look at the old cat. The travail was over—she lay on her side, beset by the new-born. There was green, inexplicable light in her eyes as he stooped over her, and when he patted her head she stretched one paw out over her kittens like an arm.

He rose stiffly and left her, turning out the light. As he went up the stairs, "Adorable life," he thought, "I know you. I know you were given only to be given away."

The house was silent again, as he tiptoed back to his room. His vigil had been unsuspected, his watch quite useless; and yet he had kept a vigil and a watch. To-morrow might have been too late for it—even now he trembled with cold. Yet, when he stood before the window, he looked long at the winter sky. The stars were still hard points of light, and he would not see them soft again, but earth would continue to turn round, in spite of all these things.